SIXTH VICTIM

C. A. MITCHELL

BOOKS

RAMPART BOOKS

Also by C. A. Mitchell

Beneath the Veils
Beneath the Lies
Beneath the Conflict
Girl in the Middle
Third Child
Sixth Victim
Double Deception
Angel
Tinker Tailor Conman
Children of the Mask
A Woman Called EVE

RAMPART BOOKS

Copywrite © C. A. Mitchell 2023

ISBN 978-1-915778-08-6

1 3 5 7 9 10 8 6 4 2

Rampart Paperback

SIXTH VICTIM

1

———

Remember that when you have a mortgage, work. Sitting in a new house day after day and waiting for that lucky star did nothing except create panic. Every day, she was getting deeper in debt, and now she was cursing herself for it. Money—that's what she needed, money. As an investigative journalist, Cecelia needed to use her brains and find a story to write about. It had to be interesting after her last and only success. Use your head, Cecelia, and think.

Cecelia had been reading an old article in *Changing Worlds*, which she found fascinating. It raised the subject of identity in the most important relationship of them all—the self. A child born as a boy, after a tragic accident, was left without a penis. A shock for everyone. The inevitable conclusion was the child would not be raised as a boy but as a girl.

Which posed the question, what did it mean to be a boy or a girl? Was it purely environmental, or was it purely the conditioning of the mind? Do sexual organs define gender?

Questions that could be answered with a child that seemed to be almost genderless.

As an experiment, the child was treated well. Furnished with a good home, warmth, food, education, and care. But one thing which was missing was perhaps the most important of all. Emotional intimacy. The child, of course, was an experiment.

The developing child was subjected to female discipline and limitations while the child's behavior was noted. Physically, the child thrived, healthy and robust. But emotionally, the child was not so balanced. Retreating into itself and displaying symptoms of depression, the child became angry and withdrawn. But was it because the child was not in the right identity? Or had it something to do with dissociation from the foster parents. The child grew up and got on with life and then disappeared.

Since her success last year, Cecelia knew she didn't belong within the newspaper business. Climbing outside of the structural parameters, she was unwanted and now alone. A familiar feeling knowing that she was different and didn't fit in.

A newspaper journalist is part of the team with a pecking order. The editor pecks at you for results, a good script, and you nibble at the words. The editor has the final say in everything, which meant she was out of a job when Claude, the new editor, took over. A pot-bellied man that hated gays and feminists and figured that she had to be one or the other. But she wasn't. If anything, she was probably asexual. Something not to be discussed was her sex life or lack of it. That was all in the past now and was to be forgotten. She was a woman who simply wanted to get on with her life and wait for that divine inspiration.

Although if someone were to come along and catch her

eye, she would reconsider her sexuality, and why not? One must always be open to change, but at least she was trying to be better and more successful. Everything in life had to do with hope. But with this house and holding on to it, she really didn't have time for her heart.

How time moves on. Her late twenties had turned into her mid-thirties. And still so much to do with her life. That first success fired up her tastebuds like nothing else, and already she was addicted. Realistically, though, the newspaper wasn't going to do that for her. The feeling of aversion was mutual when she left. She was now utterly reliant on herself, and alone.

Sitting at her laptop, staring at the empty screen. Cecelia was immersed in oblivion. Nothing was scrambling in her head to put that story down. Unfortunately, she was not a quick-thinking writer. Her skills in the past dealt with facts and not in poetry. But that wasn't a problem. These abilities can be learned, perhaps.

Staring at her desk, Cecelia waited for that original thought to surface through the haze. Spying a pile of her old newspapers, she picked up a copy out of curiosity, hoping that perhaps they weren't doing so well without her. But of course, it was still going on, reporting the latest news. And she had been replaced. Yes, well, forget about that, but it still smarted when she looked at it.

Today's news reported the finding of a third victim in a similar situation to the others. Young, always young. Another average American girl to be murdered by The Alondra Slasher.

Picking up the newspaper, Cecelia read the facts with dispassion. The first body had been found a year ago, dumped by Lake Munday. The young woman had been strangled, mutilated, and raped, then left for dead. A small black and white pixelated photograph of the girl hung next to the report. She wasn't a beauty, just average. An engaging smile, sweet, a child who was cherished and loved and was now severely missed.

'How sad,' muttered Cecelia, and then, 'Why?'

Facts, this was all there was. Age, gender, where, and when, an appraisal of how wonderful this individual had been. 'It's not enough,' muttered Cecelia, finding fault with the work of her former colleagues. It's not enough to record a death with just a list of facts.

Cecelia squinted at the grainy picture of Marcia Davis, the first victim. Black and white squares added up to make a tragedy. That people can be processed like information was just another added heartbreak for those who loved them.

The oldest daughter with four other sisters and a mother and father that were now grieving. How did they feel when they realized their child had gone missing? And then when they were told she had been murdered? In the drama of life, Cecelia rehearsed that moment of impact. 'I'm so sorry, we have found your daughter, and she's—'

Eyes staring, mouth dropped open as all the voices in your head say no, yet some part in you confirmed that secret thought. We always knew this was going to happen one day. That dreadful fear which every parent harbors had come true.

Scanning through the piece once more, her mind filtered for a practical thought. She could write the story of the victims; she knew she could. She could speak for them and give them history for their daughter, and in that way, she would never die. Marcia Davis would remain immortal, perfect, untouched. It would be something they could hold in their hearts and feel that Marcia was still living. As a writer, not a great one for now, because she would get better.

Train her ability to speak those words to describe Marcia precisely as she had been. Be alive, now go, child, and carry on with your life.

But these words could only be written through an interview with Marcia's parents. I would like to write Marcia's story. I can speak for her through my story. But first, I need information. I need to see and feel what it's like to have a great loss like yours. Tell me how it felt when you heard your daughter was dead? I will write it for you and make people understand. She was alive once and part of your family. I will be your guide to take you through your horror. But the truth is, I need to get a good book because I want to make money. I want to win literary prizes and be remembered for all time. I want to write a classic, so can I use your lives to do it?

No, she didn't think so. She couldn't rape them through her words and sling their lives to all on the public stage via the media networks.

Carefully flicking over the pages, two other victims, Virginia Campbell and Lucy Rodrigo. Seventeen and nineteen, though unremarkable, they stood out. All the victims had long hair, and all of them smiled out from their photographs.

Why did the Slasher choose them? The only notable common denominator was they were all average, nothing remarkable. Why would someone pick on any of these girls who were sensationally less than average in interest? There must be a reason.

But there had been a fourth girl; Cecelia blinked rapidly when she read this. A brief mention, nothing spectacular, no details on her rape, which was unusual. This other young woman claimed she had been attacked just last week by the Slasher, but she remained unnamed. Why? Because she was the one who got away? The lucky one who had fooled the Slasher and made her escape. There was so much more Cecelia wanted to know about this lucky woman.

What was it like to meet death in the eye and fool it? Thoughtfully, Cecelia reflected on these advantages of her escape and the drama. What would it be like? It would be like writing another story and getting applauded for it. If only she knew who this lucky woman was, if she could be called lucky. She had faced death and escaped it. This alone was a miracle. Are you reborn afresh inside with a greater need to live and do the things you had always meant to do but always put to the side?

'James, it's me, Cecelia Clark. I need help.'

That familiar friend, James Patts, was one of the detectives at the Alondra Police Department who she had met through her work.

'Cecelia, now that peculiar because I was just talking to my wife about you. How are you, girl?'

'Good. You know we've spoken about many things during our friendship?'

'Yes, we have,' hesitation took hold.

'I have to be honest with you; I want to write a story; I want to get involved, and the only way I can do it is by writing. I'm talking about The Alondra Slasher. Of course, whatever I hear will be related straight back to the police. Don't you want someone who will do your dirty undercover work for you—for free?'

With interest, James Patts reflected, amused by Cecelia's request. She was a good girl because that was how he saw her. Anxious to please, willing, and wanting to earn her place in the big wide world, a little sister. He already knew that she had wanted to be in the police force. For this reason, he liked her, and there was nothing prickly about her.

True, they had used outside help before, and it had often been rewarding. Who was the fourth victim that got away from The Alondra Slasher? And then he laughed. He wasn't breaking anything sensitive. The last victim's name had already been published in a back copy of her old newspaper, so there was nothing that could be said to be underhanded. Hadn't she been reading up on her own old newspaper's news?

'No,' Cecelia listened to James Patts, feeling the fool. 'When I quit my job, I didn't want to go back to it in any way, which even meant reading it.'

James Patts laughed again, pleased that she was human and didn't take herself too seriously.

'Well, the problem with this victim was, she wanted to make a headline for herself. She demanded to be interviewed. Reckless. Giving her details to a paper so the world would know where she was. It was one of the reasons as to why the police couldn't take her seriously. How can we protect a victim when she lets everyone know where she was? She gave away her identity, which was stupid of her. Crazy woman. Her name is Mary Ann Leigh.' Not usually a sarcastic man, James's anger towards this woman was that of incredulousness.

'Thank goodness for the environment,' Cecelia dashed to the basement, almost skidding down the steps. A pile of papers sitting in the corner waited for the exit. And she missed this while calling herself an investigative journalist? Tied with string, one never throws string away. It was unlucky. Cecelia dashed off the most recent copies and skimmed through them, wetting her thumb and fingers until she found the page.

It was here in the Friday edition, but it didn't make headline news. Nine days ago, a woman told the police she was The Alondra Slasher's latest victim.

He had his hands around my neck. I was terrified, and it was only by luck and the grace of God that I managed to escape.

There was no picture of Mary Ann Leigh, nothing to betray her anonymity. The question was, why did she do it? Poking her pen repeatedly on the article, wasn't this a bit of stupidity? How you must regret it now, Mary Ann.

The address was going to be a problem. Yet it was that unexpected result that added to the peculiarity, Cecelia found Mary Ann Leigh listed in the telephone directory. She lived just off Hubbard Street, a modest road in Alondra. Everything fell nicely into place; everything Cecelia needed was conveniently handed to her. Pick yourself a tragedy, and the story is almost written. Clapping her hands with a jig, she nearly hugged the paper, but kissed it instead. When she was happy, there was a danger she would become thrilled beyond reason.

At eleven o'clock on a bright spring morning was a good time of day to visit. Well, one can only try. Passing a flower shop came the irresistible desire to buy the poor victim some flowers. This would give her an advantage.

Entering the shop, cool to the feel and reckless with exoteric colors. Casting a scant eye on what looked to be the cheapest chrysanthemums, when a woman with myriad mermaid shades of colored hair appeared from the back of the tall electric blue delphiniums. In her hand was a large sunflower.

'Oh hi, another flower lover,' pretty blue-green eyes occupied Cecelia while two cherry-red lips upped into a smile. She looked and sounded exotic, especially with her English accent.

'No, the flowers are not for me. I am buying them for someone else,' hesitated Cecelia.

'Yes, of course you are.'

'What I mean is, I do like flowers.'

'Who doesn't like flowers, especially when someone else is buying them? Do you need any help? I can help you to choose what is best for the situation if you like.' She was hanging on to Cecelia's annoyed face and blinking and looking different. And then she walked away as if she was bored.

A sudden attack of shyness made Cecelia feel affronted by this strange and alien young woman who could have been anywhere from her teens to her early thirties. But she was pretty, in a kooky sort of way.

'Are you buying for a man or a woman?' her voice rose from between a big tub of black tulips, a bin of which sat on a shelf, while below a container of pink, the bottom tier held a container of yellow tulips.

'For a woman, definitely for a woman.' Does anyone buy flowers for a man? Cecelia stepped across, now interested.

'Is she old or young?'

'Young, of course.'

'Young, of course.' With mocking eyes, the flower lady smiled as if everything Cecelia said had to be questioned. 'Which means you would never buy for a man or an older woman?'

'No, I never said that.'

'Yes,' she grinned. 'Interesting, isn't it? What we say and don't say. Our words are not just simple words. They have a history with undertones rather like flowers. When you give flowers, you are marching into an arsenal of trouble. Send the wrong flower, and life will never be the same for you or the other person. Do you understand what I'm talking about?'

No, Cecelia didn't. She was being tricked into saying things she didn't mean. What was this mischievous woman about? A cranky magician? But again, she was interesting. 'The language of flowers?'

'Yes. It's really important. Red roses for love, and everyone loves, but there are different levels of affection. How long have you known this young woman?' the twenty-something-year-old florist was taking out one pink, one black, and one yellow tulip and putting them into her basket in her other hand. 'Do you know anything about flowers other than you like them?'

What was there to know? They grew in soil and looked pretty. Wasn't that enough? Cecelia's expression confirmed what the colorful florist already suspected.

'There is a secret world going on in front of your blind eyes. Why talk and speculate about the possibility of the multiverse,' she aired her hand, 'when there are so many worlds going on in the garden? Have you ever considered the insect world beneath our feet right now?'

'No, I haven't.'

She laughed. 'It's the best way to be—ignorant.' She looked straight into Cecelia's eyes with a mischievous grin.

Was this complete rudeness or plain bad humor? Whatever, the florist appeared to be enjoying herself at Cecelia's expense. It might be a good idea to walk out of this shop and teach this rude individual some manners.

'This basket is called a trug,' the flower person carried on taking a flower from each bin and adding it to the trug. 'Just some useless information, but the English are good at that. You must excuse me. Sometimes, I tend to get carried away. I like Americans,' adding another flower to her basket. 'They are extremely friendly people.' She raised her blue eyes to see if Cecelia was still listening. Her eyes were bright and lively and targeted with mischief, and then she smiled. 'I am here to help you get the most out of your flowers. Flowers are my life as well as good health—by the way, I make all my own clothes. I am so bohemian, and also, you must have guessed by now, I like to talk. Sorry, but I lost my cat today. And the only way I can come to terms with it is to talk. I appear to talk about anything that comes to my mind when what it really is—is that I miss my cat.'

'Oh, I'm sorry.' How a conversation can suddenly flip upside-down, Cecelia should be angry; instead, that ever-waiting compassion slid under the mantle of her temper, curled up, and purring beside her.

'Thank you. Sometimes knowing your pet was happy and that he had a good life doesn't seem enough. Her name was Petal. She was a rescue cat, yet I'd like to think it was the other way around. She rescued me. I got her when I first came to this wonderful country. She slept with me in my bed and licked me every night on the chin because she accepted me. Oh dear, I promised myself I wouldn't cry. But you know, I would have given half of my years to have her company.' She turned to wipe her eyes. 'I keep on thinking about her and how she won't be waiting to sit on my lap, kneading her paws on me anymore. To love anything is so painful.'

How helpless this woman suddenly appeared. Grief. It was always down to grief—this alone can make people behave the way they do. Grief and happiness, two of the most powerful forces in life, yet there were others. With her back again turned to Cecelia in that moment of kindness, Cecelia's hand fluttered in the air, not knowing whether to touch her for comfort. Are you okay? A stupid question to ask when it was obvious she wasn't.

'What I am doing now,' said the woman who once owned a cat called Petal, while wiping her tears away. 'Is choosing a flower from every pot. I am going to make Petal the most wonderful bouquet in the world, or perhaps it should be called a wreath?' her voice slipped again. 'But whatever. This is a celebration of my little darling's life. We shall all die one day, so while I'm alive, I've got to enjoy it. It's important to be grateful for the time we're given. Don't you think?'

Her smile was sweet, warm, as if she put her entire soul into it so that Cecelia couldn't help returning her smile.

'I meet lots of interesting people working with flowers —' for a moment, she looked preoccupied as if she were counting her thoughts. 'But once again, I am talking too much. You were telling me about your friend. Is she a friend or someone you are trying to impress?'

'I have never met her before.' Private business shouldn't be discussed, but this was a person who had just opened up her heart to her. And besides, buying flowers was not as easy as she supposed it to be. 'I thought that if I took her flowers, it would break the ice.'

'And flowers do. They make many silent communications for us mere mortals. I believe flowers have a soul, or if they don't, they should. That's the bohemian side in me. Do you have any ideas on the sort of flowers you would like to give this person?'

'No, not really. Something cheerful perhaps—something like those chrysanthemums over there.'

'Is she French, or is she dead?'

'No, neither. I don't think. I mean, she's not dead,' said Cecelia, scrunching her eyebrows in annoyance. 'Obviously, she's not dead.' Was this woman playing with her again? 'I am not going to her funeral.'

'Which means you would never go to her funeral even if she were dead?'

'No, it doesn't mean anything of the sort unless you want it to. I've come to this shop to buy flowers. I thought flowers would give me a pleasant introduction. I didn't expect to endure this questioning.'

'You're right. I asked about the young lady only because if she were French, chrysanthemums would be an insult. They're flowers for funerals, which is why you should never give chrysanthemums to a French person unless, of course, for a funeral.'

Exacerbated by this woman's sense of flippancy, Cecelia stared back hard. True, she was an English person in America, away from her homeland, and normally Cecelia would have made allowances. Still, this bubbly humor was provoking, even if she had just lost her cat. Only so much kidding around and wordplay one could have when talking. There must be another florist.

'I think I've changed my mind about the flowers. I'll buy chocolates instead.'

'Oh dear, I think I've just lost a sale.'

Cecelia shrugged, and with a blank smile, raised her indifference by moving to the door.

'I guess that's life.'

'I guess,' answered Cecelia.

'Okay. I'll quit the wise-ass remarks—isn't that what you Americans call it?'

'We actually call it good manners. I wanted to buy some nice flowers for a person I've never met, but with you, it's like a dress rehearsal for war. I never knew buying flowers could be so difficult.' Now angry, Cecelia's temper showed in sparkling sarcasm. People—young women were being murdered, and it wasn't prettily. Didn't the English, known for their eccentric sense of humor, understand what pointless tragedy was all about? But when she looked at this flower woman expecting her to show some hint of remorse, there was none, except that exasperating glint of merriment. Cecelia's hand was on the door.

'Carnations,' the flower woman called after Cecelia. 'And pink ones. Wait, I'll give you a bouquet. It will be my gift to you as a way of apology.'

Cecelia stopped. Why did she need to be so weird?

'Pink carnations represent gratitude. It should do the trick,' the flower woman walked to the heavenly paradise of flowers, confident that Cecelia would return. Without looking, she began selecting the most perfect carnation blooms she had. Long-stemmed and beautiful, like elegant ladies. She carefully wrapped them in pink tissue paper. 'By the way, my name is Phoebe; it means brightness and radiance. My namesake was also one of the Titans, and depending on which you choose to believe, she delivered Paul's epistles. It gets better. Phoebe was also a prophet. Isn't it wonderful to know the meaning of one's name? But whatever, I am a wonderful person.' She grinned again, impishly. 'You took the bulk of my grief, and you are the first person I told about Petal.'

An irresistible draw tugged Cecelia towards this maniac woman. An apology was something Cecelia admired and should be met halfway by giving this oddball a second chance. A silent exchange with Cecelia returning. She had been won over. A little smile from Phoebe, who readily took these long-stemmed blooms to her counter. Fascinated, Cecelia watched in obedience as the sure and deft hands quickly strung a stunning bouquet together.

'I can't change the way I am. I know I'm awkward and opinionated, but I'm a good person. I stand up for those who can't stand up for themselves. Usually, I am a lot better mannered than this,' she handed the bouquet to Cecelia. 'I feel I should make up to you for my outbursts. You've seen me at my worse and forgiven me. I would be interested to know how you went on with your interview. I'm pretty sure my flowers will do the trick. What do you say? A fair exchange?'

Taking the carnations out of Phoebe's hand, Cecelia assessed this strange English woman. She wasn't completely contrite because she showed spirit, and a flicker of amusement in her eyes made her attractive. A fair exchange would if this Phoebe told her about England be beneficial. England was a place where one day Cecelia would like to visit.

'I prefer to pay for them,' Cecelia went for her purse.

'Accept them as a gift,' said Phoebe, pushing the money gently away. 'At the end of the day, there are always flowers leftover. We sell them to funeral homes a lot cheaper. I'm not mean, but on this occasion, I would sooner give them to a person like you. So please, take them. And yes, I am the owner of this business, and these are my flowers.'

Cecelia's problem was that nothing in life is free; she was inclined to hold back but instead shrugged and took the flowers. If only this Phoebe weren't so glib, then perhaps they could be friends. But maybe this was defensive behavior by the flower lady.

'Thank you,' Cecelia smiled while holding the flowers as she left the premises. 'It's so kind of you.'

'You didn't tell me your name?'

She stopped, stunned by the question. 'Cecelia, it's not a name I'm fond of.'

'St Cecilia was the blind patron of music and also a

talented musician,' smiled Phoebe. 'I have a bet that you're a talented musician.'

'No, I'm afraid you're wrong.'

'Ah,' but Phoebe refused to give up. There must be something wonderful about her name. 'Then you must be a wonderful singer.'

Cecelia smiled.

'Yes, I guessed right. Bye, bye Cecelia, I hope to see you again.'

Phoebe was right about the flowers; they do have a positive effect on the mood. Looking at the pink heads now gently swaying as she walked, a good feeling came merrily to her heart; this was a beautiful gift to give. One good deed follows another, and sometimes quickly. If her plan to have Miss Leigh open up about what had happened didn't work, she would at least have circulated kindness.

'Yes, can I help you?'

The woman answering the door was unexpectedly tall. A straight, good postured young woman whose soft voice had an accent that wasn't easy to detect.

'I've come to visit Mary Ann Leigh.'

First impressions gave the notion that this tall woman didn't fit the picture Cecelia had stored vividly in her mind of a victim. At five feet eight or nine, she looked too tall to be raped. Although slender, she also looked aggressively fit. Long ash blonde hair staggered over her shoulders and down her back while striking blue eyes stared warily yet interestingly at her. It could be she hadn't spoken to anyone for a long time. One of those strange moments when Cecelia felt she had met this woman before but couldn't say when or even how.

'And you are?' she asked, with her head cocked to one side with interest.

'I am Cecelia Clark, a journalist. And the reason I am here is for your story—but before you close the door on me. I believe that every woman who has been raped has the right to speak out.'

'Now that's a hell of a controversial remark,' said Mary Ann, uncertain in her smiles but still amused. 'Would you like to come in? I also think that everyone should be heard, no matter how eccentric. Honesty counts for something in my books. I've never been interviewed by a journalist before.'

Walking off, having given Cecelia the look of approval, she left her door open, leaving Cecelia in turmoil. Should she go in and close the door to the world? For a recently raped victim, Mary Ann Leigh showed far too much trust. Closing the door, Cecelia followed, thoughtfully puzzled, behind her.

It was a feminine house, perfumed, frilled with ornaments, too fussy for Cecelia, yet still nice. The hallway wasn't dark but full of light, and colors helped this light and airy house. A pot-pourri of delicious and edible smells shouted out. Hey, I'm a female. Look at me.

'I like my peace and quiet,' she said, pointing to her carpet.

Thick and deep, like a light green lawn, which certainly kept out the noise. This was a woman who aspired to live well and not cut corners.

'I am glad of the company. Won't you come in?' she moved to the middle of the room and held her hands out decoratively.

It was a room full of the energy of space. Nice, but not the sort of room that Cecelia felt comfortable in. Was this a show house?

'Now, if you had been a man, I would not have opened

the door to you,' said Mary Ann, standing by the doorway after Cecelia had entered. 'I'm doing my best to keep my mind together, but it hasn't been easy these last nine days. You can understand my apprehension. Won't you sit down?'

Floral-covered armchairs in a duck egg-colored room, calming colors, yet not homely. The room smelled of lavender, relaxing and comforting, but staged. Busy eyes waited on Cecelia.

'You have a beautiful house.'

'Thank you,' she smiled. 'I spend most of my time here. Now, what can I get you to drink? Tea?' head cocked to one side; she smiled again while gently touching the side of her jaw, presenting herself favorably.

An oval face and beautifully made up, pale pink lipstick on a not too generous mouth. But the eyes, startling blue, the brightest blue ever. And with her long blonde hair, she should have been pretty, but she wasn't. Something was missing about her. Such a shame. But with the right balance of personality, charm, and interest, physical beauty fades to make way for personality.

'I take it the flowers are meant for me?' asked Mary Ann, looking at the bouquet.

'Yes, of course,' Cecelia held out the pink paper-wrapped arrangement of flowers. 'I was thinking about getting some yellow carnations—'

'Ah, dianthus caryophyllus, one of my favorite flowers. But does anyone know that the yellow dianthus is the flower of regret? An apt choice for me because I do regret taking that excursion that evening. I constantly think about this unfortunate decision. There was no need for me to go out that late.' Yet when Mary Ann smile, there was a falseness to it. As if the stage light of the theater were upon her. 'Yet you bought me these charming flowers, so I shall take them from you and thank you. I will take them to the kitchen and drop them into the sink for now. We can't have them dying because of our selfishness. I won't be a minute.'

Mary Ann was not the imagined victim. Walking like a gazelle, long, slender footsteps treaded surely, but conscious of herself.

'Would you like some coffee?' called out Mary Ann from the kitchen. 'I have caffeinated or decaffeinated. I drink caffeinated in the morning and then in the evening; it has to be decaf.'

'I'll have whatever you're having,' called out Cecelia, now looking about her. Being in a strange place was always disorientating.

'What was that you said?' asked Mary Ann, appearing from behind the door. Like a cheetah in the dark, she moved without sound.

'Whatever you're having. I'm easy to please,' she said, startled yet still retaining her composure. Cecelia's heart rattled quicker.

'What a gracious guest you are. Now, this is why I prefer women to men. They have much more style, more class. I won't be a minute. Cream, sugar?'

'Yes, two sugars, please.'

'And yet you are so slight, just like me, but I'm afraid I have to work at it. Gym five times a week. Well, I used to go down to the gym, but now I work out here. I'll just make the coffee. I have cookies. Would you like some? I make them myself—but not for me. You are the first person I have seen for quite a time. Have you heard of Shakespeare?' Mary Ann was again by the door and cocking her head to one side with her startling blue eyes. She was going to look after her house guest.

'Yes, I have heard of Shakespeare—'

'The Bard,' broke in Mary Ann to disappear into the hallway. 'I trained as a Shakespearian actress. I played Ophelia once in London, England. I was said to be the best.'

The victim was an actress. Now it made sense why she came back to Los Angeles. It might be a little unkind, Cecelia mused, with eyes touching on indulgent ornaments, a shepherdess, crook in hand. On the other hand, it could be Mary Ann in a China dress. A stage victim-act which would explain why Mary Ann wanted attention. The Tick-Tock of nothing played on.

Less than a minute, Mary Ann returned with a tray of coffee and cookies, fresh with happiness and doing her best to be pleasing. The cups and saucers were bright, as if Mary Ann spent her time in the kitchen buffing up the crockery.

'None for me, thanks.' Cecelia shook her head.

'Hmm,' pursed Mary Ann with more than a shadow of disapproval before putting the plate back on the table quietly like a threat. 'Now you want to talk about the rape.'

'Yes, mam, I do.' Cecelia held on to her cup and saucer in dutiful respect.

'Now let me ask you,' Mary Ann leaned forward as if to extract as much meaning as she could from this little inter-change. 'Is this the sort of thing you would say to another female, calling her mam, or did you say it believing this would please me? Because you have whether you consciously knew it or not. I studied playwriting. I am proposing to put my life into a stage play.' She held her chin up. 'But what can I write about? Nothing has happened to me. Nothing other than what happens to anyone, except now this, the rape, but at least it's something to write about. Does that sound vain?' she pulled her skirt over her knees, conscious of their slenderness.

'No,' nodded Cecelia.

'Well, what were you going to ask me? Oh, before you start, would you mind if I get my little recorder? I like to capture as much as I can about my life. I'm afraid my life has been quite dull until now. I won't be a minute.'

Usually, the procedure happens the other way around, with Cecelia taping the conversation. She had her recorder with her, but to have two recorders going simultaneously seemed a little bizarre. Besides, she was in the victim's house.

In the background, the tick of life came from an ormolu clock on the mantelpiece. Under the glass dome, the gilt brass still shone. A pretty timekeeper, but not an original. And not to Cecelia's taste. Looking about this neat house, Cecelia nodded that she had done well for herself. Nice place, nice furniture, although a little too fancy. Studied in England was an accomplishment. Yet, there were no pictures of Mary Ann on the stage. Not a vain actress. But this room, this house so unhealthily clean, something which could never be said of Cecelia. Life for her took priority above cleaning. Not lazy, no, just different values and a unique way of cataloging her possessions. She would leave them where she put them down. But she was getting better. But to clean the house every day, why? There was something on the mantel. A small trophy with an inscription. Snooping over to the mantelpiece, Cecelia's journalistic nose leaned closer to read the inscription.

To Mary Ann Leigh 2010, best Newcomer to Acting in her theater role, The Little Girl of Texas.

'Do you want to drink your coffee before we start?' Mary Ann returned carrying her tape recorder.

'I don't mind.'

Glancing at where Mary Ann had seen Cecelia looking, she smiled. 'Very well. I shall place the recorder on the table between us. My goodness, don't you have lovely hands? I love your nails. They are natural, aren't they?' taking Cecelia's fingers in her elegant hands, she dropped them with laughter and covered her lips. 'I must explain, sometimes as an actress, I need to work in other ways to pay for this life. People don't always appreciate one's talent. Yes, I know. I have trained as a fully qualified manicurist. Here, look at my nails. I do them every day. Incidentally, it was when I was on my way to see a client that the Slasher took advantage of me. I had better switch on the machine before anything else. Do you mind? Could you hold on for a minute?'

Leaning forward, a tantalizing smell of perfume emulated from Mary Ann. What was it?

A button clicked on the recorder.

'One, two, three, and now we can begin. You can start by asking me questions.'

It wasn't an order, yet this instruction provoked annoyance.

'Can you go through your movements when you left your home?'

'Why, certainly. My name is Mary Ann Leigh. I am twenty-seven years old and unmarried, although hundreds have asked me. Perhaps one day, the right man will come along. I believe, and I know it sounds old fashion that a lady should not be sallied. I nearly was that night. I am,' she smiled perfectly. 'A virgin.'

Cecelia moved uncomfortably to be offered intimate details. 'I can understand this might be difficult for you to speak about,' said Cecelia, gently dropping her gaze.

'No, it's not difficult,' interrupted Mary Ann. 'It angers me to think I put myself in such a position. Luckily for me, I am healthy and fit, so I was able to challenge him off.'

'Can you tell me how it came about?'

'He was in a car.' Holding up her hands, Mary Ann extravagant action dramatically set the scene in her head. 'I was walking along thinking about what I was going to do this evening when a car drew up by the sidewalk. You know how it happens?' she shrugged. 'He asked for directions. How to get to Temple City? I said I sure do, but you have the wrong road. You should take... and that's when he said he couldn't hear me; could I speak up? I do not shout, especially not in a public place unless, of course, for a stage part. What a fool I was to go across to him. It was all over the news about the Slasher, but it's the sort of thing that will never happen to you. Let me think of what he looks like. Good-looking, handsome men are usually not rapists of this type.' A thickening frown grooved Mary Ann's brow. 'The truth is, his good looks beguiled me, so I went closer and bent down to his window.'

Yes, I was foolish. He opened the door quicker than a fish slipping off the hook and pulled me into his car, taking me by complete surprise. I didn't scream because it happened too quickly. Holding on to me, he drove off with his car door still open. People saw what happened, but like all people these days, they become blind.

'You were lucky.'

'I was, wasn't I? I kept my presence of mind.'

'Have you given the police his description?'

'They weren't interested.'

'So, why are you telling me? I'm not the police.' Cecelia frowned.

'You're right; you're not, which is precisely why I am talking to you. I don't particularly appreciate talking to men. Men don't understand. They have no sympathy for what I have been through.'

'But they need every piece of information they can get to find him. And so far, you are the only one who has got away alive.'

She was sticky, so sticky; one of those people when they caught hold of you and stuck to you. It was creepy.

'I suppose you're right. I should do my duty, but then you won't get that story you are looking for, will you? At least not firsthand. I recognized you as soon as I answered the door. You are Cecelia Clark. Wouldn't you like another top story?'

'How did you know about me?'

'I read the newspapers; I remembered your name. You are much prettier than your photograph.'

Her surreal bright blue eyes poked into Cecelia's head to watch her. Extracting every expression skidding across her face. Then she lowered her eyes with some regret at what she was doing.

'You have to forgive me; I have an actress's temperament. I study people, and it helps me reinvent myself. It can be extremely rude, I know, but it's not meant to be unkind.'

Looking up to Mary Ann's eyes, Cecelia smiled, then looked down quickly in modesty.

2

Now back home, with much on her mind, Cecelia began writing down what she could remember of the interview. And it was complicated and long drawn out.

'How can you write my story if you don't know anything about me?' said Mary Ann, demonstrating her acting skill efficiently.

Cecelia's inward sigh, taking a breath vibrating in her chest, politely listened as the plate of cookies was again offered. A respectful smile and a shake of Cecelia's head, followed by another refusal.

The best decision Mary Ann had ever made was to study in England. Although the digs were appalling, being the only American meant she was spoiled and treated with special consideration. The best part of her experience while studying there was voice training, and the English tutors said she had a good ear for accents.

Then, Mary Ann tried out her accent; it was creepily good. She needed attention, especially Cecelia's.

'I would have stayed. I suppose I should have stayed;

because the English appreciated my acting abilities, but not back home here in America. Because once you pack your bags and tell everyone you are going, it's pride, isn't it, which prevents you from returning? Here, the values are different; Americans want glamor, they don't want true art. Now, if I had been a man, my opportunities would have been different. Don't you feel that? Aren't you affected by prejudice? How long does prettiness last? If you are not lovely anymore, you are worthless. Don't you think that? What do you think, Cecelia?'

Are you supposed to like the people you interview? When Cecelia's eyes fell away. Lack of attention was an insult. Wasn't Cecelia listening? Had she become boring? Yes, Cecelia was listening to her, but now she was thinking. What was Cecelia thinking about could be far more interesting than this woman?

Overbearing, Mary Ann claimed all of Cecelia's attention and more. There was something about this woman which she didn't like. Regardless of what had happened to Mary Ann, she was dull to the point of boring. In fact, she was vain. Her world was singularly small and uninteresting. Now Cecelia needed the bathroom.

Climbing the stairs gave some relief. On her own was a time to do some exploring to alleviate the tedium of this interview. Mary Ann's world of perfume continued above. To the left, along the landing, a pink bathroom faced opposite, and to the side was a bedroom. The door left wide open was surely inviting anyone to look in. Yellowed sunlight blew its full impact on the white and frilly. Opposite the window was a king-sized bed draped in a white matelassé fabric. Elegant and over the top. Champagne-colored carpet: the room was simplistically simple and free from clutter, a white vanity table dressed and waited hushed in reverence at the window. It was the kind of room that would not have looked out of place in a smart hotel.

Headfirst, Cecelia poured into the tranquil and waiting bedroom. On top of the vanity table was a photograph. A young black American woman and pretty too, an easy smile traveled from the picture with relaxed sincerity. Very attractive expression. Intrigued, who was this pretty girl? In this photograph, she must be roughly about fourteen or fifteen or even a little older; it was difficult to say. Picking up the picture, Cecelia was struck by the sweetness of this young girl's large brown eyes, so full of hope. It wasn't easy to believe that she and Mary Ann were friends or what part they played in each other's lives.

Snitching back downstairs, Cecelia needed to ask that question. Who was the photograph of?

'Oh yes, Sarah,' said Mary Ann when Cecelia admitted to going into the white bedroom. 'You must have gone into the wrong room.'

'Sorry, yes. I thought you said the second on the right—'

'No, I didn't tell you where the bathroom was. You saw Sarah, the best friend I ever had. But she's dead now. She died a long time ago, over thirteen years now. I still miss her, which is why I keep her photograph. I am loyal and faithful to the people I love. And I loved Sarah—I still do. She was an angel who God felt he must call for, but it was too early, and for me, sadly. But I guess the most beautiful people are often taken too quickly. I would say that God was an A-hole. But I guess another way of looking at it is that she will never grow old; she will always remain young and beautiful. Isn't that what everyone wants?'

It was difficult to elicit anything else from Mary Ann. She was holding on to the rapist's description as if it were gold dust, teasing Cecelia with another of her recollections.

Until finally, she described him. He was a white male and appeared to be family-oriented; she thought this because at the back of his car and while he had his hands around her throat; she saw a doll sitting on the back seat. This was so distressing that this man had children. Vile, evil men.

With an unbiased ear, Cecelia listened while weighing up if she believed Mary Ann or not. The truth was, James Patts and his thoughts influenced her. Another thing, Mary Ann's makeup just didn't have the persona of a victim. And another thing, how did she escape so easily?

'By the good grace of God, that's how.'

'Can you explain?' Cecelia watched, waited, and noted everything about Mary Ann's performance with her notebook in her hand.

'He was trying to strangle me; I was fighting for breath.' As if to prove this, her breathing became quick and raspy. 'I was petrified. I could feel his hot breath on my neck; I have never been so afraid as I was then. I knew he would rape and then kill me; I almost heard his words inside my head about what he wanted to do to me. If it was going to be, it was going to be. I stopped struggling because I was trying to work out what was happening. Oh, I don't know how to explain how I felt. I knew if I didn't do anything to help myself, I was going to die. It was dreadful. Unless you've been put into this danger, you will never understand.'

Her eyes, almost rabid, looked madly around, and then directly at Cecelia. She feared that Mary Ann would grab her.

'I took the only opportunity God gave me to escape. I didn't need any other hint, and I would not hang around because he would surely take his opportunity. My hands dry with fear; I opened the car door, and then I ran. I carried on running. I ran until I had no breath, and then I ran down this side alley and sat down and cried.'

And she did cry; it was shocking. Emotions were something Cecelia resisted because she didn't know what to do with them. Her hand ran over Mary Ann without touching her.

'There, there,' Cecelia whispered, resisting touching her. 'You've been unbelievably brave. Tell me more about this monster when you are ready.'

'I would say.' Mary Ann touched her eyes. 'He was about five feet ten; short brown slicked-back hair and a mustache. Caucasian and definitely America, and,' she caught up and touched that memory. 'He looked like Clark Gable; he also wore aftershave while his voice was low, and yet, sweet, and quite high toned. His hands were beautifully manicured. I would suggest he was an actor or businessman; he certainly wasn't a laborer.'

This was a good description which Cecelia could show the police, and she was sure they would appreciate it. Much of police work like journalists depended on the goodwill of informants. So, if this information was real, they had to do something for her. A telephone call to James Patts might give her an idea of what to do.

'We can't leave Mary Ann Leigh on her own, as she is obviously going through a bad time,' said Cecelia. It was seven o'clock in the evening, and James Patts had only two minutes to spare when she called.

'She has refused all help,' he finished with a cough. A bad chill was making its presence felt. 'We have offered Miss Leigh protection, but she refused. We can't bully her into accepting. You know there is only so much we can do. The lady has rights. And besides, if she managed to get away the first time, she can do it again. This lady can seriously take care of herself.'

'Perhaps that's true, but she said you offered a male officer. And what I make of it, she's terrified of men since the attack. From my meeting with her, it was plain to see she doesn't trust men.'

'I understand, Cecelia, but we then offered her a female officer, but she said no, she didn't want anyone... we are not so stupid or cruel to impose a couple of male officers. We also suggested officers sitting outside in their car. We can't do any more than that. This lady can be extremely intimidating. I don't know what the Slasher was thinking about when he decided to take her on?'

'You offered her women police officers?' now, this was a surprise.

'Yes, we did,' James Patts hiccupped a dry cough.

'Oh, perhaps Miss Leigh didn't understand what you meant.' Cecelia frowned and bit her lip. Awkward was the word that came to her. Miss Leigh could undoubtedly be awkward. 'She might not have realized the police force has female officers doing protection work?'

Another cough, James was struggling. 'Look, I tell you what I can do. I'll give you the name of a good female detective at the station; you will like her. She is into women's rights and empowering women. Her name is Halleluiah Travis—yes, you heard me right. She is a woman from the deep South and proud of it as she is of her name and birthrights. Dammit, I'm all over the map here. What I mean is, take Detective Travis seriously because she certainly takes herself that way.'

In the background, Cecelia heard Mrs. Patts telling her husband to hang up. Her concern touched on lack of sleep, and he was not going to work tomorrow. She didn't care what happened to the police department; they would just have to carry on without him. The end.

Again, that awful loneliness beamed out as Cecelia returned the receiver. A wife who cared about her husband and a man who loved his wife. It was at times like these when she felt left out. Sometimes, it would be nice to have a friend, someone she could talk to, to help exercise those demons. Yet Cecelia knew she wasn't a social person, and making friendships was a misnomer. A surprising offer of friendship with Mary Ann must be considered. But no, no, thank you. She was someone Cecelia automatically avoided. Yet, she felt sorry for this tall, angular woman with long blonde hair. Poor Mary Ann.

Daunted was how she felt going into the Alondra Police Department to talk to Halleluiah Travis. To get James Patts' praise, this woman must be someone exceptional. You will like her, James Patts assured her, which meant nothing to Cecelia. How was she going to talk to this professional detective? What did they have in common? Nothing. Someone had once accused her of being socially inept. It hurt immensely, but they were right.

The only way to cure this deficiency is to practice. Exercise charm, and work on that smile, and look really interested in what people are saying. Be nice, be friendly, and stop gritting your teeth. Cecelia bit her finger, and suddenly she realized she was biting one of her beautiful nails.

'You should look after your hands,' Mary Ann cooed, standing at the door ready to wave when she left. 'A woman with pretty hands is lucky. She'll get whatever she wants in life.'

Which, of course, wasn't true, but it was a nice thought to have. Perhaps she should put some hand cream on.

Alondra Police Department was packed when Cecelia

arrived. Other journalists waited outside for the latest reports. Another murder had happened. Late last night, a woman in her early twenties had been found murdered. A brunette with long hair was the newest victim added to the notorious list. People weren't listening to the advice; everyone believes it would never be them.

'Can I speak to Detective Travis?' Cecelia faced the officer at the desk.

'You could do, but you'll have to wait your turn. Take a seat.' The officer pointed without looking at her.

'Detective James Patts put a word in for me.'

'Did he?' the officer looked up but wasn't impressed. 'Then I guess you will still have to wait.'

Would being a member of the press affect him? Perhaps not. Perhaps she ought to turn around and go home; after all, her interest in this case only went as far as getting a good story. While her feelings toward Mary Ann were not that sincere, she took a seat and brooded about her conscience.

Two hours later, and with the feeling that she had done time for a crime, Cecelia returned to the desk. The officer on the desk had changed, and she hadn't noticed. A woman had taken the man's place.

'Excuse me,' began Cecelia, now indignant, 'but I was told to sit and wait. I've been waiting two hours.'

'Who have you been waiting for?' her dark brown eyes strode straight into Cecelia's with a direct and targeted gaze. Nothing put this short, confident, liberated woman off or intimidated her.

'I'm waiting to talk to Detective Travis.'

'And what is it you want to talk to her about?' she asked without any change of expression.

Eyeballing each other was unnerving. Her straight nose had a bump at the end, as if to suggest her blood had been mixed somewhere in her ancestry. She was proud of these parts of her gene pool; they made her the person she was. And now, her interested gaze was concerned with Cecelia and why she was asking. There was also a glint of humor in her eyes, which was rather unsettling. It was as if she were daring Cecelia.

'Are you Detective Travis?' asked Cecelia, uncertain but willing to take the chance because she didn't like being played the fool.

'I certainly am, mam. Detective Patts rang through and said you were interested in talking to me. Would you like to come to my office?'

Detective Travis, though small, was sassy and sharp. She had to be because this was a world where you fought to be acknowledged. One might call it a man's world, but there again, perhaps not. Women had that interesting edge, keen fighters in their own way. But that wasn't to say this officer had lost her femininity. Walking in front of Cecelia in her dark navy-blue trousers, she walked with a wiggle. Where did she get her confidence from? Slightly overweight, which was attractive. Her natural, kinky, dark brown hair was set in soft waves, giving her an appearance of both intelligence and attractiveness. A well-groomed, smart lady who made Cecelia feel she had just got the better of her.

Walking into her office, Cecelia was taken aback by the neatness and organization of the room. It was amazing. No one messed with this savvy babe.

'Sit down,' Detective Travis pointed to the seat on the other side of her desk. 'So, what is it you think I can do for you?'

Now sitting, this officer leaned forward with interest. It was very flattering. A slight lilt of the Southern States added not only charm but a need to get down to the nitty-gritty.

Even with no makeup, she was still pleasing, and she didn't wear jewelry either. Perhaps late thirties or early forties, there was no wedding ring. Would she say this woman was feminine? Yes, she was a dash of hot pepper and not that cat on the hot tin roof. Already and with no real reason, Cecelia felt she liked this lady and, then again, wary of her. A woman who was so different from herself.

'I've come here on Miss Mary Ann Leigh's behalf.' Cecelia was more than a little nervous, while Detective Travis's gaze did not waver.

'Ah yes, the woman who escaped the Slasher, or so she says. We have people like her who try to claim some of the attention; nevertheless, we have to deal with them. So, she's been talking to you.'

'Yes.' Cecelia felt the awkward imposition of not having any real rights to be here. A trumped-up column writer.

This confident black woman stared at Cecelia with disconcerting intelligence. She wanted facts, not fiction, and she worked hard and diligently to get results. She expected everyone else to do the same. Cecelia was impressed.

'James Patts tells me he is a friend of yours and you are a journalist. You should know now that I disapprove of journalists. In my line of work, my worries are about people and how best to serve them. My time is valuable, and I am not here to either aid a story or spin any fabulous line for everyone else to make them a fortune. I want to serve people, and I take great pride in it. I'm not saying news reporters are all bad. It's just my experience of them.'

She certainly didn't like news people.

'I'm not a news reporter. I'm a journalist.'

'Okay. Is there any difference between them?'

'To me, there is.'

'Okay, what's the difference?'

Detective Travis could be asking her about the nature of her conscience.

'I consider myself to be a journalist because I write with respect. A news reporter writes to my mind with sensation. I tell people the truth as it is. I like to think I educate my readers, and it's something I am proud of, which means I take myself seriously, especially my words. You won't get twisted, biased, and prejudicial words from me or slanting the truth to suit the newspaper. My words are written with thought and assessment. Every word I write comes with judgment.'

Making no conclusions, Detective Travis listened seriously until she'd heard this woman out.

'These days, reporters bastardize their work and sell themselves cheaply. It's easy to deceive with words and deform the truth and write history the way you want it to be written in an attempt to change the future. People find out in the end what the actual truth is. Trying to conceal the truth is only temporary. It will be out in the end. It always does. I dislike these types of people, which is why my old newspaper doesn't want anything to do with me. Yes, I am being as honest as possible. I am a journalist who is trying to write a story with caution and care. I put my interpretation on the facts and reality, giving everyone that choice on what to believe—because there will be other versions. But I believe in what I write.'

Goodness, did she really say that? Or more to the point, did she think that? Was this the person she had become full of high moral standings?

'Interesting,' nodded the detective, drawing her bottom lip in while reforming her opinion of Cecelia. 'What did you think of her story about being raped? Did you ask her any questions...?'

'The first thing I gathered about her was that she was

afraid,' stumbled Cecelia. As usual, after making her heartfelt speech, she was uncertain if she went over the top.

'Okay. So, what did she tell you? Because she must have told you something.'

'She had some difficulty talking about the rape; I felt like she didn't want to face up to it. I managed to get a brief description of the assailant.'

'Do you have it there?'

'Yes, I do.'

Holding out her hand, she expected Cecelia to hand them over instantly. Cecelia felt annoyed.

'I can do the things which as members of the law, you can't. I'm skilled at asking things in a more compassionate and sympathetic way because I am outside the circle of the law. I am the recording observer.'

'Are you saying you want to be personally involved in police work?'

Cecelia nodded.

'Now, why mam, as a friend of Detective James Patts, why didn't you join the police force? Why report instead of becoming properly and professionally involved?' in all her righteous glory, Detective Travis sat back in her chair and gloated as the jingle jangle of her answers sat tucked in her back pocket. From the grin on her face, she believed she had outwitted Cecelia.

Like a dagger, Cecelia's insecurities returned, finding their way to her side. How dare this woman attack her when she knew nothing of her life? The bile in her heart was now on her tongue and ready to be used.

'You want to know the reason I am not serving in the police force?' began Cecelia with a sudden temper. 'Because they didn't want me. I applied and was not accepted; they rejected me on the grounds of ill-health, but my willingness to serve remains. I am in the only role I can do, to find the truth and report it. Life doesn't always do us favors. You might not approve of what I do, but I do my best. I report the truth as I see it. I show people the wrongs in our society, which I believe are as valuable as any other police or detective work.'

The spirit of this meek and uninspiring woman was impressive.

'If I need to keep myself alive by selling these stories, I don't see any wrong with it. I report well because I listen. Perhaps I don't ask too many questions, and maybe that's where I go wrong. But I'm willing to learn and get it right— you won't find anyone more determined than me. And another thing, I am on your side. Well, I was, until now.'

'You hang on there, girl,' interrupted Detective Travis, undeterred by Cecelia's outburst, knowing she had upset her. 'I didn't say I didn't believe you. I'm a police officer first and a diplomat second. I'm not into the niceties of life. This is a murder investigation, and we need to catch this guy before he hurts any more young women. But it's difficult and made even tougher by women like Miss Leigh. She wants our help, but she doesn't want what we're offering. And besides, I'm not sure if she has got the full number. So, you talked to her. What did you think of her?'

'I don't have a view on whether or not I like her?' Cecelia began with uncertainty as to what this police officer was asking. 'I could see she was nervous.'

'Did you believe her story about nearly being raped?'

'I supposed I must have done because I wouldn't be here otherwise. Why? Don't you believe her?'

Pushing herself away from her desk, Detective Travis crossed to her filing cabinet.

'I go by my gut feelings. You've got to have instincts

when you're in this line of work; otherwise, you're struggling blind.'

The drawer rumbled open while agile fingers lightly ran over the top of the files as Detective Travis selected a slim, buff, blue file with noticeably short, well-groomed nails. Returning to her desk, she placed the files without undue ceremony in front of Cecelia.

'Since you have been honest with me, I'll be honest with you. These are my personal files on the victims, the ones where I put my own private thoughts. They may not be the correct views, but I work it from my angle,' said Detective Travis, poking her fingernail on a large blown-up picture of Mary Ann Leigh in a glamor pose. 'She does not fit the profile of the other victims. This woman says smart. She's got her act together, and she knows where she's going. I don't see anything about her which says she is intimidated. She is not a victim; she is a user. She is so different from the other victims.'

There was no argument about this. Mary Ann stood out proud against the natural prey.

'I've been studying the other victims, and they all have a certain personality,' continued Travis, shuffling through the photographs quickly in reference. 'Look. They're shy, gentle women beloved by their families—see their expressions. These women,' Travis turned to point at three other faces now pinned on her crazy board behind her head. 'Look at their eyes; they wouldn't hurt a fly. Cruelty is not in their vocabulary. They don't want to be known for anything special. They don't want to join the police force, army, be film stars or models, or anything else which draws attention to themselves. They don't even want to be lawyers or teachers. They just want to be wives and mothers like a large proportion of American women.'

She was right. Cecelia's eyes flickered over each murdered girl's portrait, and what was pictured in their eyes was hope and trust.

'These women want to please their men and stay home and have babies. They are the women these days that so-called feminists would be ashamed of. Good people, and if I say it myself, boring people. But this is the life they have chosen, and we have to respect them and take care of them. Yet these are the women this monster is killing.' She poked the photograph again. 'Miss Mary Ann Leigh is not one of these poor women.'

'Perhaps the Slasher got the wrong woman. He made a mistake,' suggested Cecelia.

'Maybe. Who knows?' she nodded. 'I just don't get a good feeling about her. I feel she is lying. And why do I think that?' She came over to Mary Ann's photograph, still lying on the desk, with some notes attached to her picture. 'Because Miss Mary Ann Leigh is a failed actress,' the detective read her notes. 'She has been given several opportunities to make it big. Look here, she was a hostess in a game show, delivering numbers in a tight pink dress. Hardly the most glamorous way to start your stardom. But now you are going to tell me there have been many actresses who have had a worse beginning, like Marilyn Monroe, for example. She was in a toothpaste ad.'

'But Mary Ann is still young. She's only twenty-seven. Too young to be dispatched to the shelf.'

'True. But she is pretty and blonde, and she should have made it big by now with her opportunities. And I shall tell you why?'

'Why?'

'She has that goddamn attitude like she thinks the world owes her something, and no matter what you do for her, it will never be good enough. Me, I never complain. I just keep my head down and get on with it. That sort of woman is a living whiner, a crybaby. She's always craving attention, and this is another one of those occasions—stealing the limelight of those dead women. I don't think you can go much lower than that.'

3

Back home with a cup of coffee, Cecelia went through the interview with a new set of references. Detective Travis had taken a great dislike to Mary Ann. A time waster and dishonest, and very, very vain. Perhaps she was right. But no one should judge a book by its cover. Tender in sentiment and ultra-feminine, the only consequence against Mary Ann was that she was too tall. Like a child that had sprung up too quickly, she wasn't cute anymore.

'Well,' Travis had said with a sigh. 'You want to be involved, and you look trustworthy. I guess I can talk to you, but I don't want what I tell you discussed in the media. I hope I'm all right there?'

Was this a girl thing? Had she been accepted? Whatever it was, it was fun. And a great honor which Cecelia was well aware of. It didn't surprise Cecelia that Detective Travis liked to work independently with her strong opinions and maverick attitudes.

To be included in police operations was something Cecelia had dreamed about. But now on to business. Clapping her hands quickly together, marking up a number one in the air, she was being taken seriously. Cecelia couldn't contain her excitement.

The first murder took place just over a year ago. A twenty-one-year-old, Marcia Davis had left her house for the church she attended most days, and every Sunday, she was very pious. One of her pleasures was to decorate the church with flowers. People had described her as the angel of the church. She had served as an altar girl and a member of the choir. Never spoke ill of anyone and best describe as a mortal saint. Why would anyone want to hunt, rape, and murder her? Whoever he was, he was wicked.

'Too good to be true,' Detective Travis had muttered under her breath. 'But these people exist, poor child. She was found two days later, strangled, and dumped by Lake Munday. Raped brutally. Although there wasn't any semen or DNA, the Slasher had been scrupulously clean. Poor kid. She didn't die straight away; the murderer didn't want her to. Killed by a true sadist. He painted her lips with bright red lipstick while in her hands was a note saying, of all the weird things, *she says she loves me.*'

'Poor child.'

'Yes, you can say that again. It's a wonder he left her dressed or partly. She was found by someone walking their dog in the early morning.'

Writing these notes down, Cecelia recalled the interview. A thoughtful silence had fallen between these two. Detective Travis picked up the second picture with more of her detailed notes.

'There was no evidence; the assailant just vanished. We hoped this murder was a one-off, but nearly a year to the day of Marcia Davis's murder, another woman disappeared and reappeared two days later at the other side of Lake

Munday. It was then we knew we had a serial killer. Same M.O. Jennifer Sawyer was discovered with red lips and with the same enigmatic note. *She says she loves me.* But this time, he had completely undressed her. He had become more aggressive.'

'You mean,' questioned Cecelia, 'the murderer told her to say she loved him before he killed her?'

'Can't rule that out. It might be vanity, or it might be pure torture, but I believe he promised her she would live if she said she loved him.'

'But that's wicked.'

'Yes. Whenever I come across something like this, I look at my fellow man and think, am I really related to you? But then I remind myself that these are the dregs of society, crippled minds with warped realities. These people get a kick out of killing. Quite honestly, I'm for the death penalty. We need it in this country, and if you've been a police officer and seen what I have seen, you would ask for it too. But that's my opinion. Some people take a more liberal stance and excuse the murderers by saying they must have been mentally ill when deciding to take another's life. Must have been mentally disturbed.' Detective Travis shook her head. 'I want to ask these do-gooders, what did the victims say when they were about to be murdered—please don't kill me, I don't want to die. Where is the murderer's mercy?'

An argument which Cecelia felt unable to join. Taking a life with another meant that this was no better than the murderer because who has the right to take another's life?

'I know what you're thinking,' said Detective Travis. She could see Cecelia's crisis. 'You want to be thought of as kind and compassionate. And that's exactly what these killers live on, your humanity. People like you are stupid and vain; you think that if you care about them, they will see the light and become like you and say, I'm sorry, I didn't mean what I did. I've changed, and it's all because of people like you. No, mam, these people never change. They've done what they've done, and they will say all the right words to you and promise they will never do anything like that again. And you're the type of person who wants to believe. But if they were to step back in time, they will do exactly the same things again.'

Cecelia shrugged. Could Detective Travis be right?

'Look at this woman here. Go on, look at her first.' She held Jennifer Sawyer's picture up. 'If you look closely, you will see in her eyes, and you will see her dreams. Cut off before she began life while her murderer, a low, vile creeping monster, lives on. And I hope when we find him, he gets the death penalty because, believe you me, he deserves it.'

Smiling out from the photograph, a young face, warm and generous, anticipated a good future. She wasn't asking for too much except to get married, have her children, and raise them in a good, honest way.

'She's a simple young woman,' said Detective Travis, looking down at the picture. 'Who belonged to a sewing group which, incidentally, was also linked to the church. And I know what you are going to say about that. That murderer must be someone who also belonged to the church. We spoke to everyone concerned within the church. But when the third murder happened two weeks later, it happened on the other side of town. A young sixteen-year-old was found, clothed and raped and dumped in Alondra Park near the pool.'

'By water,' suggested Cecelia.

'Yes, by water. But I don't know what the significance of

that is. There must be a message somewhere about why he always leaves them by water.'

Was there something biblical about leaving the girls by water as if they were about to be baptized, but lacking confidence, Cecelia's thoughts fell to the wayside? Such a pointless murder.

Summoned by a buzz, Detective Travis was then called away. Picking up the photographs and notes, Detective Travis put them away in her filing drawer.

Travis felt personally bad about what happened to those poor, unfortunate young women. Who on the verge of a new life had been cruelly cut down. It was wicked. Cecelia didn't dislike Detective Travis—quite the opposite. She admired her. Yet Travis didn't allow herself to be too affected. If she did, she would be no good at the job.

ALL THOSE PRETTY words about how strong Cecelia felt about doing right meant nothing. When it came to it, she could easily hide away and forget about these sick crimes. And she would have if she didn't have her house to pay for.

Then the landline rang as Cecelia walked through the door. At that point, she just felt like crawling into bed and pulling the covers over her. It had to be Travis. She had her telephone number.

'Hello, this is Cecelia Clark.'

'Hello, Cecelia. It's me, Mary Ann Leigh.'

'Mary Ann?' the question came as a snake on her tongue. When had she given Mary Ann her telephone number?

'Yes, I'm ringing to find out how you got on with the police. You went to the police, didn't you? I know you said you would, but I felt you might just be saying that to get away from me...'

'Yes, I went to the police.'

A sigh of pleasure. 'Oh, I am so glad. I wasn't too sure because we hardly know each other. I thought with the way I behaved, well, it would have been enough to put you off me. I've heard people say that I can be clingy. I must apologize for that. But if you've nearly been raped, you would understand—'

'There's no need to apologize; it must have been very frightening for you—'

'I felt bad behaving like I did to the police—I know he didn't actually rape me, but even so, when he touched me, I felt like a piece of meat. Did you tell the police how bad I was?'

'I think they could see for themselves.' How could she say that Detective Travis didn't believe her?

'Yes, I suppose so. It was hard to tell—I felt everyone was against me. You know how it is. Anyhow, it doesn't matter anymore about me. But it matters about the next victim; she might not be so lucky. What did the police say about the description? Were they pleased? They should be. At least my attack as meant something.'

And still in Cecelia's head was how had Mary Ann got her telephone number, because she knew she hadn't given it to her. 'They were pleased. It gave them something to work on.' Cecelia became thoughtful. 'My question to you is why didn't you tell them yourself?'

'Well, I told you the first time we met, I am afraid of men, especially after the attack.'

'They offered you a female officer for protection, but you refused. Why did you do this?'

'You sound like you're angry at me. Why have you

changed? I thought you understood. As I explained, I was in a bad way, and I was hysterical with fear—you would have been too. I can't keep on being blamed when I was a victim. What do they intend to do about it?'

'I don't know, I'm not the police, but I expect they will circulate the description...'

'While I think about it, there is another thing I remember about him, he wore glasses, and the reason I know this was because there were red marks on the side of his nose as if he had only just taken them off when he saw me. I think he might be vain. What do you think?'

'I shall relay this information to the police, probably tomorrow.'

'Very well, I suppose there is no haste about it.' A couple of seconds of silence followed. 'What are you doing now?'

'I'm going to get myself something to eat and then have an early night.' It was a small lie, but a necessary one. Mulling through Cecelia's mind grew doubts introduced by Detective Travis.

'Why don't you have something to eat with me? I have a chicken roasting in the oven right now. I can smell it from here, and it smells delicious. Roast potatoes and sugar beans with gravy and apple pie to finish. You must be hungry, and two make for good company. What do you say?'

'I'm about to get into the bath, that I just ran,' lied Cecelia, feeling that the supposed independence she had was being cleverly pulled from under her feet. 'I intend to have a good soak to get rid of the day's insults. Anyway, I've got an early start tomorrow, so I need to have an early night...'

'Oh, please don't abandon me, please. Don't leave me on my own. When I said goodbye to you at the door, I saw a man outside—he looked just like the Slasher. He must have found out where I live, and now he's stalking me. I think he wants to finish the job off; you know, kill me because I got away from him.'

'Are you sure it's the same man? It could be just your fears.' This was appalling. But what did Mary Ann expect her to do?

'Perhaps. Well, yes, perhaps you're right,' Mary Ann sounded scared.

'Look, the best people equipped to deal with him are the police. Get in touch with the police and tell them what you thought you saw.'

'Yes, you're right. It's probably my imagination. I'm scaring myself silly. Don't worry. I'll be all right.'

Don't worry; what a thing to say. It meant she didn't care and that one day it could happen to her. Who will she turn to if the same thing happens to her?

'You'll be all right. I can't imagine he's tracked you down. You're just scared.'

'Yes, you are right. I'm being silly.'

What was that? Someone was crying. Mary Ann was crying.

'Okay, I'll come over. I'll be there in an hour.'

'You will. Oh, Cecelia, I am so grateful.'

Emotional blackmail, Cecelia left her house resentfully. One day, she will tell these manipulating people to take a hike. Already in a bad mood, the world had taken on a darker shade of black. Instead of friendly faces, people had turned ugly. She had just turned off Verona Street, cutting through Amalia Avenue, when a man came running, while screaming towards her.

'Run,' he shouted, staring at Cecelia. 'Run. She's coming to get you—she'll kill you.' His eyes were flaring red and impassioned with madness, his vest dirty and sweaty while his face streamed rivulets of sweat. 'You've got to run. Run.' He had to make her understand because she was just standing and staring at him. Catching hold of her tight shoulders, he shook her. 'You don't want to die, do you?'

'But who am I running away from? I don't see anyone.' His wildness struck her.

'She's the devil. If she catches you, she will eat you.' He stopped, listened, and then stared ahead. He saw the devil running. Pushing Cecelia out of his way, the devil was chasing him. 'She's been killing people and eating them when they've done no wrong. Don't say I didn't warn you.'

And then he ran off, leaving some of his fear behind. Mad, he couldn't help it, while something of what he prophesied slipped into Cecelia's wellbeing and unnerved her. What was that all about?

4

'Thank you, thank you so much for coming.'

Vermillion lips spoke quickly, unreal, almost as if they were unconnected to Mary Ann. She was already at the door before Cecelia knocked.

'I feel so much better now you're here.'

Yes, thought Cecelia, passing by the two red arcs and into the warm smell of cooking. If you're going to do something, do it with a good heart, so stop being annoyed. But she was afraid now. Still, it was a relief to be where food was cooking and a house that was warm and homely. Time to relax and not mention the strange happenings. The air smelled balmy, with home-cooked food, a golden chicken no doubt cooked steadily with vegetables.

'Do you want to have a peek at the chicken? It's nearly done. It's a recipe I picked up when I was in England. They are really into roast dinners with something like dumplings; they call it Yorkshire pudding. I do it for myself when I feel down and the entire kit and caboodle.' Mary Ann opened the door to her kitchen, where a waft of hot, pungent air came forcefully through.

I did not come here for a meal; I came here because your emotional blackmail made me feel bad.

'Have a look,' said Mary Ann, bending down to open the oven door. 'Doesn't it look great?'

'Yes, it looks good.' But I'm not hungry. I don't intend to stay here for long, but to have a look around for the Slasher. He won't be here, of course, but I'm doing this to reassure you. These thoughts swelled around Cecelia's mind.

'I thought we could have a drink first.'

'No, no drink for me.'

'Why not?' Mary Ann's eyes were weapons of distress, and now she felt insulted.

'Because I'm not staying. As I tried to explain to you over the phone, I have an early start in the morning, and I need to get to bed early.'

'Honestly, I won't keep you for long.' Cocking her head to one side, Mary Ann was trying to figure this one out. 'Okay, so just have a little drink with me. You will find it relaxes you.'

One drink, and only one glass, and ten minutes at the most.

'Tell me about yourself,' demanded Mary Ann, taking the seat opposite, and then she pulled it towards Cecelia to claim her full attention.

Resentfully sipping the wine, a bigger glass than Mary Ann had promised, Cecelia wondered again why she was here, especially after the run in with the madman. Was this in the name of research so she could get that story she needed? Did she want the story or not? Yes, she did. Filtering another mouthful, she looked around the room. This room was so neat and tidy.

'There's not much to tell.' Cecelia frowned. There was a long evening ahead of her.

Not much to tell. How amusing Cecelia could be, and all the while, Mary Ann was making plans for the rest of their evening. Two people who lived on their own. Wasn't it fortunate they had met? Cecelia could be the friend she never had. Didn't Cecelia feel this way, also? No, Cecelia stared. She did not.

'I'll have a look around the area before I go,' said Cecelia, still holding her glass.

'Oh, you don't need to worry about that for now. I don't feel as frightened as I did. I feel safe with you here.'

'I will have a look before I go home,' warned Cecelia.

'Of course, but after you have eaten with me. You can't possibly come and visit without having something to eat first. That would be ridiculous. I won't allow it. Okay? So, no arguments. You are my guest, and I look after my guests. I can't bear to think of you returning home on an empty stomach; it's so offensive. Otherwise, why are you here?'

'Because you asked me to—' exploded Cecelia.

'Oh yes, you're right,' Mary Ann frowned while looking down at the floor. 'But now you are here, won't you have something to eat? Just a little. I'm not being unkind, but the truth is, you have no one to run home to, have you? You're just like me, alone.'

'I have a cat,' Cecelia lied.

'A cat? Well.' She pursed her lips. And nothing more would be said about this obvious lie.

A purge of embarrassment flushed Cecelia's cheeks, but she was remaining stubborn. 'Yes, a cat. A lonely person's friend. I understand,'

A smile of disappointment crossed Mary Ann's face.

'I suppose I shouldn't try to keep you by offering you my friendship. I should let you go.' A twist of bitterness that was sudden and ruthless. 'But let me remind you, Cecelia, it was you that came to me and not the other way around.' Bitter furrows crisscrossed her forehead. 'It's you who wants this story—that's what you told me. You led me on to believe that this came with friendship. You came with flowers. What was that all about? So now you're playing hot and cold. It's unfair how people treat me. I thought you were different. I thought you were a friend?'

'I never led you on, and I told you right from the beginning that I was here for a story.' After being frightened by the madman, it felt wonderful to be angry. 'How on earth did you get my telephone number? I never gave it to you.'

'Yes, you did. Before you left the last time. Don't you remember?'

'Yes, I remember, there is nothing wrong with my memory. And now I know you're lying and cannot be trusted. And I am going.'

Cecelia saw her flowers standing tall in a vase in pride of place on the varnished wooden bureau. It made her feel strange.

'No, please don't go,'

With grasping hands, Mary Ann hadn't expected this. Groping hands grabbed hold of Cecelia's. This was enough to spook her, especially after the madman.

'Will you please take your hands off me, otherwise—' but Cecelia didn't finish what she was saying. She didn't need to because Mary Ann's hands flew from hers as if they were on fire.

'I know, I know. I'm truly sorry. I should never have done that.'

Repentant and sorry, she had been struck by Cecelia's expression of anger and was now covered in desperation.

Hands that wanted to touch Cecelia in reassurance didn't but fluttered like embers of persecution.

'I don't know what came over me, except perhaps that I'm frantic.' From here to there, she was looking all about her, searching for something she needed. 'I feel so trapped living in this house alone. You don't know how difficult it has been since the rape; even though he didn't rape me. But the intent was still there. I know I am a laughingstock at the Alondra Police Department.'

Suddenly, Mary Ann's shoulders hung pitifully down. A tall and attractive woman like that should not be reduced to this. Once again, the tatters of humiliation had hung around Cecelia's shoulders. She knew how painful it had been when others had laughed at her. Never had there been a worse moment than that. It was an experience she didn't want to come across again. It should never happen to anyone, not even to Mary Ann.

'Please, don't do this to yourself,' Cecelia gently touched the side of Mary Ann's arm. 'Shall we say that we had a difference of opinion? You've been through a bad time, and so have I in the past.'

'You have?' grateful for any kindness which Cecelia could feed her, Mary Ann's hand fell quickly to Cecelia's arm, her eyes distraught with pity.

'Yes. It happened to me a few years ago. I have never quite forgiven myself for the depths of depravity I slipped into.'

'I can't believe that anything bad could ever have happened to you. You appear so sure of yourself, as though no one could touch you.'

'Oh, I assure you,' Cecelia laughed ironically, slowly she started shaking her head. 'I made a complete fool of myself with a man.'

'With a man.' Mary Ann's eyes turned into daggers of hate. 'I, too, have had my mistakes with men, but let's not talk about that. Because I also have been humiliated.'

'Then we've both suffered,' Cecelia smiled.

'Yes, we both have shared the feeling of what it is to be ashamed.' She inhaled a deep breath of healing. 'So, now we are friends?' Cecelia hesitated reply, caused Mary Ann distinctive pain. 'I thought you cared. I don't know why I can't make friends. I don't know what is wrong with me. There must be something about me that repels people. Look at you. You're so eager to go.'

'Well,' relented Cecelia, 'I suppose I could stay for a while. But I can't stay long—'

'Of course, you can't,' Mary Ann's eyes shined. 'But for how long we have together, let's make it a good time. There's no harm in that, I'm sure,' she stood. 'I'm just going to check the dinner; I won't be a moment. You know, it's been ages since I had a meal with a friend. You'll never know how happy you've made me.'

While the evening carried along patiently, Cecelia discovered how Mary Ann got her telephone number. When she went to the bathroom, Mary Ann used this opportunity to do her own spying. A bag left on the floor is an invitation, yes? It was ready bait for the curious. So, taking out Cecelia's notebook, Mary Ann copied her telephone number, as she didn't see any harm in that. Hadn't they both been clever? Each had been curious about the other, and nothing more should be said about their equal impropriety.

Guilt sat with Cecelia while she sat in the candlelight, eating chicken and drinking wine while smiling and nodding at Mary Ann. A nice and sophisticated evening, Mary Ann kept reminding her. In the distant background and noisily galloping towards her was the sound of manipulation roaring across the prairie; this was her punishment. You've been manipulated, do you hear—manipulated.

They chatted long into the evening, and with a listening ear and an interesting face, they touched on the Slasher. Cecelia tried hard to believe that the Slasher was in the area. But why would this rapist remain in the place to finish Mary Ann off? An entirely puzzling idea. It was then she noticed that the vermillion lips were gone, cleaned off by soap and water. The evening passed respectfully.

'You are not going away without a hug,' said Mary Ann. Smiles strangled her face. 'I appreciate everything you did for me this evening. I needed a friend, and you were there for me. Now I'm going to hug you with a kiss on each side of your cheeks. I know you aren't into demonstrations of affection, but it will do you good. It certainly does me. We Americans are not into feelings despite what they say. If everyone touched each other more often, there would be a lot less violence.'

Mary Ann was correct in her assessments. Some things have to be endured, if only for the once. But would she have chosen this woman to be her friend? She thought, smiling as she walked away. No, this was not a friend Cecelia would pick because Mary Ann was alien to her in every way.

'Take care of yourself, Cecelia, and don't be a stranger. Drop in anytime—and I mean what I say.'

It was dark. She had stayed much later than expected. At this time of night, the world took on an unfamiliar face. Lights in the other houses started extinguishing as people were heading to bed. Just your typical suburban town. Every few meters, lamp posts shone guiding lights, time for the nighttime creatures. A screech owl shot out a cry, and the pellet of noise called for others to join him. Creepy.

Was there a rapist behind these bushes? No, there wasn't. Pushing her head up to see over the bushes, the panic button was ready. Now she must do what she came here for, investigate. Well-trimmed shrubs were offended by Cecelia's probes. But the relief was great, as there was no one hiding, waiting to pounce out and take his revenge. And why? Because there wasn't any rapist after Mary Ann. As Detective Travis said, Mary Ann lacked attention. And feeling rejected, she summoned up a demon. Again, Cecelia sighed. Time to go home and have that early night she had promised herself. Yes, she needed this story, but wasting time with Mary Ann wasn't going to get it. Yet, contrarily, it had been a nice evening, but if she offered to repeat it, she wouldn't accept.

At night, it always seems a long way to go home. Alondra, a sleepy old town full of cracks and creaks, but soon she would be home. Until then, she mustn't mind her active imagination.

To leave, Cecelia had to make a promise. Against her better judgment, she promised to drop in and see Mary Ann again. Oh, the bitterness of being obliged, and it was all because she needed to make money. If only she were rich. She would have been rich if she had married Peter.

Just this morning, a postcard lay waiting in her postbox with her address and nothing more. The view was of the canal Keitzersgracht off the Amstel River, with colorful, tall Dutch hatted houses fronting the waterway, tipping their heads to catch their reflections. She held the card up with amusement. Cheerfully painted and grand enough for a master painter to depict. It could only be from Peter; she didn't know who else would send her a card like this?

The loose tokens of last night's conversation were replayed. Provoking thoughts that if she was her own mistress—why was she teased to pieces by her overdeveloped conscience? When you are made to do something you don't want to do, you resent the people who make you do it. Although again, she had enjoyed the evening, yet she resented Mary Ann for pushing her into it against her will. Yet, contrarily, it's not that she disliked Mary Ann; she could be brilliant company and very flattering—how kind, clever, and even pretty Cecelia was. Even pretty, emphasized Mary Ann, noticing how reluctance Cecelia was to accept a compliment.

'Come and have a look in the mirror.'

Grabbing hold of Cecelia's hand, Mary Ann shared the reflection.

'Pretty eyes, Cecelia. And a nose that others would die for. And lips of an angel's perfect bow.'

Flattering as well as embarrassing. But then Cecelia should have her hair dressed like this in another style.

'And your dress, it's not quite you, is it?' the face was frowning and then suddenly shocked. Away flew Mary Ann's hands. 'I'm sorry,' said Mary Ann suddenly and dramatically. 'I'm being impertinent. I had no right to tell you how you should look. You are who you are, and you are special, so special to me. I don't want to lose a good friend like you.'

It was creepy. Mary Ann could be possessive in her ways. Cecelia knew she would be driven along by this strong woman's wiles if she didn't put her foot down.

Now walking along with the shadows as companions, strange monsters stretched their legs to creep out winking eyes, listening ears, and snatching hands. Cecelia stepped up her pace. Fears which lived and festered in her imagination manifested themselves. No one was out there to seize and pull her under. But if there was, she was very vulnerable. At nighttime, the whispering voice mentioned that people go missing, especially when no one is waiting for their return.

If only she had brought a knife to stab this man in the chest, but that could be dangerous as well. There is no one there, her mind repeated. It was her own breathing she could hear and fear. No one is there, so calm down. What was Peter doing in Amsterdam?

Martial arts. That was how Mary Ann saved herself. Kickboxing was a good defense, which was an idea; she would be much more confident when walking the streets. Walking along in the night and hearing each one of her footsteps hitting the sidewalk, kickboxing was a good idea.

A cab circuiting in the night. Putting her hand out, Cecelia hailed it down. Never again would she put herself in this frightening and vulnerable situation. She would wait until the Slasher was caught before she would venture out at night again. Mary Ann was at home; she was all right.

Checking around her home, Cecelia found one of the bedroom windows was left undone. The house felt cold from fear. Yet, there was no one there. No one had entered her home while she was away, but the tension was overpowering, which was why she got the carving knife from the kitchen drawer and was now stabbing the empty spaces behind the doors and under her bed.

'Come out. I know you're there.' She stopped. What was she doing? Going slightly crazy. Being with Mary Ann had made her see life a little skew-whiff. Leave Mary Ann alone. Go get yourself another story, as this story was not panning out the way you thought it would. Things were so different when she was Clara—as if she would heed her own advice.

THE MORNING CAME with a shock of sunshine. Cecelia had forgotten to close her curtains, and now the sunlight was blinding her. Sitting up quickly, trying to fan her eyes, she grabbed hold of her alarm clock. It was okay. It was okay; she hadn't overslept. Why was she behaving like this? The last time her fears got the better of her was almost a year ago. What had she done about that? Changed her name to become someone else.

Clara, she would become Clara again. It had worked last time, which meant it could work again. Clara was the confident one who could see things clearly ahead. Ambitious and strong, and she wasn't afraid of anyone. And most of all, she wasn't afraid of herself. For now, she would have to remain as Cecelia. But as soon as she could get to it, she would legally change her name to Clara Tinder. However, changing one's name is not a simple task. It means losing all of one's history and identity. Cecelia would have to let go of her past and embrace her new name fully. But for her, it would be worth it to have a fresh start as Clara. This was something Cecelia had to do soon.

Was she unbalanced, probably? As probably this was a lifetime condition from her youth. Patterns and habits build themselves right into the matrix, but it doesn't have to be like this forever. Another program running over the top could change her life for her. But no more mind-altering medications or going to see a shrink, that's for sure. Yuk. If she was going to do her life, it had to be her way with the person she knew inside.

Mapping out her day gave a conscious handle to her reality. Go to the library and read the back issues of the local paper on the Alondra Slasher case, then check in with

Detective Travis. Reading the back news didn't shed any light on what she already knew about the murders, except for the devastating effect on the families concerned. For a man to commit so much tragedy with his wicked needs was pointless. Did he have any comprehension of the suffering he had caused?

'Is Detective Travis available?' Cecelia asked at the desk, always feeling she should confess to whatever was current at the moment. Now biting her bottom lip, she waited while the officer telephoned through. He looked up and smiled, then told her to sit and wait. How much time is spent just waiting?

After Los Angeles, this small city felt too quiet, careless, and even lazy. But living in fear was not a way to live. People are just people trying to get on with their lives. Rules are what society is made of and sticking by them for the good of everyone. A few drugs. What did it matter? It was their lives and only a problem if they took their frustration out on good people.

Out of the metropolis, life wasn't so bad, especially on a sunny afternoon. A bit of drama is what everyone needs now and again to keep life interesting. Good lives with good people. Even so, Cecelia still didn't feel like she fitted in. Too long living in the fast life.

What a relief. For less than five minutes later, Detective Travis came out to see Cecelia.

'Come on, let's go to my office,' Detective Travis smiled. It looked like good news.

And it was of sorts. They believe they might have caught the Slasher. Two nights ago, they had a tip-off from someone calling himself Mr. Vengeance, Thou Shalt be Mine, saying that he intended on striking again.

Good news? Frowned Cecelia.

'Between you and me, we have a good idea where he's living. And it wouldn't be too premature to pat ourselves on the back. We're going to get our monster.'

For some reason, Cecelia felt disappointed. Over already? Just when the excitement had started. Perhaps in this funny state of mind, Cecelia thought she would relay the good news to Mary Ann. Her telephone number was gained on callback. But good news came with a problem. No one answered. Why wasn't she answering? From what she understood, Mary Ann had become a recluse to the world, staying in because of her fears. Was she okay? Maybe the Slasher had come back to get his revenge. This meant she should visit her.

Until she reached the florist, Cecelia had forgotten about Phoebe. The exotic smells of the flower shop were wonderful, just like coming across an oasis in a concrete gray world. Behind the shop counter and singing quietly to herself, Phoebe was putting a bouquet together. Her expert hands worked quick. Sheepish now, with her tail between her legs from a promise she had made but forgotten to keep, Cecelia made herself known with a polite cough.

'Hello,' Phoebe said, selecting another bloom that was laid on the counter beside her. 'I'm in a rush. I've got several orders for a funeral, and I haven't started on them yet. It was one of the rape victims, so I'm not going to charge full price, just the value of the flowers and a little for overheads. I'm certainly not charging for my own time even though I can't really afford it, but what the heck. It's my money, and I'll do with it as I please. Would you like some more flowers?'

'Yes, I do, and this time I am going to pay for them.'

'Suit yourself, but I appreciate it. I can't carry on giving my livelihood away. Oh, don't look so worried.' Phoebe wrapped some tissue paper around the flowers. 'I can take care of myself. I like to do these things. Besides, it makes me feel good.' She shrugged. 'Who wants to be rich, anyway?' she laughed, her pretty blue-green eyes now merrily smiled. 'And another thing, what would I do with myself if I were rich? It suits me just to have enough money to do as I like and have what I want within reason.' She grinned. 'Have you ever heard of a rich Bohemian?'

Taking a towel hanging on a wall, Phoebe dried her hands. A no-nonsense moment that Cecelia found charming.

'Is this for the same friend?'

'Well, she's hardly a friend,' grimaced Cecelia.

'Okay, the same person?'

'Yes.'

'By the look on your face, I would say this is more a duty than pleasure.'

The need to tell was great. Looking about her to see if anyone was listening, Cecelia felt she could confide in Phoebe. 'I'm a journalist, and I'm writing a story on the Alondra Slasher.'

'Gosh, really? He's killed three women, you know. I'm not usually a person who is easily afraid, but this has taken hold of me. People die every day, but not usually by being murdered. These murdered women look like nice, everyday sort of people. It makes you think of getting a man just for protection,' Phoebe smiled. She had a warm, winning smile. 'Although I've had a man before, marriage is not what you think it is.'

'You were married?'

'Yes, for two years.' Phoebe bit the top of her nail. 'I was eighteen, and my parents wanted me to go to university, but

I had enough of schooling. I wanted to make money. It was a mistake, a big mistake. He was fourteen years older than me. The funny thing was, I was advised by his mother not to marry him. She told me he was abusive and that my life would be hell. And she was right. Though at the time, I thought I could change him. What an idiot. I was young, and I thought the world was beautiful, but it's not that beautiful when you're staring through two black eyes.' Phoebe stopped to reflect. 'He made my life a living hell, all right. He was possessive and convinced I was seeing other men.' She bit her bottom lip. 'And he was right. I was seeing someone else, but only after he had given me a couple of beatings.'

'How awful for you.'

'In the beginning, he was so nice to me. He promised he would always look after me—he wouldn't allow me to do any housework. I was his queen.' She smiled. 'And then that day came when this wonderful man went out to work and a monster returned. I was now a whore who deserved a good beating. The first time he struck me, I couldn't believe it happened while he couldn't believe he had beaten me. We were both in shock. But that shock passed when he beat me again.'

'I could never imagine that—'

'What? That this sort of thing goes on?' Phoebe smiled wryly. 'Yes, me too. It always happens to someone else, doesn't it? Anyhow, it doesn't matter. I had to get away from him and as far as I could, which is why I am here.'

'Did you divorce him?'

'No, unfortunately, we're still married. I'm terrified of him. I'm sure he is mentally unbalanced or something. The first time I ran away, he managed to find me. I was staying with friends—he had already been to my family's home and threatened my parents.'

'Isn't there anything you can do? Tell the police or take a court order out on him.'

Phoebe smiled. 'No one and nothing can protect you. If the man you are still married to believes he can do whatever they want, he will. And with a man like that, you are nothing more than a possession.' Tilting her head to the side, she gave Cecelia a penetrating look. 'You know, I've tried for years to figure this out. What was it that made me think I was in love with him? Is there something about me that draws such hatred from another? I don't know if I can completely blame him, though; after all, I had a part in the relationship. I must have triggered something.'

'No, I disagree with that,' said Cecelia aggressively. 'I used to think that I deserved bad things. But that's allowing these people to do whatever they like to you and not having to take responsibility for their actions.'

Phoebe smiled. 'A good way of thinking, and a positive one. But I believe some people attract bad things to themselves; call it what you like, while others dream through life. This is the reason I believe in karma; I think in my previous life I must have been extremely wicked, and now I'm being punished.'

'No, absolutely not. Why do some people get all the luck? Because they believe they deserve it, and it's not because they think they are nice people. I don't know how this luck thing works, but I am trying to go for happiness, and so should you.'

'Yes, that would be nice. I have started a new life in this country, and I'm happy here, but I still know that the day will come when he finds me, and when he does, he'll put an end to me. That's why I've changed my name back to my maiden name. My husband is called Harold Hardaker. I now call myself Phoebe Howard, but I still don't feel safe. The funny thing is, he doesn't look the type of bloke who could harm a fly, yet I still have nightmares about him. Perhaps one day, these bad dreams will fade away, and Harry will find someone he can be happy with and settle down and have a family. Perhaps with someone else, he might be different.'

'You sound like you still care about him,' Cecelia was puzzled. She was really beginning to like this feisty young woman. Her openness and generosity to others were delightful. There wasn't anything about her to dislike.

'I don't hate him, if that's what you mean,' considered Phoebe. 'I fear him, of course, but there were some special moments when we married. I just don't know what happened to him.' She shook her head. 'Insecurity, I don't know, or perhaps there is a part within him which is evil. I don't know. Have you ever been married?'

'No,' Cecelia's answer was quick. 'I often considered it. There was someone I thought I loved, but he was already married. Such a shock to find this one out. I couldn't believe he was married.'

'Life,' shrugged Phoebe. 'We stumble through it blindly, trusting and hoping. Perhaps if we knew what was going to happen in the future, we would change our minds. But everyone has their own agenda, and it's not always the same as the person they are hooked up with.'

Cecelia smiled. The more she learned about Phoebe, the more she liked her; she was not too dissimilar to herself in many ways. A quick flick at her watch warned Phoebe that it was time for Cecelia to go. Time for them to get back to their lives. They stepped out of this world into another of friendship, and it was enchanting.

Taking a few references about the person Cecelia was visiting, Phoebe selected a bouquet of pink and white carnations, delicately scented and extraordinarily lovely. It suddenly seemed a shame to give them away to someone Cecelia wasn't keen on. Phoebe smiled at Cecelia when she handed the bouquet. A price was negotiated with the help of smiles. When Cecelia left, footloose on the step with the jangle of bells in her ears, Phoebe stayed near the shop door watching Cecelia go. Such a nice person, Cecelia found herself thinking. What a different way to decide where she should live when her old jalopy broke down. It was an enjoyable interlude to the day as she strolled along the sidewalk to take a yellow cab.

On her good behavior, Cecelia rang the doorbell while rehearsing what she should say.

'Why Cecelia, fancy seeing you here. What a lovely surprise,' said Mary Ann. She was wearing white gloves. 'Come on in, come in. It's such a lovely day.' Her voice was cloudy with good manners dipped in warmness. 'I've just made a jug of lemonade. I'll get you a glass. Come and sit down. I was just thinking of you. Are they for me?'

They were.

The flowers were gratefully accepted as a pleased Mary Ann followed behind, sniffing at the flower heads, petal by petal.

'I'll put them in some water. How lovely. My little home is being filled with flowers.'

Watching Mary Ann taking the flowers through to the kitchen, she noted how cheerfully she sang to herself; Cecelia was aware of this warm domesticated scene. The house was hot and permeated with the smell of fresh lavender, which filled every room with a sense of coolness.

'I've got you a glass of lemonade.' Now handing Cecelia the glass, Mary Ann took a seat opposite her. 'Now, why do I have the pleasure of your wonderful company again?' she sipped her cooled lemon.

'I tried to telephone you just over an hour ago.'

'You did. Did you telephone the right number—I've done that before.'

'It was your number; I made certain of it,' said Cecelia, gratefully sipping the chilled drink.

'Oh, how strange, I never heard it,' she smiled and sipped her drink. 'It must be just one of those things.'

'Yes.' And yet, these instincts which everyone supposes to have at certain times were running up and taking their stations. Cecelia couldn't think why, but there was something different about Mary Ann. Her breath came in heavy stages, as if she had been running. 'You sound like you are out of breath.'

'I do?' she looked surprised. 'You're right, I've just run through the house to answer the door,' and then she smiled coyly. 'Stupid, because I thought you might be the Slasher calling on me.'

'You don't need to worry about that anymore. The police are closing in on him, but that's between you and me.'

'They think they know who it is?' with surprise, Mary Ann curled up her eyebrow. 'They think they have him, and so quickly?'

'Yes, that's the police for you. Which means you don't have to worry. You will be safe now. He will be convicted and locked behind bars forever in no time. Aren't you pleased?'

'Oh yes, I am pleased.' Mary Ann frowned. 'But are you certain they've got the right person? I'm sure I saw him two nights ago. In fact, I'm convinced of it.' Puzzled and distressed, Mary Ann found displeasure in the flowers instead. Flicking at the petals, then looking at her white gloves. 'They must have the wrong man.'

'You will be asked to attend the lineup; you'll probably see him.'

'This is ridiculous,' Mary Ann muttered to herself. A foul mood was building. 'It's not him—it can't be.'

'He's owned up to it.'

'The man who tried to rape me looked like Clark Gable, and by the way, he was scrambling to get away, which suggests that he valued his freedom. Oh dear, this is unbelievably distressing. It's really messed up my head—don't the police know what they are doing? Can't they get anything right?'

'Mary Ann,' Cecelia was surprised at her anger. 'Once they have him behind bars, you will be safe. Don't you see what this means? You will be able to get on with your life and do the things you should be doing, like going for auditions.'

'You know what this dreadful nightmare has done to me? I've lost all my confidence to go on stage. Even thinking about it makes me shake. I've never been like this before. I don't know what has happened or why it should happen to me. You have no idea.'

Surprised, Cecelia watched Mary Ann pacing the floor. She had expected elation, not temper.

'This last two weeks, my life has been a misery. Because I smile, you think I'm not suffering? I'm an actress, for goodness' sake. Not a doll or a toy with strings. No, I'm a mess inside. And for you to think that I can return to my life as if nothing has happened. It's impossible.' A temper was building, clenching fists, kicking furniture, and then she stopped in front of Cecelia. 'You don't seem to understand, or perhaps you don't want to acknowledge my distress. How can you appreciate how I feel when you've never been raped? You wait and see when it happens to you. Then you'll see how you feel. I can guarantee you won't be smiling.'

What a wicked thing to say. It was as if she was prophesying something like this to happen. 'Hopefully, I shall never be raped or even have it attempted to find out for myself.' Cecelia felt sick.

'Yes, I hope so too,' said Mary Ann, giving the armchair another kick.

Shaking with temper, Mary Ann left the room.

'Why did you bring me these?' her return came with a storm. Mary Ann held out the opened bouquet free from the pink tissue to Cecelia.

'Because you like flowers?' Cecelia frowned, now baffled.

'But why these?'

'I don't understand what you mean. You like dianthus, don't you?'

'Yes, I do.' Now she was staring hard at Cecelia and concentrating. 'Did you pick these yourself?'

What could she say? There was a threat to Mary Ann's question.

'Yes, I picked them.'

'No one else helped you?'

'No. What is this all about?' the flowers had been a gift and should not have produced accusations and questioning.

'You don't understand, do you?' sighed Mary Ann. Her eyes latched on Cecelia's.

'If you don't like them, I can take them from you. I can take them home or give them to someone else who will appreciate them.'

'No, no.' Mary Ann's temper had cracked across her brow. 'I was probably overreacting.' She held on to the flowers and stared into the petalled heads as if she didn't quite trust them. 'They are lovely; I just wish they had been one color instead of two.'

'When I saw these flowers, I thought these were the ones you would like. The flowers said happiness, fun, and they were meant kindly,' was there any point trying to be friendly to this person when everything you did was under criticism? It was depressing. 'I brought you flowers to cheer you up and make you feel happy.'

'It's the meaning attached to flowers, and I thought you were trying to say something to me.'

'To be happy, that's what my meaning was.' A little white lie came with a face now set in a sulk. 'You shouldn't try to interpret everything a person does, gives, or says to you. Life would be impossible. Accept it for what it is. A gift given with sincerity; I want you to be happy. I think life has been pretty tough on you.'

Mary Ann stared at Cecelia. 'You know, you really are a nice person.'

'I try my best,' Cecelia smiled as a flush of dishonesty made its way into Cecelia's cheeks. She shrugged. 'I wanted you to know that you don't have to worry about the Slasher. He's now locked up, and now it's time for you to get on with your life.'

'Only if they have the right man?'

Perplexed, Cecelia didn't know what to say to her except. 'I thought you would be pleased. So now you can get back to living—'

'So, you keep on saying,' muttered Mary Ann.

'Yes, so I keep on saying,' repeated Cecelia bitterly. This visit had been a great mistake; she wouldn't be doing this again, ever. 'And now the reason for my visit is over. I think I'll go.'

Immediately Cecelia's departure was halted by the

strong fingers clutching her wrist. 'Cecelia, I'm sorry. Do you see what I mean about my head being all over the place? Sometimes, I think I'm going mad. I have such bad dreams; I can't tell what is real and what isn't.'

Carefully trying to extract her wrist out of Mary Ann's hands. 'I am sorry about what happened to you. Truly sorry. And I am sorry that I added to your problems by bringing you pink and white carnations. I wanted to help, but I see what I'm doing is stirring up terrible memories for you.'

'I've ruined it, haven't I? I've made you hate me.'

'No, you haven't made me hate you,' she lied. 'I am a journalist; this is what I do. I talk to people to find out the facts of a story. There should be no personal feelings attached except considerations towards each other.'

'Yes, I can see now you don't like me.' Mary Ann's eyes were on Cecelia with ghastly concentration.

'Look, Mary Ann.' Cecelia took a deep breath and breathed out loudly. 'I know the attack has seriously damaged you,' said Cecelia tactfully. 'And it's only my opinion, but I think you need to see a doctor to get help.'

'I'm not mad, if that's what you are implying.'

'I didn't say you were. It's nothing to be ashamed of. I used a counselor myself once upon a time. It's nothing to be ashamed of,' smiled Cecelia gently. 'Now and again, we all need help, and you have had a rotten time. I'm surprised the police haven't suggested counseling before now. You need someone to talk to—'

'I can talk to you. I need a friend; that's all I need. You're not coming back, are you?'

'I didn't say I wasn't.' Why couldn't she say she was never coming back, and this was the end of whatever relationship Mary Ann cared to imagine they had?

'If I see a counselor and get myself sorted out, will you

still be my friend, please?' her eyes bored into Cecelia, all the while screwing their way into the soft covers of her soul, digging deep and deeper until they couldn't be pulled out. 'Please—'

Cecelia sighed a heavy sigh with the breath of the inevitable. There was no other answer to be made except yes. It was enough to satisfy Mary Ann and also the reason she allowed Cecelia to go.

5

———

Tonight was Cecelia's kickboxing class, but first, she stopped off at the florist just in time to see Phoebe bringing in the large bins of flowers. Phoebe nodded but carried on taking in her containers of flowers.

'Just closing up, you can come in for a moment if you like. How did you get on with the interview?' Phoebe asked, the daffodils swaying in their bin as she entered her shop.

Obviously Cecelia should help, and seeing a tray of potted plants, she carried them in after her. They were heavier than she thought.

'Thanks. Over here would be good. Mind you don't get yourself dirty.'

In silence, they brought in the rest of the plants.

'That was very kind of you,' Phoebe cocked her tricolored head to one side. 'Is there something you want to ask me?' she smiled again mischievously, as if she had already guessed the question.

'The flowers weren't well received. She was very upset when she saw the colors.'

A broad smile now took up the contours of Phoebe's mouth. What had she been up to?

'What does the flower's color mean?'

'It shouldn't mean anything if you like flowers. After all, it's not the flower's fault. I didn't think she would know; few people know the language of flowers.'

'It made my interview very difficult,' Cecelia frowned.

'Then she is very awkward and rude,' said Phoebe, going to the cash register to hit the no sale button.

Cecelia watched Phoebe collecting the notes, rolling them, and securing them with a rubber band before placing them into a blue suede bag and pulling the drawstrings together. There were lots of bills in that bag. Clearly, arranging and selling flowers was profitable.

'I feel like a drink,' said Phoebe, picking up the bag. 'Do you fancy joining me?'

'I'm going to my kickboxing class tonight,' said Cecelia, now concerned, her eyes boggling on the bag of money. Was she not going to the bank first?

'A nice hobby, I understand,' said Phoebe, slipping her arm through her casual jacket and tugging it over her slender shape.

'Don't you have security people to collect your money?'

'No. It's too much hassle. You have to get yourself registered, fill in forms, and answer all those questions which nosy people ask. Why do they need to know my age, and if I'm married or single, and what were my aliases?'

'Do they?'

'I don't know; I've never bothered to go down that route. I hate rules. Rules are for safe people so they know what they can do next in their lives. I make my rules up as I go along. You should do it too.' She smiled at Cecelia. For an eccentric English woman, she was very relaxed. 'Come and have a drink. I need a drink; you don't have to have alcohol, and you can tell me all about this woman. She sounds hysterical.'

'She might be having a breakdown after everything she's been through.'

Phoebe laughed. 'What I mean is, she sounds weird.'

'I don't think she's weird. You know, she's been through a great deal.' A sigh. 'She's trying to get a handle on her life. I feel sorry for her.'

'Do you?' the question came with a wicked look of clarity which said she didn't believe Cecelia. 'Do you always get yourself involved with strange people?' and then she looked down at herself and laughed. 'I guess so. Come and have a drink and some warmth in a down-to-earth bar. I love these places; they remind me so much of home.' Phoebe, now swinging her bag over her shoulder, was in a good mood. This was something she had done before.

How easy Cecelia felt maneuvering herself to go somewhere, not that she didn't want to. Her only excuse was to go home and get ready for class. With Phoebe, life kicked into excitement. To join her in a drink became, yes.

'Okay.'

'Good.'

They walked to Phoebe's favorite bar, chatting about nothing in particular. Yes, it was nice to have a friend.

'I've got to speak my mind,' Phoebe said when they got their drinks and were now sitting down.

A few people leaning on the counter, ordered something to eat and took their glasses to their tables. The place had a pleasant atmosphere. The dark varnished wood paneling and the gold of the taps with the sparkling glasses gave a feeling of grandeur. Everyone was an aristocrat. The atmosphere was jovial with all the convivial voices mumbling with chatter. Conversations were indistinguishable from one another. And yet they were the decoration of a good social get-together while the aroma of the beer became its perfume.

'This is who I am.' Phoebe had a beer in front of her, licking the froth from around her top lip. 'I am always forthcoming with my opinions. My grandfather was a Yorkshire man.'

This left Cecelia none the wiser about this personal history.

'About the two-colored carnations.' Phoebe leaned back while twisting the end of her predominately red-dyed hair around her finger. 'Quite honestly, I didn't think she would know the meaning.'

'What does it mean?' Cecelia leaned forward.

'From the Victorian era, a single-color bloom from a lover meant yes, while a striped one means, I can't be with you; in fact, it's a sign of rejection.'

'Is that all?'

'Honestly, if I were you, I would avoid this needy woman. I don't get any good vibes from her.'

'She's not so bad, though she has her problems.'

'From the little I've heard about her, I can tell she will pull you down. I don't like her. But that's your choice, though I think you should be careful.' Phoebe took another swig of her beer. Perhaps one glass was enough to make Phoebe drunk, because from time to time, Phoebe looked past Cecelia as if her eyesight weren't quite focused.

Then Phoebe jumped from one subject to another, and in the jump, directed the conversation to her age. Twenty-nine, while her monumental birthday was next year, then she would be thirty. Not a young woman anymore, so she couldn't fool around with life any longer. Phoebe scratched her neck. So far, she had a couple of affairs that fizzled out because it was probably her fault. One man was telling her what to do while the other had nothing to say about himself. He needed guidance from a strong woman. 'Or,' Phoebe grinned at Cecelia, 'a mother.' Whatever. Being with him was making her into a bully. So, it looked like she was going to remain an old maid. Have lots of cats and get into witchcraft.

To Cecelia's shocked face, Phoebe burst into laughter and said she was just teasing. She wasn't sure what she would do in the next five years, which was an odd way to feel since she had always envisaged where she would be and what she would do the following year. Now it was as if her life had been ended from that day onwards, and then she laughed again. 'What I mean is that every year, nineteen, twenty, etcetera, I could see myself being that age.' She shrugged. 'It just hasn't happened yet with me being thirty. But it will.'

Her passion, though, had to be flowers; she also had an interest in cultish rites. She read tea leaves, and she was also involved with herbs and recently about the moon and when it was the right time to plant. She firmly believed in reincarnation.

'I have been here before. I know I have, although I don't remember anything about my previous lives. It's that déjà vu feeling that I've done this before.' She pressed her finger hard on the table as in demonstration. 'We have two beings inside us. One that we are in constant contact with, we chat to all the time, asking questions and seeing what it thinks or feels. But there is the other one behind which acts like God, not interfering, but listening and waiting. When we die, we will leave this dimension and join the others. It's our vocation to gather as much information as possible in the harmony of the whole. Do you understand what I'm talking about?'

'Well, I have never thought as deeply as you on the subject.' Death was always an uncomfortable subject for Cecelia; she wasn't ready to embrace the proposed astral life.

By the end of the hour, Cecelia had made her mind up that she liked Phoebe, liked her a lot. Interesting, funny, and happy with a peculiar way of looking at life and its approach.

'Look, I'll walk you to your class,' said Phoebe, finishing her drink.

'Why don't you come in with me?' smiled Cecelia.

'I might even do that.' Again, she looked to the side of Cecelia. 'Oh, he's gone,' she nodded.

'Who's gone?'

'A man who kept looking across at us. He was good-looking, pity. I smiled at him, but he never smiled back, so he obviously wasn't interested in me. Never mind, it's his loss. Come on. We had better get you to your class.'

They walked together side by side, chatting about the films they saw and the ones they liked and disliked. But they both agreed they liked the classics. *Gone with the Wind* was Phoebe's favorite, while Cecelia said she loved those old Fred Astaire movies. The black and white dancing films, like *Top Hat*.

'Oh, I see what you are,' said Phoebe, pushing away, 'you are a dancing romantic,' and then she swung around and did a few dance steps, shuffling her feet in imitation tap. Embarrassing but fun.

It happened so quickly. Violently, the bag on Phoebe's arm was wrenched off, as a figure in black pushed her to the side after punching her hard. She fell backward and hit her head on the cement post.

Two, three seconds of dizzying activity that didn't register with Cecelia. Another dance routine? What was Phoebe doing? A man had run in and grabbed a reluctant dance with Phoebe. But then she heard Phoebe yell when she tumbled.

'My bag,' Phoebe cried, her mouth bleeding from the strike. 'He's got my bag.'

Looking toward the running man, the bag from Phoebe's arm was missing. In one frame of thought, the connection was made. This wasn't a dance; it was an assault.

'No, Cecelia, don't chase after him,' cried out Phoebe, still crumpled on the ground. 'It's only money.'

'But it's everything you've got,' looking back, the gray-coated man had disappeared into the shadows of unkempt shrubbery.

'Don't. Please don't. You could lose your life. Can you give me a hand to get up?'

'Are you all right?' Cecelia asked while bending down to take hold of Phoebe's hand. Her eyes were searching for any damage.

'A bit shook up, that's all. I think I might have to take up kickboxing as well to protect myself. I never saw that coming,' struggled Phoebe, getting onto her feet.

'The whole point of it was to catch us by surprise and unprepared.' Cecelia placed her hand under Phoebe's arm to haul her up when she noticed the crimson-colored stream running down Phoebe's cheek. 'Oh my god, Phoebe, you're bleeding.'

'I thought I might be. My head took quite a whack, although I'm not as dense as I look.' She tried to laugh, but her mouth was bleeding as well. Phoebe spat out a tooth into her palm. She stared at it as if it shouldn't be there. 'He punched out one of my teeth. Oh knickers, tell me how I look?' Phoebe opened her mouth for inspection.

A bloodied gap made a mischief of Phoebe's mouth. The multi-colored eccentric but still pretty face was now misshaped. She had lost one of her incisors.

'Does it look bad?' asked Phoebe, watching Cecelia's face intensely.

Impractical to lie and yet seemingly unkind to tell the truth.

'You should see a doctor. I'll get us a cab and take you to the emergency room. After that, we go to the police.'

'And what can they do for me? Tell me off for being foolish and making me worse than I already do. No, I'm going to have to write that money off. It's painful, but that's how life goes.'

'We should report it to the police. It's your duty.'

Bemused, Phoebe looked at Cecelia, questioning. Cecelia smiled.

'I'll come with you.'

'What about your class?'

'My class can wait. If I don't come with you, I have this feeling you will just go home and go to bed. You don't look right.' Staring at Phoebe's unfocused eyes, Phoebe was definitely dazed.

'There's nothing they can do for me. The thief took my money, and I won't get it back. That's life. You know, I had this feeling we were being watched this evening,' she shrugged. 'But I'm always prone to feel like that.'

'I'm getting a cab.' There weren't going to be any more arguments.

After refusing to go to the hospital, they went to the police station. Phoebe's details were taken. But just like she predicted, there was nothing they could do for her. Irresponsible to be walking around with so much money, Phoebe agreed. She had been a fool.

Details of the thief were provided in quick darts of information by Phoebe and then by Cecelia. He was about five feet ten, dark hair, slightly wavy, and dark eyes, probably brown, but they were behind dark glasses, so this was a guess. A mask covered half of his face like a Bandito had dismissed the true lines of his nose and mouth. White and strong. They judged he was in his late twenties to early forties. Again, this was still guesswork. Smart for a thief, he didn't wear jeans but the pants of a suit. A quick profile of a nondescriptive was added to the register.

'I've reported the theft, and now I'm going home,' said Phoebe, leaving the station.

'It's unwise for you to be on your own tonight. I'll stay with you?'

'Well, it would have been more of a shock if I had to spend a night in the hospital. I don't have health insurance because I'm self-employed, and besides, I'm never ill, and if I'm ill, I just mix up a few herbal concoctions for myself.'

'You can't be on your own. I wish you would take up my offer.'

The English are presumed to be reasonable, but Phoebe was far from that; she was stubborn. If it was money Phoebe was worried about, there was always the free hospital. No, absolutely not, but thank you. How could anyone be this difficult? Cecelia sighed, exasperated and annoyed, but Phoebe wouldn't be moved.

'I will be okay, I can assure you,' said Phoebe, suddenly feeling brave. Or was it just independence?

'Then, just humor me. I'm worried about you. I won't sleep tonight from worrying about you.'

'Look, there's no reason for you to be worried about me —you hardly know me. I've been stupid and foolish, and for that, I've lost one of my teeth. I've got to get on with my life, as you have with yours.'

'I'm staying with you whether you like it or not.'

It was hard for Phoebe to admit that she was grateful for Cecelia's company. She accepted the offer and acknowledged that she did not feel too well; she was not exactly sick but nauseous, so food or drink would be out of the question. Taking a couple of painkillers and putting on her nightclothes, Phoebe went to bed, her head raised by extra pillows.

Sitting in a chair by the side of Phoebe's bed, Cecelia kept an eye on her. It was not a comfortable night, but worrying about a friend was even more uncomfortable. Cecelia chose to spend her night in a chair in the sitting position with a blanket; it took some getting used to. First, though, she had tried out her first aid on Phoebe, pinching the gash together and holding it for five minutes to stop the bleeding. A couple of bandages across the wound had held the ruptured flesh together. The wound was clean and only needed sterilizing. Phoebe was going to survive. Maybe there wasn't any need for Cecelia to stay the night, but she would be happier if she did, if only for her own peace of mind.

In the morning and over the worst of the shock, Phoebe had a headache. She had slept, but it had been fitful. She was also eager to get back to her flowers.

Busy with a full-time patient, Cecelia had looked on the web about what to do for concussion. The main practical advice was that Phoebe should rest. Not a simple task for this independent English patient who thrived on doing her own thing and being her own person, especially with her flower business. Unfortunately, there was no one else to take over the reins.

This meant Cecelia would have to put her life on hold to help this eccentric woman out. Caring for Phoebe didn't stop, even when it interfered with her life. Besides, there wasn't much going on right now, anyway. The Slasher had been caught, not that it was her problem. But whatever Cecelia felt towards the murders was overrun by her need to keep an eye on her new friend.

'I will do the best I can for you,' said Cecelia, feeling the bravery of a martyr. 'I will help you get through this by being your hands and strength until I feel you can take care of yourself, but for now, you must rest.'

'But why are you doing this for me?' Phoebe frowned; her face was ghastly white. 'We hardly know each other.'

'It doesn't matter how little we know each other. I've made my decision,' said Cecelia, breathing in deeply, suddenly aware that she was changing. Inside, she was feeling different, as if walls of thoughts and opinions which had been vaunted and set in her mind forever were being pushed to the side. Growing and becoming different was good and something to embrace. She was moving towards being a person she could admire and, more importantly, someone she could live with. A person who had gone to war and found herself to be a warrior capable of sacrifice. 'I am staying with you and looking after you. You don't have anyone else who can do that for you.'

'But how can I ever repay you?'

'How can I ever repay you?' smiled Cecelia to Phoebe's puzzled face. 'I must explain that by you being ill, it's allowed me to find out about myself. Like an actor needs an audience, we are both in the show. Now, do you understand?'

'Yes, I do,' Phoebe returned Cecelia's smile. 'I've always found help unbelievably difficult to accept.'

A week passed before Cecelia judged Phoebe was well enough to work. Sitting on a comfortable chair taken from her small apartment above the shop, she looked tiny, yet spirited. Although it wasn't cold, two blankets lay over her knees on Cecelia's insistence. A strangely auspicious time for both was made to happen through a mugger.

Not used to having anything to do with flowers or any other growing plants, Cecelia found herself using her hands differently and thriving, wholeheartedly enjoying the multi-colors of flora. Its powers of healing were great. The slight depression which always overshadowed her eyes was almost forgotten. Looking after flowers and handling and greeting customers was so different from the other world she lived in. It brought with it a different kind of calm temperament. Being around petals and greenery made people on meeting, kinder and friendlier, especially when they carried a bouquet away with them. Proving nature's healing power.

While Cecelia took charge of the shop, carrying and selling, Phoebe arranged the flowers and the ordering. Some plants and flowers Phoebe ordered from Columbia and Ecuador, while the bulk came from homegrown sellers. Every day at six in the morning, the fresh deliveries arrived.

New deliveries had to be sorted straight away. The bottoms snipped and then submerged into water to prevent air bubbles from forming. Phoebe crushed aspirins to extend the life of the flowers. Aspirin helped to prevent bacteria from forming, while sugar provided the food the plants needed.

In the evening, they ate and chatted together about their lives and where they had been. For Cecelia, that was almost nowhere. On her own, from the age of eighteen, Phoebe had already traveled much of the world before she married. And here, at last, was the country where she wanted to stay.

'But what of your own country?' asked Cecelia, feeling she could never leave her home and move to an alien culture.

'Yes, I will always love England, but to me, England is my childhood, the place which nurtured me. I felt as soon as I arrived here that this was home.'

This was the first evening Cecelia permitted Phoebe to have a drink of wine. Relaxed now with her glass, Phoebe took stock of her life and how fortunate she had been. After being injured and ill, recovery was enjoyable, and the afterglow of this made the world wonderful.

'You must get on with your life,' said Phoebe, sipping her wine thoughtfully. 'You've been too good and helpful; I'm almost inclined to offer you a partnership.'

'To be honest, I thought about the flower business myself since helping out here. I've really enjoyed it.'

'So, why don't you join me? You clearly enjoy working with flowers; I see it in you. You look relaxed, and you get on well with people.'

'Yes,' Cecelia was dreaming. 'This was a surprise to me; I've always thought myself to be antisocial.' She shrugged. 'Not fitting in, if you understand what I mean.'

'Weren't you the one who believed in going for happiness?'

Cecelia grinned.

'Well, come and join me and be my partner. As a team, we get on well.'

It seemed like a super idea, and all she had to do was say yes. But in that instance, doubt cautioned, and Cecelia wavered. To be happy was too good to be true, and yet why not? But perhaps not just yet? Changing her career when she had only just been accepted as a writer was unrealistic and not practical. She would come with debts and no investments. That's what she told herself, but it was also the commitment of coming with a new identity.

'Let me write this story first and get it out of the way, and then, yes, I'll be a florist with you.'

'And I will tell you all about plants and flowers. It will be wonderful.'

'I hope so.'

'Cecelia, don't give in to your doubts. I want to be happy. It took me a couple of years to learn not to fear the future, and you mustn't either.'

6

———————

That night, returning home, Cecelia heard screaming from deep back in the darkness. Police sirens filled the night over towards the Alondra Police Department. A hungry feeling carried foreboding that all was not well in Alondra. A virus of fear spread rabidly through the pit of Cecelia's stomach, poison eking through her blood and traveling to her heart. While the jeering of angry voices was frightening, people were angry and refusing to be silenced.

Yesterday, the bodies of two young girls had been found, sisters of twelve and thirteen. A murderer had taken the two girls when they left school. How he managed to do it was a mystery. He took them in broad daylight with everyone looking. Grace and Ava were walking home together. People had noticed them but not suspecting these two would be the next victims. There were no signs of strangers. If there were, people would have been alerted. But nevertheless, it happened. He left them naked and horribly mutilated to be found two days later by a dog walker. Was this the work of the Alondra Slasher?

'God have mercy,' Cecelia muttered to herself as she turned to pass the station.

Fear was boiling and now traveled in the air, gathered from the sense of helplessness and drifting towards violence. Someone had to do something to stop this maniac from taking what he wanted. A growing crowd was coming towards her. A dark mass all lit up with torches. There's power in large numbers; it was daunting. Cecelia was almost inclined to cross herself and pray to a silent God. The trudge of war armed with demands was coming closer.

'We want John Wanton,' shouted the advancing mob. Moving like a black wave of threats in the dark, arms shaking, burning torches, threatening violence and anger by the minute as more and more people joined them. A new danger was alight in Alondra. A septic boil had been lanced, and the pus was weeping out while the wings of justice were trying to staunch it. These two extremes were coming quickly together.

'We want John Wanton,' again the call mulled with nerves and laughter.

It had to be stopped. The beating blades of a helicopter throbbed through the sky overhead, circling while a bull-horn found its voice to give strict orders.

'Desist and return home. Nothing will be done to you if you go home quietly.'

A police car screamed around the corner, filling the road with panic and trepidation. Terror was putting flesh on in the darkening skies. If these people didn't break up and return to their homes, there would be consequences.

The mob must have been several hundred strong; the police department wouldn't stand a chance if this mass of people erupted into violence. There would be bloodshed.

Every sinew, every nerve, was reacting. Cecelia's flesh

tingled hot with what to do and where to go. And yet, this crowd did not look mad. They were not out of their heads with anger. They had decided to carry out justice their way. An inevitability of taking back control produced calmness between this unity of feeling. In a way, it was understandable. A man allowed himself to do anything he pleased with their young women. He had to be punished, and now. An eye for an eye was their demand.

'Bring John Wanton out,' called out someone from the crowd. 'We don't want anyone else except him. Give him to us, and we will let everyone else go.'

'Return home,' ordered the detective in charge. 'If you attack the police, you will force us to take action.'

Voices from the crowd shouted and booed. But they would not leave until they had their man.

'You would protect a murderer? You leave us no choice,' another voice from the wall of people cried out. 'We will not leave without him. It's justice we have come for, and that's what we want.'

'He has not been tried yet, and he won't be by you.' Detective Travis's voice came from the sky. The officer on board the helicopter. 'We don't know for certain whether he's guilty or not.'

'Then give him to us, and we'll make that decision for you.' For the first time, nervous laughter quickened through the crowd.

'Don't you understand what you're doing?' it was Travis again. 'We have to carry out our investigation before justice can be served. If we don't have justice, no one will be safe.' The helicopter was doing a circuit, aware that they might also be a target for someone's frustration.

'I tell you what,' cried out someone who also spoke through a bullhorn. 'You leave the station unlocked and go home. Then you won't have to do anything, and then the justice of the people will be carried out.'

'We can't do that,' said Detective Travis, speaking through her bullhorn as she looked down at the crowd from her open door. 'We need you to stop now and return home. We understand your anger and pain, but we can't allow you to kill a person who hasn't been tried. Now go home and sleep it off.'

Three cars dashed and swerved, their screeching tires bringing them to a swift halt just before the progressing crowd. A barricade across the road, feet away in front of the still moving crowd, and waited. Several officers rushed out from their vehicles, rifles loaded and held in aim. Was there going to be another death today? Had the grim reaper not finished scything?

A child, understanding the tension, began crying. Men with rifles and in protective vests with trigger fingers twitching, waiting for the order to shoot.

At that moment, the world looked as if it was going mad. On one side was the mass of injured humanity, angry and feeling it was targeted with every fault of injustice, while the other side was ready to take aim and fire. This side that had sworn to protect those who could not defend themselves was about to attack. A deadly game was about to happen while the police protected a man who needed hanging. This was a strange and frightening world to witness, especially by the light of torches burning fiercely in the hands of the outraged.

This mass of people formed such a strange body, seamlessly joining together as a crowd of arms, heads, and legs. The dinosaur of life. And now it stood waiting.

'Oh hell,' said Detective Travis. Concern had dipped into her voice. 'Get me down, for God's sake. Put me down now.'

Was it the electric fear being beaten up by the throbbing of the helicopter turning around like a coward running off? Did the crowd, in their temper and outrage, believe they had won the victory that would leave them empty? The craft's hovering that had ripped up the dust of the day now took empty drink cans, noisily rattling them along the sidewalk, bumping, cracking, and snapping. Gunshots, it sounded like gunshots. Someone screamed. The crowd moved forward, and the sky, which once had been dark, was now shot with bullets. Fireworks on Copacabana Beach.

Then everything stopped. It happened so quickly. One man was dead, and several wounded. The crowd cried to itself while the hitmen stood still to attention. The protesters showed no fear.

'You traitors,' a voice cried out from the crowd. 'How can you live with yourselves? You would prefer to protect a raping murderer instead of defending us. May God have mercy on your souls.'

Someone had called the emergency services as two ambulances came screaming hysterically along the road. Such madness was going on that no one understood what was happening. Cecelia watched on, tightened with disbelief, standing to the side, flickered by the burning lights. This was a night to be remembered and an event to record. While the ambulance men ran to the injured, the crowds fell in different stages of shock. Cecelia took out her notebook and began recording the details. Life was going on about her while she listed the events for history.

Detective Travis was now making her way through the crowd, which stood unmoved and unyielding, showed no emotion. Five young women had been butchered for this man's appetite, some of them only children. It wasn't right that he should be protected when these children were starved of their rights.

Detective Patts was seen cutting through the dark to stride over to the standing officers, who shivered like beaten dogs while waiting for instructions. This was not a good day for them. It did not ennoble them. They were not going to receive awards for their actions. Today, they had killed innocence to protect evil. It was a day that would haunt them for the rest of their lives. It would come to be known as *The Day of Reckoning.*

'What the hell went on here?' yelled Detective Travis in her protective vest. She was moving towards Patts, ignoring the angry body of fury.

'Someone shouted out *fire* at will,' began Patts, frowning at Travis; he wanted to defuse the situation, but the way she was handling it, she was stirring up a storm.

'I have it that this is an emergency. One man is dead and another dangerously ill. Who called the order to fire?' she turned to the rigid-eyed men, who believed they had done their duty when coming under attack.

'Detective Travis,' warned Patts, trying to coax this angry woman out of the way because this was not the time to hold court. 'Let's get all the evidence first after we clear this crowd.' He shook his head slowly and grimly and eyed the men before turning to Travis. 'You can't blame these men for what happened. The fuse had been lit, and it was about to go off. They were only doing what we ask them to do, protect justice.'

Turning away from Patts, Detective Travis had seen Cecelia quietly recording the fallen figures, the medics rushing to the people injured or in shock. Everyone inciting it to happen, and when it did, it came with disbelief. Any one of them could have been killed, and even the ones they loved. They had brought their children on a march for blood.

'Did you see anything?' Detective Travis's eyes were wicked with anger, the flecks of firelight inflaming her eyes, which were now raging on Cecelia.

'I'll give you my notes when I've finished,' said Cecelia unemotionally. Her voice had become the register of events while writing this small city's history.

'What did you see?'

'People on both sides were like firecrackers waiting to go off. I agree with Detective Patts that something was bound to happen. The mood was charged and strained; it was a wonder that only one person was killed.'

'You think so?'

'Don't you? Do you believe these men came out to kill? In this case, justice asked for blood—'

'This should never have happened,' said Detective Patts, turning away, hating what had occurred. 'Why couldn't people have just gone home when they were told to? What good has come out of this?'

'I don't know.'

Cecelia watched the now soberer crowd, people hugging each other, many crying. Their anger had been fed; they had climbed a steep hill, but they hadn't found that welcoming place on the other side.

'Perhaps the only good to have come out of it is honor. I believe you should be proud of these men who stood up for justice. Anarchy has just been defeated—you can't protect these people who expect to be given what they want because they are upset,' said Patts.

'There is only one problem with that,' Detective Travis had listened to his impassioned speech.

Quickly, Cecelia turned to Travis, her eyes as big as her worries.

'I don't believe the man we have in custody is the murderer.' Like Detective Patts, Detective Travis was also shaking her head. 'This has been a bad day. If the mob had got through those doors and taken that man, many people could have been charged with murder. This entire case has been a mess.' She walked off, leaving Cecelia in deep thought.

If this was so, then the Slasher was still out there in the night waiting for his next victim. Perhaps Mary Ann had been right.

Most of the people were now making their way home. No one was being charged with anything. A wise decision had been made to allow them to go home and lick their wounds. It would never be tried again. But for the police, there would be an investigation of who shot who and why. This was going to have to be proved to the satisfaction of the coroner.

7

T he smell of gunfire left the world strangely empty. And in its vacuum crept those thoughts of an active mind. The world did not feel as safe as it used to be.

Like some enchanted dream and sleeping soundly, Cecelia, at last, awoke. The world had changed and gone with predictability. She had fallen into the madness of threats and possibilities. When had the world become so menacing? Like the sorcerer in the story of Aladdin selling his wares, new lamps for old, the world of old and tried values had now been thrown away for a box of rules given to those who claimed their new pots of rights. Everyone had rights these days. They jingled and jarred against the old trades. Where could these new practices and rough rules fit in? Nowhere. There are only so many rights to go around in a society of values. So, throw in the old rules for new rules to see if they work. A new society in the making will show how fashionable they are.

Does that mean people have to think differently and be different? Clip their wings in acknowledgment. We have a new family to accommodate. We must change, and nothing can remain the same. Perhaps old rules should be kicked into the dust every hundred years or so to go forward and not back. And is it possible for everyone to live under these new rules with no threat to their safety and sense of unfairness—It would be interesting to see if that was possible?

Cecelia hailed her cab, got into it, and slamming the door. When the car pulled off and at that incredible moment, her mind taxed her with those unthinkable scenarios. A stranger's car. Was he the Slasher?

Looking at the back of his head, Cecelia traced her ideas. Supposing he was the murderer. Would she get home safely? Bartering her life for the desire to get home in comfort. Trust, she had to trust this stranger to take her home for a few dollars.

And she, watching the road ahead of him, was he trusting her as much as she had to trust him? Did he trust she wouldn't stab him in the back and rob him of his day's takings?

Distrust had crept into the car when Cecelia stepped in.

Just as she opened her door, Cecelia could hear the telephone ringing, pouring out its bells, calling around the house for someone to answer.

'I'm just coming, hang on, hang on, already,' she closed the door quickly behind her and dropped her bags in the hallway. Cecelia hurried across the room. Hand hovering about to dip and grab when the ringing stopped. She sighed in exasperation. It was probably Phoebe to see if she got home, okay? She would give her a buzz when she sorted herself out. It was good to be home after such a strange evening. Just before she left the scene of violence and fear, struggling to understand what had happened. A woman had screamed, crying that the monster was still living, and she had been one a woman he had attempted to rape but had got away.

It changed the mob's mood, which had accepted defeat, licking its wounds, wondering what had happened. Art Perry, Jo Young, and Scott Rogers decided they would fulfill their thwarted mission. The guns they carried, which were only meant to threaten and show, were now in their hands. Three brave and defiant men stood shoulder to shoulder, strong boulders of outrage and gaining momentum. Their courage gathering strength as people moved out of their paths when seeing the guns in their hands. Tonight, someone else was going to die. Solomon's law, a tooth for a tooth.

It was the hunter's instinct to smell danger. The fifteen marksmen keeping their station had seen the three-man mutiny. Hackles stood; the smell of revenge howled in the night. This was the time to finish their job. Fingers wet from anticipation gripped the black metal and quivered.

'What's going on?' said Detective Patts, coming across to the huntsman. He had heard and sniffed the scent, and there was a kill ready to be claimed. Scanning the skyline, three of the horsemen were coming out of the smoke. No one else must die tonight; death had been fed, but not silenced. 'Everyone, keep your barrels down.' Worried now, Patts sensed the world hoping for peace.

But all three sets of eyes pierced with hatred were shot with survival. They were ready and untamed.

Art Perry lifted his gun to take out one of this line of men. Which one should he take? His barrel traversed along the line of his hatred.

'Art Perry,' cried out Detective Patts while running in front of the men. 'Put your gun down. All of you, put your guns down. There will be no more deaths today.'

The explosive sound of a gun echoed in his ears as he felt the thud of a bullet hitting his body. Detective Patts fell to the ground, his face now crumbling. He held out his hands to hold on to his life, but he was falling. It was that shock on his face that said no, this could not be happening. He thought he could defuse anger, but vanity proved him wrong. His life had compacted and was stolen while his eyes closed to the world.

No one realized what had happened for those lingering seconds until Art Perry threw his gun down and turned to run. He had hit the wrong man. Even though his weapon had discharged, he never meant to hit anyone. Now there was blood running onto the tarmac. He ran in fear.

The two other men who had stood by his side felt the weight of their guns and dropped them.

Cecelia was shocked by what had happened, but with the cold eye of an observer, she found herself still writing down how life was going on for these people.

'Someone get a medic,' ordered Detective Travis, as she ran towards her fallen colleague with her face set in arid determination. Her eyes quickly ran over Detective Patts to assess the damage done. She pulled off her body armor and fell to her knees. 'It'll be okay, Dan, you'll be fine,' she took off her jacket and wound it into a pillow to place beneath his head. 'Just stay with us, William. We're going to get you to the hospital. You are going to be just fine.'

Footsteps from behind with bags were running to the fallen officer. Two, then three medics fell to the scene, checking Patts' reactions and treating where he had been wounded.

Travis was in the way now, stepping back, her lips whispering prayers for a man she admired. For nearly four years, she and Patts had worked alongside each other. He had been the one who smoothed her way, knowing that if she ever had any problems, she could always go to him. Detective Patts was a good man, a friend, and a father figure to them all. This man could not die.

'Get those three men,' shouted Detective Travis, reclaiming order out of the chaos. 'I want them in cuffs and locked up now. Come on, men; move it.'

Cecelia had written that the world had gone into slow motion. Everyone seemed to belong to a different timeline. If it had not been such a tragedy, it could have been described as a comic. People started running into one another. Several people were arrested, and many more from the remaining crowd had their names taken. The police were going to do this properly from now on. If this police officer died, then they were going to pay.

Cecelia arrived home intact, yet her mind was fractured with these awful memories of the evening. When death arrives, it comes with nothing to bargain with or anyone to trade places with. It's yours, and yours alone. But who can it take if the person it had come for is already dead? It looks around, and it's not fussy. And those eyes had stared at her first before turning away. One day, those eyes would remain on her. She had tried to get these images out of her head while she got herself a small glass of brandy. It was only now she shook.

Now, with the brandy in her hand, Cecelia went to see who had called. But the telephone rang again and was heralding her need to answer it.

'Phoebe,' Cecelia said when she picked up the receiver. 'I'm home now.'

'I am glad.' But it was not Phoebe who answered. It was Mary Ann.

'Mary Ann,' Cecelia threw her hand to her lips. For the

last few days, she had forgotten about this woman. Again, that feeling of guilt smothered her. She had neglected this woman. 'How are you?'

'How are you?' she spoke these words as if it was an insinuation. 'I have been worried about you. I've been ringing you every day. I thought something had happened to you. You promised to let me know how you are, but you've obviously forgotten about me.'

'I've been busy—you know I'm a journalist?'

'But that isn't an excuse for bad manners. When someone says they are going to call you, you expect them to do so. As I explained before, I was worried about you. I know you don't have anyone else in your life. You are like me, all alone and friendless.'

Hit by accusations, they popped in Cecelia's ears, hitting her face and asking for something she could not give, at least not to her, her friendship.

'But you are not on your own, are you? Not anymore. You have a male friend, don't you?' again, it was a struggle to find the right defenses. 'I thought he was looking after you—'

'Oh, you mean William. I look after myself. And yes, he is good to me, and I know he will make me happy. But he isn't everything in my life. I am still entitled to have friends. You are still important in my life. I care a lot about you, Cecelia, and William knows this; he is not jealous of you. You will like him when you meet him. But first, tell me where you have been. This is not a safe world for anyone.'

'I've been away getting the story on the victims.' So why did she have to explain anything to Mary Ann?

'You mean you have been out of town?' she was surprised. Her voice suggested that she didn't believe Cecelia.

'Yes. These are the things that a journalist has to do.'

'Like you interviewed me?'

'I suppose so.'

'And did you take flowers this time?' her voice was smiling.

'No, not this time. I didn't think the interview called for it.'

'You mean, I was special.'

'Why are you asking me all these questions? Don't you believe me?'

'Oh, I'm sorry, Cecelia. I didn't mean my concerns to come across as an inquisition. You are, of course, free to do as you like and go where you want. I was just worried about you. Where was it you went?'

'Did you ring up just to check up on me? Because if you did, I don't like it. I find it stifling.'

'You are right, you are absolutely right, but it's been such a bad time for me. I'm on my own all the time, and I thought I would call you. You know it's so nice to hear your voice. And you are right. I am selfish. I just don't want anything bad to happen to you. I heard what was happening on the television. Did you hear about it?'

What was this? 'Yes, I did.'

'It's very frightening. I can't believe people were taking it upon themselves to give their own justice here in Alondra. How did you hear about it, Cecelia?'

This was too much. 'I was going home when I saw it happening.'

'You were there. You mean you were out there when the riot was going on?'

'Yes, I was there.'

'Do you know how dangerous that was?'

'What are you trying to do to me, Mary Ann? Make me as fearful as you so that I won't be able to go out as well?'

'You're right. It's my neurosis coming out again. How you must hate me?'

'No, no, I don't hate you,' now Cecelia was frowning. Everything had to be redirected back to Mary Ann because if she wasn't involved somehow in the conversation, she didn't exist.

'Oh, please, Cecelia, don't be angry at me. I can't help the way I am. You don't have to live with me, but I do. I can't just walk away from me. Please forgive me, please.'

Staring ahead, the certainty of Mary Ann's self-indulgence denied Cecelia from having any interest in her own life. Again, it reminded her of her mother, Tina, the what-about-me person. And yet again, Cecelia knew how she would be.

'It's okay; I'm not angry at you. You haven't done anything wrong. There is no need for you to cry.' It had become a rehearsed platitude.

'Cecelia, you are so good to me when I don't deserve it. I'm so lucky and grateful you came to visit me that day. You are such a special person to me. So, you were in Alondra then?'

'Why do you ask?' Cecelia's back tightened at the question.

'No reason. I thought if you were, you could have visited me.'

What was it about Mary Ann's voice, which was so annoying? She used her well-trained reed with effect, the innocent high tone stung by the accusation. Almost whining, but not quite. And then the sting in the tail wheedling through. You neglected me. How could you?

'Even if I were in Alondra, it wouldn't have mattered. I work, Mary Ann; you should realize this by now.'

'Of course, I know you work. I know how important your job is to you, as I understand that I'm not important in your life and that I care more for you than you do for me. But that's how it is, isn't it? I accept all of that. I just thought if you were passing, you could have come in and spared a couple of minutes with me. But I know you are hunting down the rapist all on your own—'

'Mary Ann, I said nothing of the—'

'No, you're right. It's me again overreacting. Oh, Cecelia, do you think I'm losing it?' the moan of crying was being produced. 'No wonder you don't like me. I've never been the same since the attack. I'm imagining all sorts of strange things that he might be waiting in the house for me some-where, and now I'm terrified of going around my house—what is happening to me, Cecelia? Why am I behaving like this? I feel like I'm losing control, and I'm terrified.'

'Mary Ann,' Cecelia stopped her in the middle of her tirade. 'Why don't you take up that offer from the police? You can have a female officer come and stay with you. I should imagine the offer is still open.'

'Do you never listen to me? Haven't I told you not just once, but at least three times? I don't want a stranger moving into my house, snooping around, and taking notes, recording everything I do and say. I can't believe how insen-sitive you've become when you know you're the only person I can tolerate. Why can't you come and move in with me for a little while until I feel better? I don't think it's not too much to ask. If the tables were turned, I would do it for you. I'm sure you've done that to help others in the past.'

'What I do with my time is my business, Mary Ann. I don't have to account to you about anything. If you telephone me just to make me feel bad, then we should end this telephone call—'

'Don't you see what I mean?' again, the sound of tears had started. Such an effective weapon. 'I'm coming apart—this is not me; you should know this is not me. And please don't say that I should have a female police officer come and stay with me—I can't do it. I just can't do it. My mind won't take it. Won't you please just move in with me, if only for a few days? Please, Cecelia, don't say anything yet. Just consider it. Just consider helping me out, and I will be good, I promise you. No, don't say anything yet. All that I ask is that you keep it in your mind.'

On the other end of the phone, Cecelia was shaking her head. No, no, no. You are trying to trap me.

'You will be free to do whatever you want. You can come and go as you please, and no questions will be asked,' carried on Mary Ann, planning out Cecelia's life and future for her with her needy and hopeful voice. It was suffocating.

'I will do all the cooking. You can eat whatever and whenever you want. I believe I am well versed in the type of food you eat. I have paid great attention to everything you say and dislike—'

'Mary Ann—'

'No, please don't say anything yet. Just listen to me. It's an idea and a chance, and it will work if you think about it, Cecelia. Just listen, Cecelia, and think about what I'm saying, don't give me an answer right now. Think about it, please. Just do that for me. And if you decide you don't want to take up my offer, I will understand. What I ask from you, for now, is that you just consider it. Please. Just say you will consider it?'

'I will consider it, Mary Ann,' said Cecelia, ending the call, already knowing what her answer will be. But for the meantime, she had stolen herself some more time. Some time to spend on finding a good excuse for why she couldn't stay with her. But the walls were closing in on her to make that choice of giving over a week of her life; it was impossible. It was exhausting. This woman was tiring her out, yet she still felt beholden to her. Shaking her head after taking a few deep breaths, Cecelia telephoned Phoebe.

'I heard the news about Alondra; I saw it was live on television. Are you all right?' asked Phoebe. 'It must have been frightening for you.'

'Yes, I'm okay, but you don't expect this sort of thing to happen here.' Cecelia was thinking things over. The last conversation was still playing on her head. A big woman like Mary Ann should be able to handle herself. There was no reason for her to be afraid, as there was no reason she should feel responsible for this tall, angular woman, whose beautiful speaking voice ran circles around her.

'Detective James Patts, the Detective you spoke of with great affection, is in a critical condition. He took a bullet near his heart, but he should make a full recovery. A brave man, risking himself to protect his men.' Then she paused in reflection. 'I think He deserves the Los Angeles Police Medal for Valor.' continued Phoebe.

'He deserves it, all right? So, is he pulling through? When I saw him fall, everything went silent. No one could believe that a good man like James Patts would be shot. It was one of those dreadful world-shattering moments when you know that everything from now on will be different.'

'Oh, you poor girl, it must have been difficult for you,' said Phoebe. 'There were many photographs of him through the years, all attributing him as being a good and fair man. It's the type of news which is broadcasted all over the world. Such a good man. What are you going to do now?'

'I'm actually so shattered, I don't know what to do with myself.'

'Yes, I can imagine. Get yourself a hot drink, have a bath, and go to bed?'

'Yes, I think I will. Thank you for telling me about Detective Patts. I'll call you tomorrow to see how you are?'

'No, Cecelia, you've done enough for me. One of my regulars came by a couple of hours ago, just after you left. She said she had gone past my shop earlier and saw you working while I was sitting there. She reckoned something must have happened to me.'

'That was kind of her to stop by.'

'Yes, it was. I felt spoiled. She would have stopped by then, but she had a dental appointment. So, there's no need to worry about me. I have some good friends around here.'

Warmed by the idea, Cecelia smiled. There are many good people in Alondra who are eclipsed by a few undesirables.

8

Returning to her project, the first people Cecelia intended to interview were Marcia Davis's family. They lived on the other side of Alondra, just on the edge of Alondra and Rosand. Recently, Mrs. Davis had suffered a stroke and become bedridden and blind. But the family held onto their faith, which kept them together. Two weeks after the death of their daughter, they moved.

A dog inside immediately began barking when Cecelia rang the bell. Laying alongside the yapping, the grip of waiting pulled on Cecelia's muscles and bones. The door was wrenched open to the disturber of their peace. A man of average height and indeterminable age with straight, pushed-back gray hair stood staring at Cecelia.

'Hello,' smiled Cecelia, holding out her hand. 'My name is Cecelia Clark, and I am a journalist. I wondered if you would talk to me about what happened to your daughter.'

As usual, her hand was left untouched while a pair of watery blue eyes scrutinized her defensively, as if she were another one of those enemies from without. It struck

Cecelia with horror to understand that Mr. Davis had been crying.

'Who is it, Arnie?' a voice cried out from a room at the back. Mr. Davis turned to look from where the voice came.

And then the door crashed open hard, and out came a young mixed-breed dog, bounding and jumping with enthusiasm. An eager and wet, cold nose pushed up Cecelia's skirt. Get down, stop it doggie—please.

'You're all right, miss,' said Mr. Davis, nodding to Cecelia as he ran his long fingers through the dog's coarse, thick hair. 'If you weren't, Scamp would be at your throat by now. You had better come in then.'

Around her legs, Scamp's rusty-colored fur twisted its way before running off back to its mistress. His tail wagging confidently.

'Arnie, who is it?'

'Just coming, mother,' said Mr. Davis, closing the door carefully behind Cecelia. 'You've got to be introduced to Mrs. Davis before you do anything else. Here Scamp,' Mr. Davis bent down, holding his fingers to the responding and excited mutt. 'Take the visitor to mother. You had better watch that tail. When Scamp gets excited, his tail is a lethal weapon.'

It was not a cold welcome, but neither was it a warm one. The inevitable, well, you had better come in, came from Mr. Davis with that awful summons of dried-out grief. There was nothing that could be done to them which hadn't already been done.

Passing into the veiled gray light with the stale smell of warmth provided a barrier for the house as if cold were its fearful enemy. It was unnaturally warm while April was still waiting outside. Filling her nose, the heated smell of medicine and sickness also came winding in like a wafer to see who this unknown visitor was.

'Go on, in there—' pointed Mr. Davis.

The parted door was lit with a bright light that stung the eyes to make it known that anyone who entered the room was on display. An enormous bed was in the middle of the room, covered with blankets and piled high with pillows for a woman whose eyes were wide open but blind to the world.

'Arnie, is it a woman? She smells like a woman. Am I right? Is it a woman? What is she like?' her voice was creakily unreal, as though it had been left in the oven and dried out.

'Yes, mother. It's a woman.'

'Yes, I guessed so. Tell me what she's like? You need to be my eyes now.' The small, shriveled up woman, an energetic spirit dancing in the covers, wanted instant satisfaction. 'Is she pretty?'

'Let me tell you about her before you go on making up your mind.'

'Well, get on with it then.'

Appraised by Mr. Davis's eyes as he went up and down Cecelia's body, it was intrusive and uncomfortable but had to be endured if she wanted the interview.

'I would say she is somewhere between five feet two and five feet four.'

'And—'

'I'm getting to it,' nodded Mr. Davis to his blind wife. 'She has long brown hair, a little wavy but not too curled, and it reaches just beneath her shoulders. She has real pale skin and I would say—'

Scamp came across and with his nose, again lifting Cecelia's skirt, his wet nose roaming up her legs. A trophy to be examined to see if they caught themselves a good one.

'Her nose is straight and good; her lips are not too big and pouty, but not too thin either, or by the looks of her,' he stood back. 'I would say she has never had any work done on her. She is not one of your glamorous types and pretty plain, too.'

A flush as heavy as her embarrassment rushed into Cecelia's cheeks.

'She is not and never will be as pretty as you, mother,' said Mr. Davis, nodding gently at the woman in the bed.

The woman in the bed was a scarecrow whose once blonde hair had turned yellow, and when she opened her mouth, there were only half of her teeth left. And now, so skinny, her flesh was hanging from her body. About to say how insulted she felt when Cecelia looked at Mr. Davis, staring at his wife. It was that pure expression of love. If he saw his wife as beautiful after all they had been through, then she was beautiful. His love for her made her beautiful.

'Pleased to meet you,' said Cecelia, coming forward. 'And I want to express how sorry—'

An iron clasp was gripped around her arm, and the face of wrath stared into Cecelia's eyes.

'What's that she's saying, Arnie?' squawked the little woman in bed.

'She thought she might have awakened you—'

'Wakened me,' she chuckled. 'I might be blind, but I'm not dead yet. So why are you here, child?'

Cecelia glanced at Mr. Davis, and his warning eyes were upon her. And then he nodded and again as he looked at his wife.

'She's just come from John Hopkins hospital; haven't you Miss Clark, you know, she's got a message from our daughter Marcia to let us know how well she is doing. Isn't that right, Miss Clark?'

What was he talking about? His daughter was dead. Then that awful realization hit her. Mrs. Davis knew nothing about the murder. Quickly, Cecelia nodded.

'From our Marcia, tell me, girl, what did our daughter say?' a little of sparkling life rejoined this woman to her earthly host. 'Is she enjoying herself in the hospital? Well, I knew there wasn't anything that Marcia couldn't do. Such an angel of a daughter. You will never get anyone as wonderful as our dear Marcia. She will make a wonderful doctor.'

'She takes after her mother,' said Cecelia, trying to play the same game. A quick, answerable look from Mr. Davis confirmed she had given the correct response.

'So, go on, what did she have to say?' beat Mrs. Davis.

'That she is sorry she hasn't been home for a while, but she has been given a student's place rather later in the year. She was made the exception. Such a wonderful opportunity, but they could see her genius. And now she is proving herself by studying to catch up.'

Mrs. Davis, smiling, leaned back into her pillows. 'You tell Marcia the next time you see her not to worry. We are both thinking of her, and she is doing what she thinks is right. Don't we have a fine daughter, Arnie? Are you not as proud of her as I am?'

'Oh yes, mother. I am so proud of her, but it's you she takes after, not me. God gave you all the good qualities.'

In her laughter, a cough built up strength and broke into spasms of distress.

'Time we should leave, mother,' said Mr. Davis, touching Cecelia gently.

'Give her something to drink and eat. Make her welcome,' said Mrs. Davis between fits of coughing. 'You'll have to forgive me. I haven't been well. One day when I get better, I will visit Marcia myself.'

Mr. Davis opened the door and ushered Cecelia out before returning to his wife.

Outside, Cecelia's discomfort was intense. Was it right to keep Mrs. Davis in the dark about her daughter's murder when she had nearly and clumsily broken the unwanted news to her?

'Go into the kitchen,' Mr. Davis said, pushing Cecelia in the direction. 'I'll give you a cup of coffee, and then we will talk. I won't be five minutes. I just need to see to my wife.'

She had walked into two people's life bringing her thoughtless needs and insensitive reasons to them. This day, life trod stupidly on gentle people. When had she become one of them? An intruder in their lives. But in the silence of the oppressed, Cecelia could hear Mr. Davis talking to his wife, cooing her down with pretty words, the sort of things all women would like to hear.

'Drink this, my darling. I told you that our Marcia would always do well. We will visit her in Baltimore—we'll find the money; don't you worry about it. We'll take the plane and surprise her. But perhaps not this year; give her a chance to get herself establish and by next summer—Well, sleep my darling, I need to look after our guest.'

She should not be here; she was that flame in a paper house, and with just one word, she could destroy their lives. The smell of living had its roots in death.

It was a kitchen that had lost heart feeding the people. A mug was resting on the draining board, waiting to shrug off the debris of water. Beside it lay some hospital equipment. A thermometer sat in a measuring cup while a kidney basin contained a swab to clean a dried-out mouth. A kettle sat dirty and unloved, waiting to be filled. Suddenly Cecelia saw a soluble reason for her intrusion by making herself useful. The kettle needed filling with water to start the process, the old stove needed pushing into igniting. Mr. Davis arrived at that moment when the flames took life.

'I see you've made yourself at home,' a slight smile almost glimmered from some dormant appreciation. He stood for two, three seconds as if he did not know what to do next. Winking away the sadness, he was determined to be strong.

Cecelia smiled self-consciously in return. This house was steeped in heavy sadness, and it was as if happiness had forgotten its way and stayed outside. At times like this, Cecelia wondered if she should carry on in journalism. But people are people, and everyone has their story to tell, and if she didn't, their lives would be lost to history and be unaccountable.

'Sit down,' Mr. Davis said, nodding towards a chair, his mouth grim and set in disappointment and ready for more unhappiness. 'And I'll make you some coffee. Do you take sugar?'

'Yes, please, two.'

'Two,' he said, smiling as if this finding her taste for sugar funny. 'Same as our Marcia.' and then he shrugged again as the inevitable grief came pouring back.

She had come here for an interview, but for the life of her, Cecelia didn't know if she could go through with it. It would be like performing an operation with no anesthetic or painkillers when this man had already suffered enough.

'Well, you've seen my wife.' He was spooning coffee into two mugs with his back to Cecelia. Deep in his thoughts, he was already stirring the cup with no water.

'Yes, I'm sorry,' she muttered to herself. She now deeply regretted she had stirred up more misery.

'And you must have figured that she doesn't know anything about Marcia?'

'Yes,' Cecelia whispered again under her breath.

'And she can't know about her,' he said. Looking up, he caught Cecelia's eyes again. 'It would kill her if she did. Marcia was everything to her, as she was to me. We had two children, a boy and a girl. Three years ago, our son was taken from us. He was stabbed for no reason except that he was in the wrong place at the wrong time. Rodin was a good boy, one of the best. He never took drugs. There was no reason for him to take them, but he was killed by someone for money for their fix.'

'I'm sorry,' muttered Cecelia, wishing now profusely that she had never come.

'Two children, we lost two children. We thought we were lucky when God gave us a son. He would have been thirty-seven now if he had been alive. Our Marcia would have been twenty. We didn't think we could have any more, and then our little girl came along.' He smiled. 'After seven miscarriages, Marcia was God's little miracle for us, and we thanked Him. But what I didn't bank on was that our blessings would be taken away.'

Overwhelmed by Mr. Davis's huge grief, Cecelia again wished she had never entered this house of remembrance.

'After we lost our son three years ago, Mary took all her grief inside. I should have realized what was happening to her, but I didn't. I lost my son, my only son, for nothing. It was so pointless. A person gets angry and believes they have the right to take away someone else's life to get what they want. Have these people no ethics, no values? Are they not taught to care for other people's lives as they would their own?'

He stared at Cecelia. Did he expect her to answer him? She had no answers for him except to write his story. That was the only way she could give him his justice, to shout out at the outrage. He shook his head again and returned to his story.

'The murderer is serving time now for how long, I don't know. It doesn't matter to me anymore.' The kettle rattling on the hob reminded Mr. Davis of where he was. Without letting it boil, he took the kettle and poured the heated water into the mugs. 'You need a lot of energy to be angry and take revenge, but that all fell to the side when we lost our Marcia. The grief, you see, nearly killed my Mary. She had a fit, and you can see what is left of her now. If you could have seen Mary when we married.' His hand went to his eyes. 'This is all my fault. She should have married someone else; he was wealthy, and he would have looked after her and provided for her better than me.'

Her instincts demanded that she stand and go across to Mr. Davis to put that much-needed arm of comfort around him, but that feeling, the recorder of knowledge, warned her to wait and listen; there are many ways of giving kindness, and this was one of them.

Again, Mr. Davis shook his head. 'It was always me Mary said she wanted to marry, not Richard. A man who had everything to offer. But what did I have to give?' he opened his hands in front of him. 'Look, you can see what I've got, nothing but this awful grief.'

'You gave her your love, which is more than most people have in their lives,' said Cecelia, forced to speak for this man who could not speak for himself. 'What I saw when I went into your wife's room is a fortunate woman. She has been fed well with love. Perhaps you didn't have your children for long, but God gave you these wonderful spirits. I'm not telling you to be thankful.'

His head slipped down while listening to Cecelia.

'It's important you recognized what you were given, if only for a short time.'

He turned with questioning eyes. 'That's the sort of thing Marcia would have said. Perhaps you are a messenger from our dear girl. The father said we shall hear from Marcia and that she will always be around us. And you have come as the bearer of her thoughts.'

It was not possible to be what he wanted her to be. Cecelia hadn't wanted to hear his pain and had supplied something like a tourniquet to stifle it. A few kind words were all it took.

'I heard the police believe they have caught Marcia's murderer,' started Mr. Davis.

'Yes.'

'I would like to meet him just to talk to him, just once, to know why. I would not have been able to ask that a week ago.' Mr. Davis's heavy, sad eyes once again strayed to Cecelia's face. 'I just don't understand what sort of person would ever think about taking another's life. Perhaps this man doesn't know why himself? But that doesn't seem to matter anymore. If I can keep this news from my wife, I will die happy. You can see for yourself she is not a well woman; it's just a question of time.' His eyes glistened. 'I don't want to lose her, but God would be merciful if he took her.'

Why had she imagined she would get a clinical extraction of facts with no mess, unpleasantness, or display of emotions? Maybe because this would be convenient, or simply what she hoped for. But when life gets torn on the inside, a jagged hernia is wrenched out.

'I'm really sorry I came.' Cecelia knew she had to leave. 'I feel as if I've done more harm to your grief than good.'

'Where are you going?' genuine surprise stood out from

his eyes. 'I thought you came for a story. I cannot help my anger or cover my pain.'

'Yes, I came for the story, but I am doing you harm.'

'Do you know how many people have come to visit us since we lost Marcia? Not one. No one wants to be around unhappiness. They feel it's catching. But Mary needs people. She needs the compassion and understanding of society, but except for the police and the father, no one else has come to see how we are. And do you know how lonely this makes me feel?'

Biting her bottom lip, Cecelia stood in the room like a naughty child who deserves to be told off.

'Like we are lepers.' Hard as ice, his eyes were gripping Cecelia's. 'When I leave Mary asleep to get our groceries, I enter a world alien to ours. People greet each other and laugh. They are there for today while we are still trapped in yesterday. They don't want to get personal with unhappiness —oh yes, they want to read about it in the papers or hear about it on the television news, but they don't want to meet or do anything about it. Yes, I am bitter, and sometimes, God forgives me. I have wished the same for them. But with you coming here today, admittedly, it wasn't actually pleasant, but you gave something back. You listened, you were a witness to our injustice, you said you would write about it. Well, you write about it, missy. You make people understand what we've gone through, and then they'll learn something about grief.'

His voice had become stronger while his anger, which had been kept under control, was now released.

'People must know the truth. They must come to understand that it could happen to them. We are a society. We need to care for each other. So, you will stay and write our story. You will, won't you?'

9

———

Now back home, Cecelia began writing up her notes. Mr. Davis was prepared for all of her questions; she could be as brutal as she wanted. It was not the questions which would injure him; it was indifference. He and Mary had become ghosts to the world.

But he was nervous about the interview, as he was going to talk about a private life which was meshed with fancies and ideals, and preserved in ice, never to age or become ugly. In fact, the beautiful fairytale. To get to the murderer, Mr. Davis was prepared to crack the ice. From the back of the kitchen cupboard, he took out a small bottle of bourbon and poured a healthy shot of it into his cup. Did Cecelia want any? He held the bottle up in offer. No, she did not. He stirred his cup and laid the spoon by the side. One sip and then two sips. Then he wiped the back of his hand across his mouth. Arms on the table, he cradled the mug. This drink was the genie that unlocked all dark thoughts.

As far as he knew, Marcia was still a virgin. Of course, at her age, she was interested in men. And she had an on and off relationship with Tony Hare.

Tony Hare was a new name and one which could be relevant. Cecelia underlined it.

'Marcia stopped dating him,' continued Mr. Davis, now looking into the pith of the wood as if to raise the molecules from the grain with a stare. 'When she discovered he had gotten Meghan Dark pregnant. It was a great shock for her, especially hearing those whispers, but she had to know the truth from him. Tony Hare could not deny it. As far as she was concerned, they were finished. Marcia had values, even though she cried her heart out. He asked her to forgive him. Perhaps she might have done if he hadn't tried to get totally out of the responsibility. Tony told Marcia that Meghan had tricked him.' Mr. Davis stopped talking to look into the journey of his thoughts. Was there anything he could have done to prevent this from happening?

At the side of Tony Hare's name, Cecelia had written "potential murderer?" but what about the other women?

'We spoke about Tony and the child, which was due to arrive four months later. Marcia always came to me when she had doubts or problems,' said Mr. Davis, reflecting on that past conversation. 'I asked her if she cared about him. You know it's difficult when it's about the heart. Each of us errs in life, but not everything is forgivable. In the scripture lessons, we learn to forgive the sinners. And this is something that is easier said than done, but it can be done through love. Marcia said to me, dad, I care about him. I love him. But I have no rights to loving him anymore because there's a child involved. He has to do right by Meghan, and now I must have nothing more to do with their lives.'

'Do you think she tricked him?' said Cecelia, ringing around Tony Hare's name. 'It might not be his child. She might have laid with someone else.'

'This is a mortal's battle with trust, something we all must make. Finally, I believe Marcia couldn't trust him. That's what love is about. It didn't matter about Meghan's history; the problem was Tony Hare. If he had slept only once with Meghan, it was enough for Marcia. She said that she couldn't be bound to a man who shares himself. Marcia was a good and forgiving girl, but her standards were high, and I admired her for that, but it always comes at a price.'

'What happened to Tony Hare?' Cecelia asked, swiftly looking up from her notebook. Her mind now on the idea that maybe Tony Hare was Marcia's murderer.

'He wouldn't leave Marcia alone; he was always begging her to forgive him. Following her, aping her footsteps, she didn't say anything to me, but I believe she feared him. Marcia forgave him; of course, she even told him to get on with his life and be happy. But she was firm with him when she told him she could have anything more to do with him. I believe he broke Marcia's heart. She wouldn't speak about him after that. Instead, she took to going to church regularly.'

Church, another reference which Cecelia as a likely meeting place for the murderer.

'Gone was our sweet child. Her natural joy turned to devotions. She had always been a church server, but now she was taking on extra duties, visiting people, especially the parish's sick. It gave her something good to believe in. And she was always good with her mother, reading to her, feeding her, giving Mary her medicine. And that night when she disappeared, I waited up for her, but she never came home. On that same day, when I was pacing the room, alert to any slight sounds at the front door, that knock came. I instantly knew this wasn't Marcia. I knew before I opened the door that our visitors were the police. When I opened the door, the look on their faces told me straight away that it was bad news. It was the same look that they had when they come to tell me about Rodin. I wanted to curse them and tell them to go away and never return. A tidal wave of bad tidings, and once more, I prepared myself for grief.'

Holding on to her pen, Cecelia stopped to read that expression fixed inexorably on Mr. Davis's face. This was the story she should write about. What one wicked person's fleshed desires had on other people's lives.

'Inside, I bore rivers of blood and tears. I cursed humanity and demanded the devil to destroy everyone else's love. I looked up to my God and asked why, what had I done? Am I so important that you should take your revenge out on me?' Mr. Davis shook his head, lost in comprehension. 'Do you know why He has taken out His wrath on me?'

Cecelia shook her head. A God like that is not to be trusted. She lowered her head from his stark eyes.

'But the hardest task was to come. I had to pretend to Mary that everything was fine with our Marcia. I told my darling that Marcia had got that place at the hospital, the one she had always wanted. I had to lie to my darling and tell her the world was good when it was not.'

Mr. Davis looked at Cecelia for acknowledgment.

'Do you understand anything about this because I don't? What had Marcia done to anyone? Or Rodin. Why were we punished because this is torment?' Mr. Davis looked down. 'I lied to Mary. It was the first time I had done that. I had broken one of my marriage vows to the woman I love most in the world, the woman who was also my best friend.'

'You lied to protect her,' said Cecelia, yet again coming to Mr. Davis's defense. 'It was a good lie because you didn't want to hurt her.'

'Is keeping the truth from her, doing her more harm than good?'

An earnest question that needed an answer. Not for the first time, Cecelia found she needed to reach deep inside to give Mr. Davis that necessary balm.

'I think we hold too much importance in truth.' Cecelia searched herself for something to help him. 'True truth is beautiful, but only when it doesn't harm. How many times has another type of honesty been substituted?' what was he expecting her to tell him? 'If you love someone, you do what you think is best for them, and that is the real truth.'

'Yes, you're right.'

Leaving Mr. Davis was difficult, and Cecelia felt she should visit again. But she had already made a problem like this with Mary Ann, and she didn't intend doing it again. There are some people whose loneliness is unbearable. The best way she could help was to write for him.

Spooked, this was how she felt. The interview had been a strain, and trying to disengage her feelings at the door was nigh impossible.

During in the gradually darkening evening, Cecelia felt the ghosts of the Slasher's victims catching up and following her to keep her company. A few days before Marcia was murdered, she had confessed to her father that she thought she was being followed. Mr. Davis offered to walk her to the evening mass. But no, she didn't want him leaving her mother. And mother to Marcia always came first.

Oh, how Mr. Davis regretted not accompanying her now. And then that night, just before her murder, she told her father that it was Tony Hare who had been pursuing her. She had waited for him around the corner in the dark and caught him. He told her he was in love with her and that what she was doing to him was punishing. He had pleaded with her and said he couldn't live without her in his life.

'I think,' said Mr. Davis, staring at someone who should have been standing by his side instead of this ghost. 'That she considered getting back with him. I don't know for sure. But she loved him, and I am certain about that.'

'So, what happened to Tony Hare when he found out that Marcia had been murdered?'

Could this be the man who had murdered not only Marcia but also all the other girls? These facts could be stretched to cover every possibility.

'Tony disappeared, and no one has seen him since the night he came to see me. He told me he had waited until the police had left. You understand my priority was Mary, and I didn't want Mary to know anything about it. I didn't want her seeing Tony. She never liked him or trusted him. Anyway, she thought our daughter was too good for him.'

Mr. Davis took a deep breath and wavered his eyes to the side. There was a world of regret in his breast. Again, in her notebook, Cecelia summoned those words—so difficult to find the feelings to express, and emotions are more powerful than facts. Everyday feelings are lived after accepting the facts. There were no words Cecelia could write for him, except Mr. Davis looked sad.

'When the doorbell went again,' continued Mr. Davis, another thought had accidentally dropped in. 'I thought the police had returned, and I was preparing to tell them to leave Mary and me alone. But it wasn't the police; it was Tony. He had been crying, no, not just crying, sobbing, and he was troubled. At first, it was difficult to feel any pity for him. After all, it was us who had lost our only daughter, and he could always find himself another partner. But I invited him in. He refused to enter. It was as if he were spooked about something. Bad luck, maybe? When people believe they have bad luck, they know they can pass it along. And we've had our fair share of bad luck. I said, come in, man, you've had a shock as big as ours. We need to take comfort from each other. I was in shock. Yet, it hadn't quite sunk into me that our Marcia was gone. My main concern was not to upset Mary, and I figured any more bad news would kill her.'

Listening dutifully, Cecelia entered the scene.

'We stood just inside the house,' continued Mr. Davis. 'This was the first time we had met. I often saw him sitting in his car, waiting for Marcia to leave the house for their date. A smart-looking man, I thought. No wonder she'd picked him. Yet, that day, he wouldn't sit down. He appeared nervous and frightened, and there was something bad going on in his mind. When he told me he was sorry, I asked him, for what? What was there to forgive? And then he babbled on about it would never have happened to Marcia if it wasn't for him. I didn't understand what he meant, and I still don't understand. When I tried to put my arm around him to comfort him, he backed away and told me not to touch him because he was evil and that he couldn't stop washing himself after it had happened. I was confused by his behavior; I didn't know what to do for him. He stayed for less than ten minutes. And that was the last time I saw him.'

'Did you tell the police about Tony Hare?'

'No, no. I was worried about Mary. If I told them about Tony Hare, they would be nosing around us.'

This is not your business, wrote Cecelia as a note to herself on her notepad. You are here to write the facts and not solve the case. That's up to the police. You could end up making things worse.

'What does this Tony Hare look like?' asked Cecelia, without looking up from her notes.

'Oh, he's a handsome man, all right, there's no doubt about that. All the girls were after him, but he chose Marcia. And she was flattered because she knew she wasn't a beauty. But she's a good and strong girl; she was not afraid to say what was on her mind—I'm not saying she is tactless,' and then he smiled. 'I like to think she takes after me.'

Again, Cecelia underlined, handsome.

'And was he Marcia's age?'

'No, he was a few years older and a basketball player. When he was younger, he played for the Inter-Hoops Basketball League. He was spotted by a talent scout for the Las Vegas Acres just over a year ago. The future looked good for him. At twenty-four, he could have made a great deal of money. Not that money was what Marcia was interested in, although it's always comforting.' Mr. Davis stopped to reflect. 'But then he had an injury, knee cartilage. He could still walk after the injury, but for basketball, that was out. A great shame for him, and he was, of course, disappointed and angry that life had thrown him a curveball.'

Mr. Davis spoke slowly as he thoughtfully directing his eyes to moments in time while Cecelia built her own picture. Her thoughts were not evidence, as they weren't governed by facts or proof. It was just over a year ago when Marcia Davis was found, and it coincided with Tony Hare's accident. If the murderer was still on the loose, she had to do her duty and hand in her findings as she had promised. And she would do this first thing tomorrow after she had carefully edited her piece.

The offer of bourbon would have been appreciated now, and with her head full of questions and answers, Cecelia wasn't going to get any sleep tonight unless she had a drink.

At the back of her kitchen cabinet was a bottle of vodka, and it hadn't been opened. Not her favorite drink, but any port in a storm. Now what to have with an unpleasant drink to disguise the taste? Why on earth had she bought it in the first place was a mystery when it didn't suit her taste?

Orange juice, Cecelia nearly always had some in her refrigerator, but on looking inside, her hunt was bare, but there was some grapefruit juice. This would have to do. So, adding the juice to an ample measure of vodka, Cecelia forwent the ice.

Taking a drink on an empty stomach was not the smartest thing to do, especially as she was completely reliant on her abilities. Imagine not remembering to eat, and now not feeling hungry, she began looking through her cupboards. She had heard so much pointless horror and sadness that her appetite had suffered. Why can some people eat for comfort while others like her found food in times of stress unpalatable? These were questions on which she would not sit around and pontificate. It's the way some people are. What was there in the house to crave her hunger?

Some oatmeal. Thank goodness for oatmeal. She could eat this soft and comforting food any day of the week and skip the supposedly good dinner. And the great thing about this grain is that it doesn't take hours to prepare, easy to eat, and hot and ready in less than five minutes.

From out of the microwave, and bubbling hot, was her oatmeal. Too hot to handle, Cecelia held the bowl with a kitchen towel. Now she felt her hunger. Putting the dish on the kitchen table and with a spoon in hand, Cecelia engaged with it to her mouth. It was at this point when the telephone rang.

Only a few people would ring her at this time of the day.

Detective Patts was still in hospital while Detective Travis, Cecelia, she felt sure, had better things to do. Phoebe, it could be Phoebe, but somehow, she doubted it. The only other person was Mary Ann. Staring at the ringing telephone, Cecelia waited in anticipation. Finally, instinct said it was Mary Ann.

Then the ringing stopped. It was a relief. A mouthful of hot oatmeal followed by a good mouthful of vodka. The vodka with the grapefruit was bitter and took some swallowing, but it was doable. It didn't take long to finish the oatmeal and the Vodka. Perhaps another one, yes, another would do nicely. She had been remarkably good just lately and was nearly on her way to becoming teetotal.

The measure from the second glass was not the same as the first. Again, size having command to how generous she felt, and at this point she knew she should be kind to herself.

Drowning her mouth with the alcohol, Cecelia relaxed. While her head was swimming with alcohol, her thoughts were not easily converted to sensible ideas. Why do righteous people like Mr. and Mrs. Davis become the subject of bad luck? Take Rachel Blaine, whose only acquisition was to sleep her way to the top, and whisper words of, 'your family or friends won't accept me because of my class.' And to prove her wrong, he married her. What had Rachel ever done for society? There were many others like her, dressed in money gained from pillage and robbery, and these people are deemed gods. Money always goes to money. Who was it that said that? Probably jealous that they couldn't do what these rich villains did. Nor are these people afraid to use religion for protection. Cecelia grinned. She was just at that stage of intoxication, which was delightful. It amused her to put the world to rights.

Then the telephone rang again, worming itself into the house, demanding her attention. She knew who it was going to be. Striding across the floor, Cecelia snarled as she picked up the receiver.

'Yes,' Cecelia snapped aggressively. 'What do you want?'

'Cecelia, it's me, Peter. It took a while, but I found you, so I thought I would call to see if you were all right.'

She had not heard his voice for over a year.

'Sorry, Peter, I didn't expect you to call.'

'Apparently not,' he chuckled. Strange to hear good humor coming from this dark man.

But what did he want?

'You haven't answered my question? Are you okay because you don't sound it?'

'Grouchy, I suppose. I haven't been sleeping well just lately.' Then, pushing her ear to the receiver, she listened, wondering where he was and hoping he was nowhere nearby. 'What made you call?'

'Yes, what made me call? I had a feeling I ought to. Did you get my postcards?'

'Yes, I did. You mean the one showing you were in Holland on the waterfront, Keizersgracht? Are you there now—'

'No, I'm not.'

Listening close to the crackling from the line, a cold knife wavered up and down. Was he here?

'I've just completed a bit of business for myself for a change. It then came to me I don't know a lot about you. Do you have a middle name?'

'Yes, I do.'

'Then perhaps you would like to share it with me.'

'Marie,' Cecelia bit her bottom lip.

'Marie, what a charming name.'

'Thank you. I like it better than Cecelia.'

'No, I mean, Cecelia is a lovely name, and incredibly musical, and it suits you well.'

Musical? Peter called her name musical. It was the same thing Phoebe had said. Did he know about her friendship with Phoebe because, if he did, he could be jealous?

'Where are you?' Cecelia asked quickly.

'You know it's difficult for me to discuss my business.'

'Are you in this country?'

'Suffices to say that I am not.'

What a relief, Cecelia collapsed inwardly by three inches.

'Well, it's been nice to talk to you,' said Peter in a voice that suggested he was smiling. 'We should do this another time. Take care of yourself, Cecelia Marie.'

'And you take care of yourself, Peter' even with the drink, Cecelia felt herself shaking while replacing the receiver. But what a surprise for Peter to call, and why? And such a quick conversation, if any. He was a man she would never understand. But now he knew where she was.

10

Last night, one of those freak weather storms arrived that come under the banner of climate change. The wind pushed its face against her bedroom window, banging and clattering to come in. Are these the ghosts of previous lives? Although Cecelia liked a magnificent storm, it had arrived at the wrong time. The noisy weather through the night was enough to disturb Cecelia's good night's sleep. Just on the point when she should have risen from her slumbers, Cecelia went into a deeper yet serene sleep.

On one of those late-night discussions, after the shop had closed and she and Phoebe were sitting across the table from each other, they would talk about numerous subjects. Their experiences in life, jobs they had done, and the things which interested them the most. Phoebe was always much more versed in these subjects, having traveled, seen, and read more; Cecelia's best subject to bring to the discussion was her mental health. It was littered with unhealthy parcels, some of which were funny, but most of them embarrassing. The worst being the shame of what she had said to her father. This was something of which she could never forgive herself. This frank memory was never touched on, and she had dug it deep into the dark side of her memory.

Late, late, late again. She was always late. And now angry with herself. Running around almost in circles to make up for lost time. Cecelia turned on the radio, a habit which she had picked up from Phoebe. Running naked from the shower, she put her basin of oatmeal into the microwave while getting dressed. Now in her underwear, Cecelia tried to eat it without burning her lips. Her blood pressure should be excellent from eating this cereal if it wasn't for the alcohol. And still buzzing through her head was the fact that Peter had not only rung her but found out where she was. She felt unsafe.

In the background, the too cheerful a voice kept on repeating the same words. Murder and murderer. The murderer had been murdered; it didn't make sense until Alondra was mentioned.

Scooping up the last of her oatmeal, John Wanton had been murdered by another criminal, Art Perry. How this could have happened was still being investigated. Had the murderer been placed in the same prison as John Wanton by design? The correctional officers were changing over when he was said to have made his break. He was reported to have shouted out he was going for one man.

'Now all the women and people of Alondra can sleep tonight,' he cried out before grabbing his arm and plunging a knife deep into his victim. He had killed John Wanton. It was a noble gesture, though not a just one.

With her hands to her mouth in a state of shock, Cecelia held her own prayers. What was happening in Alondra was madness. Evil had gone amok, and no one, it appeared, could contain it. Lone vigilantes now believed they had the right to judge and carried out their own sentence on others.

'I take it you heard,' said Detective Travis when Cecelia entered her office.

'Yes,' she stared, wide-eyed.

'Well, John Wanton certainly wouldn't have been standing trial even if he had owned up to the murders.'

'What do you mean?' frowned Cecelia.

'We have just found out that John Wanton was not our murderer, and Wanton or the Slasher did not kill Grace and Ava. The M.O. was not the same, and there was other evidence left at the crime scene.' She nodded. Standing up from her wooden office chair made comfortable with a soft pillow, she made her way to her filing cabinet. Taking hold of the handle, she pulled out the second drawer. This was populated with her conspiracies. Detective Travis looked up. Her neat, manicured nails ran across the tops of her folders for the black file that held the suspected murderer's details. John Wanton. Bringing it to the table, Travis sat down at her desk and pointed to the chair opposite where Cecelia was to sit.

All questions were sealed on Cecelia's lips. So, John Wanton was not the Slasher?

Taking a deep breath, Detective Travis looked up from the envelope, then sighed and shook her head slowly.

'John Wanton was just a man craving to be acknowledged. This is a sick world.'

It didn't make any sense. Why would he do that? If someone owned up to something, why couldn't it be for something good?

'Everyone thought we had our man except me,' began Detective Travis. 'I always had my doubts,' she pulled in her lips to pluck at her thoughts. 'The reason why he knew everything about the murders was because John Wanton had worked in the county mortuary. He retired last year and became bored. His ex-colleagues knew he was unhappy about his retirement, so they allowed him to come and have a quick chat. But no one knew what he was up to or why he was interested and asking certain questions. To them, he was just old John.'

'It doesn't sound credible,' muttered Cecelia, staring at Detective Travis's lips.

'It doesn't, does it? But it gets worse. When they heard he was the murderer, his colleagues were understandably shocked. But they didn't put one and one together to make two. Perhaps they felt they were guilty as well. They assumed he had come to gloat over the victims that he had murdered. Sometimes, you just wonder about the intelligence level of some people. You just hope and pray that they are on your side and not against you. Sometimes, though, it might be better if they were on the other side.'

This time when Travis shook her head and raised her shoulders, it was with experience.

'Sentimentalism is always a big mistake; it was for him. What makes a man want to confess to not just murder but rape? You're the writer, and you should know or at least invent something which can mildly come up with the answer. Are these men just fools?'

'I don't know,' said Cecelia. 'Except you passed on it just now, loneliness. Loneliness and being overlooked are accountable for a great deal of unhappiness.'

'I guess you're right, which makes these people dangerous.' She stood again and returned to the file to her drawers. 'And I can add something else to your list. Being impulsive by jumping the gun, especially when the pressure is pushed down. The law is always under a great deal of pressure to solve cases, especially when it concerns a mad murderer. This is the time when the police make mistakes by pushing the jigsaw pieces into places where they don't fit, but they'll always fit if you push hard enough.'

'So, the murderer is still at large?'

'Yes, and he has had time to rethink and set up some more victims.'

'Yes,' returned Cecelia reflectively. She had almost forgotten her notes made at the Davis's household. 'I think I might have some ideas as to who the murderer might be.'

'I'm at the bottom of my ideas, so I'm quite open to proposals for suspects, as homicide hasn't been successful until now with its investigations.'

From her brown leather briefcase, Cecelia produced the notes she had made from the Davis interview. But then she held back on her thoughts by keeping a duplicate of her original notes. A professional journalist does not disclose everything. Cecelia passed them across to Travis's waiting hand and watched as Detective Travis's eyes traveled hungrily and quickly through it.

'Interesting,' she said, placing the notes on her desk. 'So, Mr. Davis was concealing information—I should have guessed.'

'He was protecting his wife.'

'Yes, I heard about his wife.'

Had she no heart? Did Detective Travis fail to understand that Mrs. Davis was so ill and Mr. Davis was doing all he could to protect her? Wouldn't we all do that? Then Cecelia saw the strong reserve on Travis's lips. To this police officer, everyone was a potential criminal.

'This is the first time we have had a likely suspect.'

'You mean, you think Tony Hare could be the murderer?'

'I feel more sure of him than I did of John Wanton,

stupid man. Paid with his life, though.' She picked up a black folder and pushed Cecelia's notes into it.

It was just as well she had her own revised copy.

Picking up her office phone, Detective Travis rang through. 'I want a man called Tony Hare brought in for questioning. He was once a basketball player in the Inter-Hoop Basketball League.' Detective Travis stood and looked across at Cecelia; she hadn't finished with her yet. 'Do you have any more information on him? Where he might live or work?' her question was aimed accusingly at Cecelia.

'No,' she shook her head. Her eyes filling with fear of what she might have caused. She suddenly realized her views could put a man in prison because of something she was not happy about. Her opinions came with responsibilities. But isn't that what she wanted? To be taken seriously.

'No, we don't,' Travis replied. 'But what we know—hang on there.' She went to the folder again and pulled out Cecelia's notes. 'He is Caucasian; height about five feet ten, give or take an inch or two. Said to be good-looking, with dark brown hair—there may be a picture of him somewhere on the internet. I seem to remember a rookie officer was going on about basketball; I'll tell him to have a look.'

A quick reply followed.

'I'll tell him to get on to it right away. I want a picture of Tony Hare, and then we'll at least have some idea of what he looks like.' She replaced the receiver with a smile.

'It might not be him,' said Cecelia, rushing to protect herself.

'Then he won't mind being questioned,' a smart answer which made Travis smile. 'But I have a good feeling about him,' she nodded, tapping the file with something like good luck.

'What about Mary Ann?'

'What about her?'

'She gave you a description of the man who attacked her.'

'No, rephrase the sentence. It was you who gave the police a description of the supposed assailant who was thought to have attacked her.'

For some unknown reason, Detective Travis did not like Mary Ann Leigh; this knowledge was written across her face.

'Look, Miss Clark, you are not in the police force; and you have a limited knowledge of the law.' when Travis smiled this time, it was without meaning. 'But there are similar resemblances to Miss Leigh's attacker.' She tapped the file again in consideration. 'You never know, this might be the same man. The rapist might well have attacked her.'

'I believe she was attacked,' said Cecelia, almost as if sulking.

'Then you are a good and faithful friend.' Travis stared at her. 'I'm not going to beat about the bush. I don't like the woman, and I don't trust her. And I think you should stay well clear of her.'

'Why don't you trust her?'

'Instinct, and I can't give you any good reasons other than that. Now, if you don't mind Miss Clark, I have to get on with some work,' she stood. 'This case has been a mess right from the start. There are a lot of things which have to be sorted out. And John Wanton is one of them. It's not been a good day for the police force. Our jobs are hard enough without people wasting our time. Damn. I'm going to have to talk to the media about this affair.'

Already Detective Travis was at the door, eager to show Cecelia out. That drowsy smile this time said she was tired. Long days and sleepless nights were taking their toll on her.

'I want to say thank you for what you've done. Interviewing Mr. Davis has proved successful; it's given us another lead.' She shook her head. 'This case is not going well. It's more like a kaleidoscope of disasters all crashing into each other.'

Cecelia walked out of the building and into the brilliant sunshine, unhappy with how the discussion had gone. True, she was not a big fan of Mary Ann, but this did not mean she should be ignored. Sometimes Cecelia's thoughts led to unfair accusations about Detective Travis, and it was all to do with Mary Ann. Sentiments from both parties, which Cecelia was thinking about now, can be unreliable.

No one mentioned anything about James Patts and how he was. The life of crime could be fast-moving while the injured fell by the wayside. Perhaps she ought to visit him.

11

It was getting expensive, taking taxis, while the idea of driving herself lacked that necessary appeal. So much pleasanter to sit in the back seat while someone else did the driving. More time to reflect and arrange her thoughts instead of watching the road and preparing for someone else's bad driving. Tossing a coin in the air to get the best out of two of three as to Cecelia's answer on whether she should take a cab or go by car, it fell cryptically on the downside of her driving there.

Damn, since when did she ever take advice from luck? Never. Ordering a cab, Cecelia thought about that necessary interview with her bank manager for a larger overdraft. When she becomes rich, as she would one day, this bit of spending would be nothing. Cecelia flicked across her knees. Time to forget about these trifling events in her life and leave the worrying. It was time to enjoy life and move on to a more positive way of thinking. Yes, she nodded. One day, she would be rich. It was only a question of time. But when?

Detective James Patts was still in the intensive care unit.

His once large body, all six feet two of him, was lost in the hospital bed. Drained of color, he was not the man Cecelia remembered. The trappings of position, the robes of office had been stripped away, exposing his vulnerability. He looked so alien. A reminder to everyone, and especially Cecelia, of her own fallible pose. Last night was still raw in her mind.

He was asleep and dreaming his induced sterile dreams. A big man in every way. It didn't seem right for him to be reduced to this.

She had come with a small carton of white and black grapes, not knowing which he would prefer. To Cecelia, it seemed the safest bet to bring a mixed box. With swept and washed floors in this white disinfected room, a large metal bed held James Patts. His warm smile and big gruff voice were now sleeping. The white scratched metal boxes to the side of him registered his details. Summing up James Patts' humanity. Somewhere inside that lean body, a good man was sleeping.

Staring at this man of character, Cecelia wondered if she should go when he blinked his eyes open and ranged them on Cecelia.

'I've come to visit you,' Cecelia said, quickly coming towards him with one of those *too* healthy a smile. 'And I've brought you some grapes.'

There were hundreds of get-well cards around the room that suddenly came into view.

'It's good to see you,' James Patts replied, his voice weak and hardly discernible.

'They told me I should only stay with you for a short while,' Cecelia said anxiously, wanting to please but now worried.

'Take no notice of the nurses; they don't know what's

good for me. I know they mean well, but they don't know me.' Raising his eyebrows, he moved his eyes to a chair that was there for a visitor. 'Pull up the chair,' he whispered. 'It's good to have company.'

'Has anyone else been to visit you?' Cecelia asked.

'My wife, of course. She was here for the first two days. And now, she's not well herself. It was the shock.' He had some trouble focusing. 'I don't know what they've given me, but I'm out for the count most of the time.'

'Something I should imagine for the pain. Are you in pain now?'

'No. I suppose it's better to be doped up and out of it most of the time.' He smiled gently at Cecelia. 'I guess I should be thankful I'm still alive.'

Cecelia smiled back at James. Why would anyone want to kill such a nice man? 'Has anyone from the police force visited you?'

'Nope, not that I can remember, but I guess they're busy. So, tell me. What happened to Arthur Perry? I like to put in a good word for him. It wasn't his fault. He didn't mean what he did.'

'What, trying to kill you? I think you should take that personally.' James Patts had received no news of what had happened just two nights ago. Was it a good idea to tell him that Art Perry was dead? James Patts was still weak and vulnerable.

'All three of them are good people.' His warm blue-gray eyes were taking their cognizance of her. 'By the look in your eyes, I would say you know something which you're not telling me. Am I right? Come on, Cecelia; you are not doing me any favors by keeping things away from me. On the contrary, denying me information is making me stressed.'

'I don't know what to tell you.' She squirmed uncomfortably, now weighing up the merits of him knowing.

'The truth is, I'm a big boy. I might have been shot and nearly lost my life, but I'm still a police officer, and I hope a good one. My work is important to me, so tell me what's happened—it's about Art Perry, isn't it? As soon as I mentioned his name, I saw your face flinch.'

James leaned his head forward, waiting to be told, and by the way he was looking, she would not be surprised if he attempted to disconnect himself from all those hospital tubes and wires to get out of bed.

'The situation moved quickly after that night. Art Perry went to jail, and the same one as John Wanton—'

'Oh my God.'

'Yes. And somehow, he managed to get to John Wanton last night. No one knows how it happened.'

'It was something I feared when I came to my senses. Last night should never have happened. He was not an evil man.' The dark lines on his whitened face were denser not only because of his pallor but because he had lost weight. 'I've been thinking about him a great deal. Lena wouldn't tell me what had happened. She pretended she didn't know—'

'It's only just happened.'

His eyes hawked straight to Cecelia's.

'So, you know?'

'Yes.'

'Then tell me what happened?'

'Art Perry got a knife and stabbed John Wanton in the stomach and then in the throat and killed him. Then he turned the knife on himself.'

'So, he's dead as well?'

'Yes. He cried out when he turned the knife on himself

that he was doing this for all the women in Alondra, so they would never be afraid anymore.' She didn't add that it was a pointless death; James Patts would find this out later when he was stronger and able to cope with the news. What everyone wanted for James now was to carry on living.

'Oh,' James Patts shook his head. 'This was what I was afraid of, that he would try to do something like that. Such a tragedy,' his eyes blurred over with thought. 'But he wasn't alone. He was helped, of course?'

'Detective Travis has set up an investigation to find Art Perry's accomplices.'

'She will never find out who it is. I know these people. When they get it into their head what justice comprises, they slam the door tight shut. There is no way anyone will penetrate that invisible barrier.'

A police officer was making his way back to health, pulling away at the sickness to get to the man he was. Silently and unconsciously, Cecelia watched him as her finger strayed quietly to her mouth; new thoughts were drawn and busily considered.

'What is going on inside that silent head of yours?' asked James Patts. 'Something is bothering you; tell me what it is.'

Awakening to his instructions, Cecelia knew she wouldn't be able to keep her thoughts intact for long. It would help her unburden herself if he had not fallen to pieces when she gave him that last bit of news.

'I don't know what you think about Mary Ann Leigh.' This woman who had been often in her mind came out from the shadows.

'Think about her. I don't know that much about her except what was written in the case notes. I looked her up when you showed an interest in her. Detective Travis had taken on the case; I was dealing with some other case at the time. You know, you would have made a fine law officer.' He smiled proudly at Cecelia.

'Thank you,' she whispered. If she had been in the police force, she would have been different, stronger instead of flawed. But life chooses its own journeys.

'So, you want to know my opinion of her from what I've read?'

The healthy color of blood pinkened his face. He was returning to life. His eyes brightened, and his cheeks were filling. This was what his life was all about, being of service to others. Behind him and to the side were the conditions of his life. Heart stronger, blood pressure high, but not deadly. He was registering on all the beacons of health.

'Each of us has our personal opinions, and I know Detective Travis has vastly different views to mine. That's not to say she is wrong, because we will get to the truth between us. But sometimes, the truth can be a bit more difficult.' His eyes catching Cecelia's eyes smiled. 'I'm not so sure of this woman, Mary Ann. I feel she is playing with us, and I don't like it. I suspect Detective Travis doesn't like it either. Detective Travis, you will probably have found is a no-nonsense woman who thrives on facts.'

'You think Mary Ann has made it up about being raped?'

'No, I didn't say that. It's just that I can't put my finger on the game she's playing.' He watched Cecelia to see if he was on the right track. He was still working his way through the challenging storms. 'Have you met her in person?'

She nodded.

'I haven't. What do you think of her?'

'To be honest, I'm uncertain whether or not I like her. She makes me feel guilty when I don't contact her. It feels something like emotional blackmail.'

'Here is some advice, keep away from her.'

'She calls me—'

'You gave her your telephone number?'

'No, I wouldn't be so stupid as to do that.' Cecelia frowned, now more annoyed. She might be new at this game, but she wasn't stupid. 'She took my telephone number from my bag when I went to the bathroom—' Again, Cecelia reminded herself of her choice. When she went to the bathroom, she left her bag to show Mary Ann, she trusted her. Believing this would open her up about what happened.

'Cecelia, take my advice—Leave her alone. What did you say when you found she had your number? What did she do? Did she ring your home number?'

'Yes,' Cecelia lowered her head.

'Have you told Detective Travis?'

'I nearly did.' Her eyes quickly darted out to see what he was thinking.

'And—'

'Oh, this is such a bitch. How can I be angry at her when I did the same thing?'

'What do you mean?'

'I snooped around her house.'

The surprise was that James Patts burst out laughing.

'Two little girls were playing at spies. Oh, Cecelia, perhaps it was just as well you didn't join the police force; we'd always be running to get you out of trouble.'

It had taken courage and trust to bring her concerns to James Patts, and now he was laughing at her. A big sulk cleaved to her cheeks. If she gave into it now, she could never get out to face the world with confidence. And he had seen it.

'What is it now, Cecelia? Have I upset you?'

'It's nothing,' she began believing now he would find something else to laugh at her for.

But he waited for her to continue.

'It was this portrait I found in the bedroom. It's been haunting me. It's a photograph of a young black female. I would say from the picture that she was about fifteen or sixteen when it was taken.'

'And that bothers you?'

'Yes,' replied Cecelia, stopping until she was coaxed to move on.

'Do you want to tell me why?' his eyes softened, realizing she was struggling.

'I think it must be me feeling this way; you know, being sentimental and stuff. The girl is dead, and yet Mary Ann still carries a place for her. It's so sad. It shows loyalty, to still keep someone with you.' She looked up. Was he going to laugh at her again? No, he was waiting for her to continue. Pushing against the anguish, Cecelia struggled to carry on. 'I think it's this which keeps me coming back to Mary Ann to see if she is all right. She looked so strange when I told her I found the picture of Sarah, and with much regret that it hurt me to see this in her.'

'She is an actress, Cecelia.'

'Yes, I know. But I felt this was not an act. She is lonely—'

'Yes, and lonely people take advantage of others.'

'It reminded me of my father just before he killed himself.'

'Ah, I see.' James Patts leaned back into his pillows. 'Now I see where you're coming from. So, you're afraid Mary Ann will do the same?'

'Yes, I am. I don't know. I don't know what goes on in other people's heads.'

'Well, then you have a choice. You can't walk through life trying to be considerate to everyone. For most people, this is a pretty tough world. A world which means in this case, you've got to put yourself first.'

'Like you did when Art Perry shot you?'

'I'm a big man. I can take a bullet or two, but you can't.'

It was in the taxi returning home that Cecelia considered her thoughts. Again, she felt guilty for passing Tony Hare's details across. It was not so simple, neither can it be argued that it was just information. She had fingered Tony Hare with suspicion and brought him to the attention of the police as the likely murderer. And then this followed almost naturally into the interview with Mr. Davis. Someone else who she felt sorry for.

James Patts recalled Mr. Davis being overprotective of his wife after losing their child. They didn't get to do a proper interview with the couple, which was another failure. But the man's fears about his wife outweighed their investigation. A quick judgment had to be made. Mr. Davis and his wife were vulnerable; they had suffered enough. People clam up when too much pressure is applied. But Cecelia had accomplished the interview when the police had to capitulate. Well done. Perhaps they could make her an honorary police officer yet.

If this was a compliment, Cecelia felt uneasy about taking it. It smacked of patronization. And here was another time when she thought she wasn't being taken seriously.

Getting out of the cab after paying him a too bigger tip was another example of how stupid she was. She should not have bought herself the house; it was too big a commitment, and now she was forced into examining everything she did as an extension of payment. First, the cabs, and then a week of her life suspended to help Phoebe out. None of this she could afford, monetarily. This was no life worrying about how she had put herself into debt with no security. While at the same time, James Patts had turned the screw tighter by telling her she had done this by choice and willingly. Which wasn't the truth, well, not completely. Commitment has an entire world of meaning.

How angry she was with herself. Whatever she did always failed. She was stupid, stupid, stupid. Slamming the door behind her hard as she strode into the middle of the room, it was then she burst into tears. Shattered glass. Everything in her life was smashed. While in the background, she could hear her mother laughing at her. It had to get worse, didn't it? She had to be humiliated even more, as everything of worth and good was expunged of significance.

'Serves you right for thinking you're superior. Serves you right.'

A hundred tears and a hundred sobs had cost her tiredness. Curling up into a ball, she fell asleep on the sofa from exhaustion until the telephone rang. The house was eclipsed in darkness, and for those two or three seconds, she thought she was dead.

Without thinking, and still exhausted from crying, Cecelia took hold of the receiver.

'Cecelia?' the voice repeated when she didn't answer. 'Are you all right? It's me, Mary Ann.'

'Yes, I am fine, Mary Ann. What is it you want?'

'Well, I heard about the news—you know the rapist-murderer on the television. He's still on the loose. It's frightening, isn't it? I just wondered if you were okay. You don't need to say anything more than if you are well. I just wanted to see if you are home and safe.'

'Yes, I'm fine, thank you.'

There were a few seconds of silence.

'You are not okay, are you? Something has upset you. I can tell. Your voice sounds different.'

'Really, I am fine, and thank you very much for being worried about me.' Then Cecelia listened; she was curious. There was a strange echo behind Mary Ann. Was she in her bathroom?

'Do you want to talk about it? I mean, you can come and visit me, if you like. It's late, but it doesn't matter because I hardly sleep at night, especially with the Slasher still around.'

'What time is it?'

'It's just turned ten. Did I wake you?'

'I fell asleep on the sofa. I took a couple of painkillers and laid down,' she lied. Why was she always lying to Mary Ann? 'So, I'm glad you woke me. I would have slept here all night if you hadn't called.'

'There you are. I'm good for something. But you're feeling better now, aren't you? Would you like to come and visit me? You can stay the night if you want?'

'Mary Ann, I have tried to explain how busy I am.'

'Yes, I know. I'm so sorry, Cecelia. I always seem to upset you when it's far from what I want to do. I simply called to see if you were okay. I'm sorry.'

'Please don't be sorry. You're making me into a monster when I'm trying to explain how important my work is. I really need to work now, especially—well, it doesn't matter. Sometimes, you just don't want to understand my side of the story.'

'I do, I do. And it is all my fault. I know how I can get sometimes. It's been such a trying time, made worse by the argument I had with him.'

With him? Who was she talking about?

'It's my paranoia about the rapist believing that he's

stalking me and about to pounce out on me at any moment. Well, it has affected William.'

'William?'

'My boyfriend. I haven't been so nice to him—in fact, I haven't been nice to anyone just lately, have I?'

'I wouldn't put it like that.'

'Wouldn't you?' she almost laughed. 'Then, I would. As always, you are too kind to me.'

Kind? Mary Ann thinks I'm kind. Well, she's not sitting in my head and hearing my thoughts. People are usually kind in order to get something they want.

'You can be real hard on yourself, Cecelia. I have found you to be a good person.'

Cecelia could almost see Mary Ann smiling.

'I can tell this by the way you talk to me. And you've been good to me when most people have lost their patience. And I realize there is nothing harder than kindness to battle against.'

Tears bubbled up in Cecelia's eyes.

'Well, it's getting late, and just to let you know that no matter what happens, I'll always be your friend—I might have a few problems myself.' She laughed, lightly mocking herself. 'But people like us should stick together.'

This was the time for Cecelia to respond, but she was unable as tears were now rolling down her cheeks.

'Life isn't that bad, Cecelia, you should know that—we both should know it. It's been such a dreadful time, but I won't bore you again with my silly troubles.'

'How are you?' it came out quickly with no time for Cecelia to think about it.

'Me? Oh, I'm fine now. William and I have had a long talk about it. He says he is taking a month off work to come and live with me and help me get over this bad patch. I've been a bitch to him.'

'He sounds wonderfully kind.'

'Yes, he is, and tolerant,' she laughed again. 'I am so lucky to have someone like him. I wish you could have someone like William, too. It makes you feel wonderful. If you get someone like William in your life, Cecelia, don't turn him away. Don't do a number on him because you will lose him. Just some advice.'

What had happened to Mary Ann? She had changed from bad to good. It was nice to hear, and in a silly way, Cecelia found herself envying her. To have someone who could love her for herself would be something like a miracle.

'Are you still there, Cecelia? I can hear you thinking.'

'Yes, I'm still here.'

'Are you reviewing my character as something approaching likable?'

How did she know?

Laughter again from the receiver.

'I'm glad you've got someone like William. You deserve him, and he deserves you.'

'He said we are like peas in a pod. We say the same words together all the time; it's frightening. I looked in the mirror the other day and was shocked to see how alike we looked. Well, not quite. He has dark hair and sometimes a bit of stubble, which I definitely have not—it was William that pointed this out to me. But he is older than me by four years, which is a nice space between us. You must meet him one day. I know you will like him.'

This was a changed woman. Laughing and happy. William coming into her life was the best thing to happen to Mary Ann.

'Yes, I would like to meet him. He sounds like fun,' smiled Cecelia lightly. He sounded too good to be true.

'I'm going to go now before you get sick of me. Now I want you to get yourself something to eat because knowing you; you've probably not eaten. Do you have some bread in the house?'

'No, I've got oatmeal.'

'Oatmeal? Well, that's different. I can order you a pizza and have it delivered. It will be my treat.'

'No, I would sooner have oatmeal.'

'Comfort eater, I understand. But you need to eat to help you feel better, and as someone said on the silver screen, *tomorrow is another day.*'

'Yes,' said Cecelia, seeing Vivien Leigh's silhouette across the flaming skyline. 'Tomorrow is another day.'

'Wash your face and have a cup of cocoa and get yourself snuggled down in bed. Everything will be a lot better tomorrow. All you have to do is click your heels together three times and say...'

'There's no place like home.' Cecelia laughed.

'Okay, Dorothy. Now get yourself something to eat and ready for bed.' There was a pause, as though suddenly Mary Ann had lost confidence. 'I don't suppose you would like me to ring you tomorrow to find out how you are?'

'That would be nice.'

'Oh Cecelia, does this mean we're still friends?'

Cecelia smiled and shrugged. 'I don't see why not. Yes, we are.'

12

Despite everything that had happened, Cecelia slept well and out for the count. It must have been the heavy crying.

To be healthy and enjoying life is not a novelty; it happens to many people. But there is a new type of smart cell phone, PC people, with smart jobs through their newly politically correct degrees who have created their own kind of sensitivity, called indifference. Who plugs into life, which has been perfectly constructed for them. These people born at the last moment and are now sweeping the old generation away. To hell with these people, people who haven't suffered, who don't plan to either, but still busily making certain they have furnished their own nests with the best. These are the fast, new kind, the continental smart cars which whizz around town, proving how clever they are. But their days are numbered, even now.

A couple of months ago, Cecelia had experienced activity from one of these smarties. Out from the blue, she came like a sudden haze overhead, which clouded her reality like a storm that had pulled her crashing down with it. There was no good asking how she got there because she was stranded, and if she didn't do something about it, she would be stuck until the full duration passed. That could be weeks, months. Literary, she couldn't afford to wallow in this ghetto, she had to get out, and therapy was the help she ran to. She had a house and a life to pay for.

Not trusting herself to drive there, Cecelia took a handy cab. Worry about money was the least of her problems. Without her health, she wouldn't be able to do anything.

The tall woman of about twenty-five was waiting for her. Her eyes flicked over at Cecelia. Casually, she was already working out her number.

Nice dress, registered Cecelia quietly to herself. But shame about the legs. Needs to go on a little diet and work out a lot.

'If you would like to go through,' directed the five-foot-eight modern American Asian woman, dwarfing Cecelia in volume and height. 'My name is Stacey. Please take a seat.'

Her well-padded office chair sighed as she sat down. Cecelia couldn't help feeling sorry for the chair.

'And what can I do for you?' she asked.

A newly passed graduate from a therapy course lasting four months, and she knew it all. She knew how to sort out the world and the people who were complaining, just like Cecelia. Cecelia was whining and complaining. What was the matter with her? Had she been spoiled? There was nothing wrong with her. She would sort her out. Cecelia, you can walk, talk, and get yourself something to eat. You can make eye contact. Isn't that enough for you? There is nothing wrong with you except that you're whining. If I figured this one out, so should have you. As long as you are paying my wages, look at me; I'm not complaining at all, am I?

Where had the other therapist gone? The kind one who understood. The man who had become crusty with years of experience and could guide her through his knowledge so she could find her own way out.

Cutaway the old views and tackle the world with a new purpose. This new therapist had now made eye contact with Cecelia, and she felt good. She was in control not only of her life, but had been given charge of Cecelia's. Here was her office, and this was her computer. She found herself to be important. She listened while Cecelia outlined her problem, chin in hand. This didn't only boost her confidence, but it was fun. Her dark brown eyes were entertained, and she had made it.

So, everyone gets down when they don't get what they want, and this applied to herself. You've got to decide about how you want to be.

Cecelia listened to the empty but smug face, who had reached nearly twenty-six without experiencing a thing. A therapist was meant to help their clients and not themselves at Cecelia's expense. Yet Stacey was the proof for what it was to be right. Cecelia wouldn't be like this if she had money. She wouldn't be sitting here; she would have gone to someone else and got some better treatment. But there again, if she had money, she probably wouldn't be ill.

And then the twenty-five, twenty-six-year-old yawned. This was the ultimate insult when Cecelia explained that after she had lost her father, she had tried suicide. While that lazy, derisory smile that clung to her lips as wet sheets on a windy day, whose mind hadn't bothered to consult her mouth, spoke.

'So, why are you still here?' she asked, tapping at her computer making her notes.

'Yes, why am I still alive?'

A dangerous question to ask a person who had suicidal tendencies.

Of course, Cecelia paid for this session of abuse. She had no choice. But there were some things she could do in life, and that was giving Stacey Swayne a good reference.

Today was about getting an interview with Jennifer Sawyer's parents. She was thought to be the second of the victims. Hands tied behind her back; vermillion red lipstick painted on her lips with a note. *She told me she loved me.*

Jennifer Sawyer had been left on the banks of the Alondra golf course's large pool. Naked, raped, and dumped. A used-up body, a comment of the murderer's indifference. No semen had been found, which suggested the Slasher didn't go all the way.

And like Marcia Davis, Jennifer Sawyer was also a virgin, whose entire life seemed holier than thou. These days an almost impossible state of grace, but the murderer had managed to select only virgins and not the prostitutes. Murdered young women who had never known carnal knowledge or sexual love. They would take with them the hatred and abuse of a man who had no respect for them. Again, it was a shame.

Being kind to herself was what Cecelia needed. Taking time dressing and making certain she had something to eat. This morning, she would have a bath instead of a shower and wear a dress, although she would have preferred wearing trousers. But if she were visiting to get an interview with strict religious people, looking boyish and cocky certainly would not go down well.

A morning that started slowly, Cecelia took more time than necessary to get ready. Now and again, her eyes went to the telephone. Mary Ann said she would ring this morning. What had happened? It was now gone eleven, and if she didn't leave soon, it would be too late to make it for the interview.

Another ten minutes had passed, and still no call. It was mystifying. At twenty past eleven, she left.

It hung in her mind as she sat in the cab. What had happened to the promise Mary Ann had made? Repeatedly, Cecelia wondered if she was okay or was she going through another one of those suicidal episodes. But Mary Ann had William. She must not worry about her; she would be all right; it was herself she should be worried about.

The Sawyer family had now moved out of Alondra to the border between Roseland and Alondra. Perhaps best described as being right off the beaten track. A lonely place where no one could get to them. They had three other girls who needed their protection. A place where dust balls passed on their way to their own heaven.

It was not the best-looking house along the road. The less flashy, the better. This family didn't want to attract attention.

Someone was sitting on the porch watching the cab as it came bouncing up the long driveway. The woman was peeling carrots and dropping them into a large silver bucket. Putting her hand up to her eyes, she shielded them while watching. Two young girls played with a dog. They too looked up, and upon seeing the car, began running back to their mother. They looked terrified.

Coming across to her fledglings, the mother ushered them into the house. Apron on and frowning, the mother crossed her arms to enlarge her determination that visitors were not wanted. We have made our home on the outskirts of yours, so please don't enter. To reiterate, visitors are not welcome.

Any moment now, Cecelia expected the father to come

out with a rifle in his arms and waving it with the purposeful intention of aiming. But this didn't happen, and there was nothing except the chirping and buzzing of insects.

Once paid and out, the cab turned and was off along the driveway, heading back to town. What next, she thought, looking at this angry woman? Interviews with the parents of murdered children would never be easy. Cecelia found a nervous smile for the frowning woman and put her own concerns on the back boiler.

'Hello,' she continued smiling, stretching out her hand this time in greeting. 'My name is Cecelia Clark, and I've come a long way to see you all,' she carried on smiling. The woman stood still on the porch and continued frowning. 'I take it you are Mrs. Sawyer.' Each step was taking her closer to the mother. She had now reached the porch and was staring up at her unattractive scowl.

'You have it right.' A strained voice as if it had been taxed by smoking instead of the weariness and tears of life. Stay away, these eyes were saying. The porch was her territory, and she was guarding it.

'I am a freelance investigative journalist,' Cecelia added quickly. 'So, I'm my own boss.'

'You should have kept in your cab; it's going to be a long walk back for you.'

'Francine,' a man stepped out of the house, wiping his hands on an old cloth. 'Give the woman a chance. Let's hear what's she has come here to say.' He nodded to his wife before turning to Cecelia. 'What did you say your name was?'

'I'm Cecelia Clark,' she tried to carry on smiling, but her lips were loosening.

'Well, Miss Clark, what can I do for you? We might be in

the middle of nowhere, but we still believe in good manners. Get the young lady a drink, Francine.'

'You don't need to,' hurried in Cecelia. 'I've bought a bottle of water.'

'No, we'll get you a drink. We're well-mannered, like I said. And we'll listen to what you've got to say. We shall also make sure that you get yourself a cab for your return. Francine, go make some coffee.'

'You don't have to. I don't want anyone putting themselves out for me.' She liked the man but wasn't certain of his wife.

'Are you going to tell us why you're here, then?'

'As I said, I am a journalist, and I'm doing a story on the Alondra Slasher. I've already spoken to Mr. Sawyer about his daughter, and I thought I would talk to you about your loss and how it has affected you.'

A quick whistle of breath taken through his nose made Cecelia grasp the difficulty of her suggestion.

'I think you might find it therapeutic in that you may have some input in catching the killer,' her voice was drowning, and her eyes were darting rapidly here and there. She was making no sense. How could she? What they had been through was the worse trial any parents could go through. These moments were leading up to his answer, with eyes that couldn't believe what she was asking.

'You want me to tell you what happened to my daughter?' at last, his thoughts were out. 'Read the newspapers for yourself.'

'That is exactly what I have done,' Cecelia said, fighting from her own corner. 'But I am sure that your daughter is more than just a statistic.'

'You come out here with your fancy words and think I will be impressed because I'm not. You think being clever makes you feel more while us simple folk won't have missed losing one of our kin because we've got others?'

'I didn't say that.' It was a shock how he could misinterpret her offer. She had come here to give him help. To put across to those other people who had not been touched by grief that, once upon a time, they had a daughter called Jennifer who had a life which was uniquely hers. No one could take that little time away.

'You want to make some money out of my daughter's life? Everyone wants a piece. Even after she's dead. Well, I tell you what, why don't you help yourself to a piece of our loss? Take some sadness back with you and share it with others. What do we get? Because we sure can't get her back.'

'Your right. I'm sorry,' for it was true. She was using their loss to make money, and why not? These days, everyone was living off the death of others, even their own loved ones, because it was profitable.

'No one knows what our Jennifer was like.'

'You're right. I'm sorry.' Cecelia's steady eyes concentrated on Mr. Sawyer's face, looking to see where she could repair the damage. She was now feeling so sorry for him.

'One of the sweetest girls you will ever come across. But of course, I know this is what everyone says about their daughters. But it's not the same. It's never the same, is it? She was our daughter—we loved her, and she loved us. I held her as a baby in my arms, and you know it's the sweetest feeling to hold your very own child. Something so young and vulnerable. She was our first child, and there is nothing like holding your firstborn in your arms. It's true you can feel for others and their love and loss, but it's never the same, is it? It can never be the same.'

'I can do that for you. I can use my fancy words to write about Jennifer and put fresh light into her memory and make her live again. You haven't lost her; you will never lose her once I have dressed her in clothes of love.'

His face, gaunt with pain and suffering as the circle of loss was still going on. But here was a promise, a chance to renew her life, resurrect his Jennifer into eternal beauty. Something he could hold on to.

'I will do my best to bring her back to you in the only way I can, by words.'

'Francine,' said Mr. Sawyer, grabbing Cecelia's hand to bring her into the house. 'This is Cecelia Clark, our visitor.'

'I know that,' said Mrs. Sawyer, standing by the kitchen table.

A large table for a large family and not too dissimilar from the table at the Davises. Suddenly Cecelia was struck with a weird sensation that she had been here before, yet nothing was recognizable. As if this was a replay of something which was going to be entirely different. Had she been here in some other time? Or was there a divine being pulling her strings?

'I can guess what she wants.' Mrs. Sawyer's eyes were hard on Cecelia, the eyes of the relentless. 'She is another one of those bone pickers, the kind that turns the carcass over to see if there's any flesh left for their breakfast.'

'Bring us some coffee,' said Mr. Sawyer, exchanging looks that perhaps once had said love but now hate. 'We will be sitting on the porch. Come on, Miss Clark. We'll sit out there.' He pointed to the door for Cecelia to follow him.

The once white fleeting clouds had disappeared to leave a bright-eyed sun heating this sacred earth. A bee buzzed as it passed by, looking for blossoms.

'Take a seat, Miss Clark. We can have our discussion out here on our own. You'll have to forgive my wife; our loss took away her heart. It's easier for you to forgive her than for her to forgive herself.'

The door swung open, and Mrs. Sawyer looking about the porch and found a spare chair to put the tray of coffee on it. Saying nothing, she returned to the house, leaving behind a solid wall of distrust and hate. She hated everything.

The purr of the insect life was comforting, but not so the green parrots, for there were at least six waiting in the trees. She remembered seeing these birds waiting about the Sawyer's home. These green birds of disaster came like a spooky omen. Several stories traveled along with these birds that they had migrated from Mexico, where they are surprisingly endangered. The other tale accompanying them is that they escaped in 1969 from an East Colorado Boulevard pet shop when it was on fire. Attractive birds, but they were also extremely noisy.

Now in the depth of the late afternoon, Cecelia found herself sitting in Mrs. Sawyer's wooden rocking chair, a homemade cushion fitting her comfort. How many evenings had Mr. and Mrs. Sawyer sat out here on the porch together to watch the changing horizon? Only now, keeping their thoughts to themselves. Nature brings its kindness as well as its wrath.

There is always time to have a few moments to oneself. And then again, Cecelia wondered about Mary Ann and if she was okay. Her thoughts passed on to James Patts; he might never return to active duty with the police again; his wife would be pleased. And then to Phoebe, in her garden of flowers; it was a wonder she could part with any of them.

'Tell me something about your daughter,' began Cecelia. 'Give me an understanding of what she was like, the things she liked to do, and how she was with everyone and the way she looked. Those special moments when you would catch her looking and thinking and when she doesn't know you're watching her.'

His eyes moved to those thoughts of when she was here, laughing and sad, thoughtful and witty. She existed, lived, and was loved. Now, though, she had made a great hole in their lives that could never be fixed. Again Cecelia's eyes watched him.

Was it the delight of Cecelia's imagination to picture these thoughts in Mr. Sawyer? Perhaps. It was his eyes that said he was looking about the place for Jennifer. Now turning his head in response, she had called and come to him, stepping out of the ghostly shadows. Jennifer had been waiting for him. He had heard her, and now he smiled.

Daddy, have you missed me? Those questions we imagine would be said by those we love when the energy of their being is just shadows. A tear fell away from the corner of his eye. How could she ask him if he missed her? He was always missing her. Yesterday was such a long time ago.

'We had a feral bitch once come and land herself in our garden shed,' said Mr. Sawyer as if he awoke from a dream. A different person had been recalled from a memory of a much younger man. 'She wanted somewhere to unload her puppies and judged our house to be the safest place. Six pups, and from the looks of it, different fathers, but one of them was dead. Well, that's what I thought.'

Cecelia was about to be treated to a treasured memory of his daughter; it was an honor; as he had told no one else about it.

'When I picked this little piece of life up, it made no movement. I was just about to take it out to dispose of it when Jennifer stopped me. She asked if she could see it. I wanted to protect her; she had a sensitive heart. It's gone, I told her. There is nothing more to be done for it. She heard about the puppies and had come to the outhouse bringing the bitch some meat, knowing that the mother would be hungry. Jennifer was twelve years old, and from her birthday money, she brought the mother some food. A strong-willed little lady, she would not let me go until she got the puppy. Leave the pup to me, daddy, she said.'

It looked as if he had a tear in his eye as he gently shook his head.

'She looked at me with big eyes as she held out her hands to take the puppy from me. I remember that look on her face; yes, she was determined. She had great and admirable strength. I tried to explain that the puppy was dead, but she wouldn't have it. I'll bring it back to life even if it is dead. She was an angel. She took hold of the pup, wrapped it in a piece of blanket which she had with her, and then she began breathing life back into it—I could have sworn it was dead.' He placed his hand to his mouth to breathe through it, just as she might have done for the pup. 'Oh, I miss her. I miss the sound of her voice—she had a lovely voice, you know. She was in the church choir, and she could sing like an angel. Oh, my Jennifer. Why did He have to take and kill my beautiful little girl?'

Jennifer Sawyer was not an academic. Instead of these skills, she was given other talents. She could bake like the devil, and no one could resist her bread and pies. She could make her own clothes as well—she had a promising future ahead of her. But for all of that, she just wanted to get married and set up her own home.

'Was she a virgin?' asked Cecelia before blushing. Mr. Sawyer turned quickly, sharp eyes almost in anger. 'I'm sorry to ask, but I think this might be an important factor. You don't have to answer if you don't want to.'

'My Jennifer was a virgin. She believed in keeping herself pure for when she married. She used to say when she was married, she would make her husband happy—she was a traditionalist, and there is nothing wrong with that.' His eyes were defensive.

'Of course,' Cecelia mumbled.

'She wanted to do everything right, and she would have made a wonderful mother. She told me she wanted six children.' He suddenly looked down. 'She thought Francine, and I were happy. We were happy, but now we don't talk to each other. Oh, how I hate her murderer with a passion. When they find him, I shall ask for the death penalty, and I hope he burns in hell.'

It made Cecelia envious to see such fervor from a father to his daughter. But is it only in death that anger forms its sorrow and that regret understands remorse? Had her own father felt like that for her? No. Her father had been broken by his wife and become a wafer of a man. Her father had been too gentle for this life. He had nothing to defend himself with when the hyena of death found him.

Crumpled with gray and tortured, Mr. Sawyer covered his eyes with his hand. 'To be a good person, you are supposed to forgive those that trespass on you. But I can't. I rage at God and ask Him why he took Jennifer, and for what reason? Lord, you could have stopped this from happening. You could have sent one of your angels and taken Jennifer in your grace. Instead, you turned your back on her. Did you hear her screaming when he stripped off her clothes? Did you think it was okay for him to take her the way he did? Did you God, did you?'

It was with compassion that made Cecelia want to stretch out to him, but she thought he would attack her if she tried. Holding back, she could see his eyes were crazed with thoughts.

For a long time, they sat in silence. She couldn't say how long had passed, except the warm sun was losing its strength. Inside the house, Cecelia knew she wasn't welcome. With a look of death, a young child of about six was staring out of the window.

'If I need to talk to you again, would you mind if I came back?'

'We'll have to see about that,' replied Mr. Sawyer, recovering some of his indifference and aloofness by climbing back into his protective shell from the hostile world.

'I'll call you.' Cecelia attempted to be light and cheerful.

'You'll have a problem with that. We don't have a telephone, and we will not get one to accommodate the outside world.'

Lowering her head, Cecelia said she understood. Because she did, she had opened up their festering wounds again with no balm to heal. The trust which everyone takes for granted from the harmony of life had been broken. If she were taking something away from them, she needed to give something back, and her words were all she had to offer.

The Sawyers had left everything to start afresh with a family without that missing member. It was the only way they could survive, but it hadn't worked because the ghost of Jennifer had followed them to Roseland. She would not leave them alone. She was looking for something from them, but they hadn't figured out what she wanted.

A life for a death. Cecelia had to do something for these people, leave something of significance for them to move on with their lives, especially for their children. This had to be her mission to dig down, get to the bare skeleton of her soul, and then understand and feel like they felt. But to understand suffering, a person has to suffer. It cannot be done on the perimeters of a blessed seashore, with golden sands and sweeping blue skies, but by the humbling of the soul. Perhaps in telling of the pains of others, she too would also find some peace and even forgiveness for herself.

13

Having traveled only a few kilometers and conscious of the incurring debt made against her, she looked out of the cab window. It was then it occurred to Cecelia she was near to Mary Ann's house. It would be a good idea to stop off and visit her and reduce some of her debt. The rest of the way, she would walk, cut through the roads, and then catch the bus. Because that question kept on returning; why hadn't Mary Ann telephoned?

'I've changed my mind,' said Cecelia, tapping on the dividing window. 'Can you stop the car now?' one person's fortune is another person's debt. For his trouble, once again, she paid him too handsomely. He took the tip with the look that this was due to him. But it was handing over money, which she couldn't afford. The price of her penance. Was it always going to be like this, paying atonement for the things she did from need? Changing her mind was her choice.

I must change my name to Clara. Being Clara, I was different, much more sure of myself. I had more pride and self-respect, thought Cecelia.

Watching the cab pull off, Cecelia stopped for a moment and listened to the sound of the road. It was quiet, quieter than normal. A little breeze scooted up the road, picking up and lazily turning over leaves in curiosity with all the time in the world.

Some two hundred yards away and moving swiftly, a man walked with determination from the opposite direction. Something about him made her slow down. With his head lowered, he looked awkward and even embarrassed by the way he held himself. Wearing a woolen navy jacket with a scarf wrapped around his neck, which covered half of his face. He appeared uncomfortable. Was it this that made him look uneasy? Or was it the reason he was here? Suddenly, he changed direction. He was heading for Mary Ann's house.

So, this must be her new beau, smiled Cecelia, pleased to see an actual person was looking out for her. It was a relief that the responsibility was not completely hers. So, this must be William. If he saw her, he might be embarrassed. Stopping for a moment, Cecelia pretended to look for something in her bag. If she were a smoker, she could delay by pretending to look for a cigarette and light up. It would have been useful. But she was not. Keeping her head down, she rolled her eyes upward. Like a ballroom dancer, he swirled to the side, stepping nimbly onto the path of Mary Ann's house. He looked nervous.

What was this man doing? He was evasive, yet how interesting he was. Alert and worried, as if fearing that he would be caught, she must keep out of his way just in case she giggled to herself. Not a powerful man, but strength is deceptive. There is no need to carry a ton of muscles to damage an opponent.

Swiftly, she saw him running to the door, and then he turned to look straight towards her. Did it matter if he had the key to the house? Was it really any of her business? But upon seeing her figure hanging around, he leaped off the doorstep and dashed away. Why?

Oh, what a shame. Was he so shy that he didn't want her to see he was Mary Ann's William? He should know she wished them both happiness. Perhaps she had been a little jealous, but if Mary Ann could find happiness, then she was pleased for them both. But where was he now? Had she really frightened him away? Frowning, Cecelia walked thoughtfully to Mary Ann's door.

This was so awkward. What was she doing here? To see if Mary Ann was okay, and it was perfectly acceptable to care about someone.

Touching her hair and straightening her dress, she agreed she looked fine. One, two, three, and then press the doorbell, take a step backward, and wait for the door to be opened.

I was just passing, so I thought I would look in; Cecelia rehearsed. Just to say hello. I hope I'm not interrupting anything. She smiled when she thought about William and why a man of his age should get embarrassed when visiting the woman he loved. But he would return once she had left; Cecelia was certain about this. These two definitely suited each other, Cecelia thought wryly. In truth, she had never had a successful relationship, but this was down to her habit of rebuffing men. Learn to trust and take the chance. Mary Ann had.

The door remained closed. To Cecelia's sensitivity, the house felt empty, as if no one was home. How can no one be at home when Mary Ann can't leave the house? No, she had to be there. She was tied to the place. But the question remained. Should she press the doorbell again? Perhaps Mary Ann didn't want to see anyone, not even her. Just one more press of the doorbell, and then she'd go. The door opened.

Mary Ann was in her housecoat with a pair of dark glasses. Her hair was swept up in a towel, supplying the answer that she had been in the bath.

'Mary Ann, I'm sorry. I didn't realize—'

'I wasn't in the bath; I was lying down. I had a bad migraine.'

'Oh dear, I'm sorry. I didn't mean to wake you. I'll leave and let you rest.'

'No. I'm feeling much better now. Please come in; it's good to see you.'

Walking ahead of Mary Ann into the dark hallway, Cecelia felt uncomfortable. Something was not right; secrets were being kept, and it must have something to do with William. Now she understood. This was a grand affair. Had Mary Ann telephoned William to come and spend a very intimate evening with her? Absurd as it appears, had she frightened William away?

'Go into the living room, and I'll put the light on for you.'

It was not dark outside, but the curtains were pulled. A new vase of red roses was arranged on the small table. The scene of a lover's nest and she had intervened.

'I came to see how you were and to thank you for last night's kindness.'

She wanted to apologize for scaring William off, but she could see Mary Ann's thoughts were somewhere else. As Mary Ann tightened her long housecoat and made sure her towel was all right. Cecelia could see there was something wrong. The dark glasses slipped forward when she turned on the light, and in that swift glance, Cecelia saw Mary Ann's eyes were red and sore. Again, muttering to herself the apologies she felt for this friend.

'I had only just risen from my bed,' said Mary Ann, securing her dark glasses once more. 'I didn't realize it was so late. Rather like you,' she smiled.

'Such a lovely surprise to see you,' she touched her glasses to make certain they were still fixed on her face. And then she smiled, which was disconcerting when only half her face was showing. 'I would have been on my own if you had not visited.'

But you invited William.

'I'll go and heat some water for a cup of coffee, if it's not too late for you? Coffee doesn't keep me awake, but I understand it does for many people. I can make you some cocoa if you like. Yes, I think I'll have cocoa too. I won't be a minute,' she said, leaving the room.

Still frowning with conscious discomfort from having intruded, the desire to be absolved of her sins was accumulating. But what exactly was she looking for? A look, an expression, or something for Mary Ann to tell her she was forgiven, Cecelia followed her into the kitchen with this need. The kitchen was also in darkness until Mary Ann flicked the switch, and the room came flickering into sense.

'I had an interview with the Sawyers, the parents of Jennifer Sawyer,' said Cecelia, following in the footsteps of her host.

Spinning like a top, Mary Ann whizzed around. She hadn't realized that Cecelia had followed her. Cecelia took a step back, scolded by the way Mary Ann looked at her. But, by the backdoor, a coat lay across a chair, a dark navy-blue coat resting as if taken off in a hurry. So Mary Ann was not alone. The keen senses of the guilty had worked out the mystery.

So, he had sneaked through to the backdoor so he wouldn't be seen entering. A smile crept through Cecelia's lips into a knowledgeable smile. Not needing to wonder or look what Cecelia was smiling about, Mary Ann understood she had seen the coat.

'It's William's,' Mary Ann looked at the coat. 'I'm afraid it's me that makes him hide; it makes him nervous. He's told me so.' she smiled, trusting Cecelia understood.

'Oh please, there is no reason for you to explain, and there I believed I had frightened him away.'

'So, it was you. It makes sense now. William came dashing in saying he had been spotted?' Mary Ann took off her dark glasses to reveal her bright blue eyes, amazing to look at but defective. An unnatural color, but what an amazing effect.

It must have been Cecelia's startlement at coming across such sharp, bright eyes again.

'Yes, I'm a freak,' Mary Ann said, stroking a pacifying hand across her cheek. 'A curse and a bonus, you can't have both in this world. I have a condition called Waardenburg syndrome. People stare at me, but for all the wrong reasons.'

'Because the color of your eyes is beautiful.'

'How kind.'

But this time, her delicate eyes were stained with soreness.

'I told William he didn't need to hide, but he has taken on board not to be seen. Poor man, I hope he doesn't become neurotic like me. And now you are wondering what I am talking about.'

'Is he here?'

'Yes, he's upstairs taking a bath. Did you want to meet him?'

'No, not now, perhaps another time.' She was already embarrassed by the deception. 'But why don't you want others to know you have a male friend?'

'Oh Cecelia, I thought you, of all the people, would understand. I didn't think I needed to explain it to you.' Mary Ann's eyes searched Cecelia's face. 'But I see I do. Don't you remember I was almost raped five weeks ago? I know it's not the same as Marcia Davis or Jennifer Sawyer or the others because I managed to escape, but for me, it was still traumatic.'

'Yes, but I still don't understand.'

'I told the police I was raped, which suggests that a person who has just recently been assaulted will have nothing to do with men. So, you understand how having a man in my life would look when they already believe I made up my attack.'

'I think I understand,' Cecelia slowly nodded her agreement.

'Do you? I don't know how to prove to anyone that I was raped except you. Not to be believed is like saying it didn't happen. I tell them I'm terrified, and I can't cope. And all the police tell me is that they will send someone to protect me, which at this moment is like being rapped again. Do you understand what I'm saying?'

'I don't know what to suggest. Except to forget about what other people think, you can't control their thoughts.'

'Yes, I know, and I'm not trying to. But to the police, I am not supposed to have a male friend. But I trust William. We are not having sex, if that's what you're worried about. You won't tell anyone about him, will you?'

'Of course not. Look, I'm going to leave you two alone, and I'll speak to you later.'

'No, no, please don't go.'

'I can't stay here while William is in the house. I know when I'm not wanted.'

'Please stay. I would sooner have you than him. I won't be a minute. I'll tell him he's got to leave—'

'Don't be an idiot, Mary Ann. I'm just a friend. But, on the other hand, this man could be somebody you could spend the rest of your life with—and I'm happy for you.' She was making her way to the front door, her ticket to freedom.

'I don't want you to go, don't you understand?' Mary Ann's footsteps thudded frantically behind her.

'Yes, and you are kind, but I've got to get back home. There are things I need to do.' Her hand was on the handle, ready to open.

'Please, Cecelia, don't go. I've been on my own for days. You came to visit me because you cared about me. If you go now, I know you won't come back,' and now she was holding on to her arm. 'You won't come back, will you? I know you won't. You promised always to be my friend.'

'The truth, Mary Ann, is I'm busy. This is not to be taken personally—it's just one of those things. People move on with their lives, which you're doing, and it's good for you. I'm happy for you.'

'No. My friendship with you is important. I shall tell him to get out of my life if I can't have you.'

Cecelia stopped; this was a shocking statement to make. 'Well, that's your decision, Mary Ann. But I've got to move on with my life.'

Spoiled and possessive; perhaps in the past, Mary Ann got whatever she wanted. But this had nothing to do with her when she had her own life to lead. Dramatic behavior was just another of Mary Ann's tactics. But this time, it was not working with her.

'But you came to visit me,' cried Mary Ann.

'You're right. I did. I came to see if you were okay—and you are okay, Mary Ann. This is a job to me—'

'Did our friendship mean nothing?'

A hundred things were said in that one exchange, a hundred thoughts in the space of a second. Cecelia shook her head at Mary Ann; she would never come dancing to her again. The balloon had popped, the string binding them together had been severed. She was free. An extraordinary gift of liberation, the serfdom for life did no longer apply. Incredible, but how necessary.

'Take care of yourself,' Cecelia smiled, leaving the house.

In her own way, Mary Ann was another Tina, another intimidating bully who demanded total control by telling her what to say, do, and even think. The same as Tina had done to dad. In that instance, when Cecelia left her parent's home, she vowed never to return. This time, it would not be repeated. But make no mistake, there were people like Tina everywhere, and she would not be another statistic like her father. Cecelia had learned this from his destructive mistakes.

Although it was a relief walking out of the house, the phantoms of fear were climbing all over her, asking if she had done the right thing. Who knows anything until that chance is taken?

Already the light was fading as the long shadows started marching across the ground beside her.

Not for the first time had Cecelia decided which side she was going to take. There was no returning with apologies. No more guilty trips or waiting to be forgiven. For Cecelia, this was one of the biggest things she had ever done in her life. Getting through it would be a personal triumph.

Had she expected Mary Ann to call after her? Perhaps. But perhaps Mary Ann was as proud as her. No one was pleading for her to return. Although Cecelia knew Mary Ann's eyes were watching her as she walked away, and at that moment, hating her, yet returning now meant she would never be free of her. It wasn't easy to do when making someone unhappy. Yet, this was pride and freedom and doing what she wanted. Carry on walking; an inner voice was growing and becoming louder. There is no turning back now, Cecelia. You know that, don't you?

Behind in the growing darkness, a door closed, and Cecelia was released from the spell.

14

'Cecelia, what are you doing here?' Phoebe answered the door, smiling yet surprised.

'I have done something which I should have done a long time ago.' She was trembling.

'You better come in. You look like you've fought a ghost.'

'I feel like a ghost,' replied Cecelia, giggling.

The pungent smell of hundreds of flowers competed with each other as she entered the shop.

'You had better come upstairs; you look like you could do with a drink. I've got some brandy; I'll have a glass with you to keep you company, and then you can tell me all about it.' Laughter was infectious, even if from nerves; Phoebe was happy to see her friend.

Cheerful in this house, the smell of flowers, like before, chased the two when they mounted the stairs. Even the worn carpet, which had seen so many feet climb it, said welcome. Being with Phoebe was uncomplicated and even homely, such an amiable person to be around.

Climbing to the higher floors brought with it another dimension of scents. The crisp smell of cucumber and tomatoes perfumed the air, and suddenly Cecelia found an appetite that she had not known before. Was this going to be an evening of firsts?

'I'm hungry now,' confessed Cecelia. 'I could smell the aromas of your salad.'

'And you need feeding,' grinned Phoebe, nodding. Going through into the kitchen with pleasure. 'Tell me what you would like? I have everything here that a vegetarian stomach craves for, and plenty of it. Mung beans, alfalfa, nuts, and fruit, as well as the more traditional ingredients. It's possible to exist and get complete nourishment on this with perhaps a steak thrown in now and again.'

So different. Phoebe was unique to everyone else Cecelia knew. Her kooky trousers were made by herself because she had one leg shorter than the other, not that Cecelia would have noticed. I am being myself, so take me for what I am.

But was she pretty, it was difficult to say? Phoebe moved too quickly for an adequate description. And perhaps it was this liveliness and enthusiasm for life which was so attractive. The fun she found in almost everything Phoebe did and touched and saw made her a captivating and interesting character.

Between the cucumber and the Romaine lettuce, Cecelia told Phoebe what happened with Mary Ann. This was greeted with a round of approval before sipping the brandy and water.

'Bravo, bravo!' Phoebe clapped her hands, stamping her feet to induce the sound of an audience.

The noise, fuss, and excitement prompted Cecelia to stand and take a bow. Phoebe's fingertips called out for a wolf whistle as this great friendship cemented.

What is this love for a person of the same gender that binds itself with promises that surpass any other love, even for one's children? Like twins formed from one cell, cleft from the beginning, and now returning to each other with gravity's swinging pendulum, so many experiences were yet to be had. But, at last, they had found each other.

'I believe there are people out there,' said Phoebe, now calmer and on a note of discipline marbled with the truth. 'Who gives up on themselves to satisfy another's feelings?' Phoebe smiled and looked up from her glass. 'I used to think it was from weakness that I caved in, but now I believe it's from a person's temperament. These bullies have some sort of detecting instinct, and they home in on other's gentleness. They instinctively know that we don't want to upset them. People like us are well-mannered, kind, and thoughtful.'

Phoebe paused for a moment to align her thoughts.

'While they are the wicked witches from the west who intuitively sniff people out like us. We smell sweet, caring people and believe they won't do us any harm.' Again, Phoebe convinced herself that she had worked out the correct answer. 'It took me over two years to understand this. Two years of beatings, two years of believing I deserved it because he told me I did. What happened to me? I used to wonder if I had always been like this. Whenever we made up, I thanked God that Harry still loved me because he had forgiven me. I must have been mad. But now, every morning, I thank God that I'm free of him. Harry never loved me because he couldn't understand what actual love was about.'

It was fun being with Phoebe, and Cecelia felt great happiness as they chatted like sisters. Eating and drinking, planning and plotting, they exchanged thoughts. Talking to Phoebe was often like talking with herself, a self she had forgotten existed and only dreamed of.

Her father should have walked out on Tina, and he

should have turned his back and left. But would he have taken her with him? Each of us caves in one way or another because it's easy. I'll stay for my daughter. I'll stay for another reason, and one day, I will leave. But it never happens.

'I know,' said Phoebe, going to the side where the brandy bottle stood. The cork came off with a pop. 'We should go out together and make more friends. Make our lives bigger. For nearly eight years of my life, I've been too busy running away.' She shrugged. 'To be honest, I've been afraid of doing anything too grand in case my husband found me. But life is too precious to live in fear. The human body is fragile, and every day we take chances with our lives. We must live life as if it is the last moment of our existence. To feel everything we are, the bad and the good. There is nothing to be ashamed of. And if that giant, nebulous creature called God is waiting out there, then when he's ready, we will return to him because I believe we all go back to the beginning. Then we can say to him, yes, I've had a grand time, and I've been happy. I've done everything I wanted to do. But, gosh, I must be drunk.'

Wonderful to hear Phoebe talking like that, but she was right. Why should people like her and Phoebe have to suffer? 'Why don't you divorce him, and then you would be rid of him altogether?' The last piece of cucumber was still lying on the plate, but not for long.

'Yes, it's a good idea. I'm sure he wouldn't be a monster with the right someone else. I think it must be something to do with me,' she shrugged again. 'I never figured out why he loved and hated me. In the end, I think it was easier for him just to hate me.'

Her animated face slowed down like a steam train

coming into the station. 'And then I think he must have been so damn unhappy to find pleasure in hurting me.'

Phoebe was right. For to understand how someone thinks, it's necessary to imbibe some of their soul.

'I don't care how Mary Ann feels, because if I worry,' began Cecelia more firmly, 'I might go back to her with another apology.'

'Which is just what she is hoping for, and I should know that; I was always apologizing to Harold after he beat me. It sounds idiotic when I think about it now, but he made me believe no one wanted me and I was so lucky to have him. I think I'll have another brandy. Do you want one?'

Cecelia picked up her mug and looked inside. There was enough.

'I'll top up your cup. This is a celebration. We are free people in a free world. Isn't it wonderful?'

A liberating night deserved a party, and one came running to them ad hoc. Sitting and chatting and finishing off the brandy. They talked into the night about everything.

'Why don't you stay the night?' suggested Phoebe. 'We can share my bed, and I promise you I don't snore. I've never woken myself with it. Do you snore?'

'Who knows? I've never spent the night with anyone, but I'll have to go home in the morning.' Even as Cecelia said this, she had already decided about staying with Phoebe. It would be like an adult sleepover.

How the house came up was probably something that was lying on Cecelia's mind. Phoebe had a spare toothbrush for Cecelia. While Cecelia talked, Phoebe became quiet.

'Why don't you move in with me for a while? Put the house up for rent, and you can make some money that way. It should be enough for you to pay off your mortgage and help to contribute towards your living cost. I won't charge you for living here; really, it'll be fun. When you can, you can always help in the shop. Don't you see—it all makes sense. And we get on famously, haven't you noticed? We will also be able to protect each other from the Slasher. What do you think?'

'I don't know. It's a big step to take, so I'll need to think about it.'

But it would certainly sort out all her problems that have been giving her headaches and making her stressed and depressed. Watching Phoebe clear away the plates from the miss-shaped meal. Phoebe caught Cecelia looking at her; it ended with them poking their tongues out at each other. This was the friend Cecelia had always craved for.

Yet why not? Why not move in with Phoebe? It would be fun, and they would be there for each other. To refuse this offer suddenly seemed stupid.

'Okay, I will. I hope I know what I am letting myself in for?'

'Brilliant. There's another small room which houses my junk. I can sort it out and get you a bed. It would be cozy having you staying with me. We will have such larks,' and then she smiled gently. 'To be honest, this face here,' Phoebe pointed to her chin, 'has been showing a bit of bravado; I haven't felt safe since the Slasher attacks started.' With her mask off, Phoebe's vulnerability was apparent.

'I think it will be good for us both,' said Cecelia, tempted to put her hand over Phoebe's.

'Yes, and if there is anyone you want to bring back, you must think of this as your home for how long you need it.'

'Thank you.' Phoebe's kindness was almost overwhelming.

Then Cecelia couldn't help staring at Phoebe's head.

'You've only just noticed,' laughed Phoebe, her pretty

blue eyes merry with happiness smiled. The red, blue, and green had now reverted to light brown hair. 'I thought it would be a sensible change.'

Come tomorrow, as the two chatted into the night. Cecelia would inquire about putting her property up for rent. Such a decision like this had taken a great deal of weight off her. Finally, she had a friend, someone like family. Someone who would help her.

SOMETIMES, life needs immediate action, while everything else must be put on hold until the problem is sorted. After considering doing the renting out herself, it seemed easier to go through a locally certified property manager. It meant paying a fee, but it also meant she could get on with her life.

'One day,' Phoebe said while they were reading the housing literature. 'I am going to own my house. I'm going to put in a bid for this house. It's in an ideal situation off the main highway. And not only that, but I also love this old building.'

Later the following day, they used Phoebe's old jalopy to collect Cecelia's stuff for her stay. This was the first day of a wonderful adventure. It could have been a scene from a Hollywood movie. The endearing old truck was just about roadworthy as it bounced along the road stacked with Cecelia's possessions. Two enthusiastic women were running up and down the stairs, coordinating their fetching and carrying. Excited voices raised high with the plans they were making. Never having been to summer school, but this was how Cecelia imagined it would be.

It was a surprisingly well-sized apartment above the shop, large and generous, and a great host for Cecelia's belongings. She had collected quite a few bits since acquiring her property. Single chairs, the odd pillow, somewhere to put her umbrella, and an ashtray for those who still smoked had snuck in, intending to stay forever. Of course, it would be best if you had these glasses, and no one does anything without a lampstand. True, most of these items came from a second-hand shop, but they were picked with love.

'There are solutions to everything,' said Phoebe, picking up another box.

Planning to move on with her life is such a frightening and final thing. Although she had stayed that week with Phoebe, it was with always knowing she had her home to return to. But Phoebe was also changing her life.

Three days passed during this adventure while the world stood outside and watched. Perhaps Life stood intentionally out of the way to give these two a break. Because on the fourth day and switching on the local radio, they heard that The Alondra Slasher had once again taken a new victim.

Seventeen-year-old Cindy Clayton had been found in the same place as Marcia Davis just over a year ago. And no one had witnessed anything out of the ordinary. What happened was scary.

The previous sightings of a man in dark clothes hanging around schools and colleges just two days ago came to nothing; he had simply vanished. Everyone was on the lookout for him, but it was like looking for a phantom with only flimsy pieces of information available. The only way to tackle this problem was to prevent young women from going out on their own. They would either have to go in groups or have a man present.

'He's only going for virgins; but how does he know

they're virgins?' Phoebe touched the side of her head where the injury was. Still conscious of the area where Cecelia had no other choice but to shave Phoebe's hair. Her bald patch was now covered with a beanie which she had made while recuperating. But, of course, nothing would be simple with Phoebe. Spangled silk pieces with checked cotton bits fashioned her hat.

'Who knows,' said Cecelia. 'Perhaps the Slasher is a priest. He gets to know them when they come to confession.' An interesting thought was gathering momentum. 'Perhaps he's just lucky, or perhaps he knows the girls he talks to. I don't know. It seems like rapists and murderers can easily alter their profiles.'

'I suppose, but I've spent too long being scared. I know if my husband finds me, he will certainly kill me. He once told me I belong to him, and if I ever left, he would hunt me down and take my life. That's why I can't let him know where I am. The police can only put someone away after the crime has been committed. Do you want to see a photograph of my husband?'

'Yes, of course.'

From the table near her bed, Phoebe took out a photograph. Cecelia had been prepared to hate him on sight, believing she would see a recognizable monster, but it wasn't in the picture. Instead, she saw a rather nice and gentle-looking guy. Was Phoebe sure this was the same man who was her husband?

'Yes, I can say it for you,' smiled Phoebe with irony. 'He is handsome with inherited wealth. On paper, this should be a marriage made in heaven. At least, it should have been for me. He told me he was a virgin like me. People refuse to believe that he hit me. They'd always say you are lucky to have a man like him. He looked a thoroughly nice man.'

Holding his picture in her hands, Cecelia found it difficult to believe that under those eyes slept a monster. Dark wavy hair, finely shaped nose, soft and with full pink lips, a face that could draw faintness from every female heart.

'Well, it just proves that sometimes the outside is not the same as the inside. Why did he pick you?' it came out without thinking.

But it sparked off another of Phoebe's laughs.

'I have often asked the same question myself.' Her eyes twinkled. 'Obviously, my beauty and even possibly my interesting wit attracted him.'

'I'm sorry, I didn't mean that.'

'No, that's okay. I used to wonder why he was still free. When we went out together, I'd see the girls looking at him and then looking at me. It was a wonderful feeling until I got married, although to be honest, he didn't beat me straight away; it was when we came back from our honeymoon that he first struck me.'

Together, they had cleared out the small room, which would now be the new bedroom. Phoebe bought a bed for Cecelia. After dragging the heavy mattress up the stairs, they were now sitting on it.

'I don't hate Harry anymore. For me, that's a waste of energy. I just don't understand him or why he would want to make not only my life miserable but his as well.'

Although Phoebe's scars from their marriage weren't visible, her pain came from deep within.

'In the first year of our marriage, I went to the police, asking for help. They were helpful in that they listened to me. I showed the bruises where he had hit me. Then they told me I had to pack my bags after giving me an address for a women's refuge. So, I moved, hoping to start afresh. What I didn't reckon on was that Harry would follow me.'

Although this wasn't an amusing story, Phoebe started laughing nervously. It was as if this was the funniest story to be told.

'Harry followed me to the police station, and when I left, he talked to them. Such a clever move.'

'He must have suspected you were up to something.'

'Yes, and I was stupid to doubt his intelligence, but he was kind enough to tell me about the interview. He liked to dabble with reality, including my history of mental illness, especially in self-harming. He told them I would throw myself downstairs—'

'You're kidding me.'

'No, and he got away with it. He wasn't going to let me go. I was his punchbag, and now I was doing this to myself. Another year went by before I realized that if I stayed, I would be dead, which would make it a kind of suicide. One day, I know he will find and kill me. I read it in the tea leaves once that I was going to die early and with a violent death.'

15

The days passing were to be remembered as one of those wonderful holidays when young women reverted to their childhood. They were trying on each other's clothes, for they were nearly the same height and size. Talk about kooky Cecelia looked eccentric in Phoebe's clothes while Phoebe paled into a person who could pass with no one remembering her. Astonishing to see Phoebe as herself, but that's how she must appear to others. Through the night, they would creep into the kitchen to make waffles with plenty of maple syrup. It was fun.

But of course, there always has to be an end to everything. And that day came for these two little girls to rejoin the world of adults. Fantasy had lost its nebulous fibers, and the dream had broken. It was now time to awaken. Time to make money, which, for Cecelia, meant writing. Today, she would go to the Alondra Police Department to find out about this latest murder.

A body had been found dug deep in the perimeters of Elmansor Park baseball field. A new baseball stand was being erected, so more training could be done. The digger had pulled up a man's leg. Forensic revealed the death happened over a year ago, as they had also determined the man's age when he was murdered as about twenty-three to twenty-five. The fractured skull showed he had died from massive trauma to his head, and from the markings, it suggested an axe was the weapon.

Knocking on Detective Travis's door, Cecelia was told to enter. The police detective was going through some documents and frowning.

'You write very well,' Detective Travis said, without looking up. 'It's a pity young rookies aren't shown how to write good notes. Adequate, I suppose, but they expect officers to learn on the job most of the time. Which, to my mind, is not good enough.' Travis was wearing thin gold-rimmed glasses, making her look like an English professor. 'I'm getting a better picture of the people you interviewed, especially that of Mr. Davis, from your notes.'

Was this a compliment? From Detective Travis, perhaps it was.

'We're waiting for the body to be identified. I put my bottom dollar on it being Tony Hare. And if it is, then he didn't run away from his responsibilities. He was murdered. And making an uncalculated guess, I would say that the arrow points at Mr. Davis being his murderer. There isn't anyone else with any real motive for the murder.'

'You don't know for sure it is Tony Hare or if Mr. Davis killed him.'

'No, I don't. But I'll wait until the evidence proves it. It was from your notes which drew my attention to it. I want to congratulate you. You've done a damn good job.'

If Detective Travis needed to succeed, why did it have to be someone as vulnerable as Mr. Davis?

Words became dangerous. Suffering from guilt, Cecelia nearly bumped into Phoebe, coming out of her shop with more flowers. Her poker-dotted and striped beanie sat comfortably on her head.

'You're back again. What's the hurry?' she blinked. Her eyelashes had long extensions, and when she blinked, they fluttered like butterflies; she looked just like a wide-eyed rag doll.

'I need to visit someone. I think I might have done him a great deal of damage. I'll call you when I find out what has happened,' said Cecelia, too seriously for Phoebe's liking.

'Oh, before you go. You had a telephone call from the property manager. He thinks he's found someone interested in renting your property, and he just needs to agree to the rent.'

In Phoebe's hands, the blue petalled irises rendered a beautiful picture of serenity. Against her pale white skin, and her expression could have been executed on Delft pottery. But, for the first time in years, Phoebe looked happy and at peace with the world.

'I don't know when I'll be back. Do you think you could deal with it?'

'Yes, I can,' Phoebe was surprised. 'Is there anything you want me to say?'

'No,' grinned Cecelia. 'Except get me the best price you can,' and then she stopped in reflection. 'Without losing the client.'

'Am I not a businesswoman? Do I not always get the best out of a bargain?'

The banter between them was fun; they got on so well together. 'Yep.'

Wouldn't it be wonderful? Cecelia's excited thoughts chased her up the steps two at a time to go into partnership together? It would be a far better life than journalism. But, unfortunately, her written words had got a person into trouble, even if they were guilty. Her mind quickly reminded her to change from jeans to a skirt out of respect for the couple.

'I don't know when I'll be back,' Cecelia said, still tackling the stairs.

'I was thinking of doing something with chicken tonight. Something not too heavy like chicken and fruit salad. What do you think?' Phoebe smiled at Cecelia, rushing around. 'I'll do something with chicken then.'

Rushing everywhere, Phoebe stood at the door to say her goodbyes. A customer wanted flowers. In such a hurry, the man had to stand out of her way. No time for a hug; things needed to be done.

'Okay.' Cecelia spared a hand for goodbye.

The sun was shining, and the world looked happy and optimistic; everyone wants flowers on a day like this.

An ambulance waited outside the Davises house. Lights still flashed as the paramedics were busying themselves, trying to assess the sick woman's condition. With the doors open, Cecelia walked in, edging nervously to the obvious conclusion that an angel had come calling for Mary Davis. The tide of death was pulling her away.

From the doorway, she watched Mr. Davis staring down at her small body, drained of blood, and fighting for life. Shoulders bent in helplessness while his sweetheart lay dying. Mr. Davis's grief superseded his will to live.

Breathing lightly with the help of oxygen, her hours of existence were numbered in minutes. It was now up to him to decide whether his wife should go to the hospital to be made comfortable. The paramedics had taken her blood pressure and just finished checking her heart. Her sleep was deep, and she wasn't aware of what was going on.

An intimate scene of someone struggling to hold on to their life. And there was Mr. Davis's grief inestimably flowing out and covering the room. All the days of his life had never prepared him for her death. His darling was leaving him. Every second she was drifting further away to the shore of the dead. Nothing could solace him, not even their dead children. He was being abandoned.

From the chaotic whispers and gestures, the paramedics were now leaving the room. Let her be, Mr. Davis had told them; she is better off here with me. I won't leave her.

No one noticed Cecelia staring from the doorway, only stepping back when the two paramedics passed. They were going to their next callout.

'Mr. Davis,' Cecelia stepped forward into the living mural. 'It's me, Cecelia Clark. I need to talk to you.'

He didn't move; he didn't turn to look at her, but perhaps he didn't care. Gently and carefully coming across, Cecelia stood beside him to help him keep his vigil. Mary had crept into herself to become a child whose complete efforts in life were just made by breathing. Side by side, they watched her.

'It's just a question of time,' Mr. Davis's hoarse voice said he had been crying. 'She had another stroke this morning and hasn't come out of it. I know she's fighting to stay with me. But I can't let her hang on like this. She's suffering.' It comforted him to have Cecelia keeping the vigil with him.

To Cecelia's eyes, it looked like Mary was asleep, a tired child sleeping.

'They wanted to take her to the hospital. But I couldn't do that to her. To die in some unknown bed, she would be afraid. People don't care in those places—'

If only Cecelia could tell him that people care and that all life is precious, these people are always busy.

'I don't know what to do anymore or how I'm going to

live without my Mary. The last question she asked me was when our girl was coming home. Soon, I told her, soon. But then she smiled at me, a funny kind of smile; I had never seen her smile like that before. She knows about our Marcia. She told me she was looking forward to seeing her soon. She knows she's dead.'

'Perhaps she was delirious.'

'No, no, she wasn't delirious. The look in her eyes told me she knew.' Turning to Cecelia as if he had just registered she was standing beside him. 'Days, hours, minutes. That's all they've given her. This year she would be sixty-three, but she looks a lot older than that. Come,' he said, walking out of the room. 'She's asleep. I need to sort out my plans for what I'm going to do without her.'

Sadness and tragedy could feel so heavy, Cecelia followed Mr. Davis into the kitchen.

'Thank you for being here,' he said, sitting down heavily. 'I would have been alone without you.'

'It's nothing,' Cecelia muttered under her breath, and then even quieter, 'I'm sorry.'

'Mary was supposed to have a few more years with me. Of course, I'm not ready to die yet, but there again, who is?'

How to broach her thoughts and the message she had come with. Shuffling her feet, he must have picked up on how agitated she was.

'You came here on your own?'

'Yes.'

'Why?'

She had to find the courage to tell him and to tell him now. If he didn't find out from her, he would find out another way, and it might not be so friendly.

'You've got something to tell me.' He was frowning, but not afraid. 'Come on, girl, tell me what's on your mind.'

Haunted eyes. There was nothing she could say to him now that would upset him anymore. He had gone past all the horrors of living.

'A body has been found on Elmansor Park baseball field,' Cecelia hurried out.

'And what is that to do with me?'

'I just thought you ought to know.'

'Yes, so now I know.'

'The police suspect it's the body of Tony Hare,' Cecelia faithfully recorded.

And now he smiled. The curling of his lip showed he was pleased. 'And today of all days. It's almost prophetic.'

'Yes,' she muttered, feeling in some way that she was to blame for Tony Hare's death. But she was just the bearer of ill tidings. A man was losing everything, and she had come to find out if he was guilty or not.

'Is that why you are here, to tell me the police have found his body? Is there anything else you've come to tell me?'

'Yes.'

'Well, go on, that's what you're here for.'

'They think it was you who killed Tony Hare.'

He laughed. He thought this was funny. 'I can see how everything adds up. It's obvious that I'm the likeliest suspect because of Marcia.' Mr. Davis was looking at Cecelia seriously. 'But how did this come about? It seems to me a mighty strange coincidence for the police to have stumbled on me.'

'I think it's my fault.' Biting her bottom lip, Cecelia felt she could cry. 'I mentioned your daughter Marcia had once been in love with Tony Hare and he had come to you when she was killed before vanishing. I'm so sorry. I don't know what possessed me to write those things.'

'Perhaps you thought I was guilty of his death. But never mind, it doesn't matter anymore. Nothing matters anymore.'

'But you might go to prison because of me.' Now distracted with worry, Cecelia needed his forgiveness even more.

'Quite honestly, I don't care if I do. It's all the same to me, but at least I will be in good company.'

Was he giving up on everything? He didn't know how sorry she was.

'Look, young lady, it's just another problem landing on my shoulders. Perhaps God figured I could take it. Whatever. It just doesn't matter anymore. I'm not going up to His place. I'm doomed to go down. You know, it strikes me I was an excellent candidate for bad luck. I didn't complain because I had my Mary. I thought if I complained, they would take her away from me and give me all those empty things that wealth can buy. But, if I could choose again, I'd choose exactly this same old life. So, I'm not going to fight.'

What could she do for him? What could she give him or say to him to make him happier? But he was accepting fate like a man prepared for execution. Suddenly, he was losing Mary, and it didn't matter if he was guilty or not. His life had been emptied of everything he loved. They could lay him on a bed and stick a needle in him for all he cared, as life must be important to want to hang on to it.

'I am all tuckered out,' he began. 'I'm just waiting for Mary, and she won't be hanging around for long.'

There was nothing she could say to stop him from thinking like this. It was like a replay of her old self when she was stalked with depression; what an ugly word. Shock was always a good strategy to get those tempers working.

'Did you kill Tony Hare?' if he said no, she would do everything she could to get him off.

His first response was a smile. 'What do you think? I take you as my judge and jury. You tell me what you think?'

She would have liked to say she didn't think he would commit such a crime, but who knows what a man would do to avenge his family, especially his daughter?

'I'm going to check on Mary. Do you want to come with me? Perhaps you can talk to her, make up a story to tell her about Marcia. Tell her how happy Marcia is. That would be a kindness I'd appreciate. Would you do that for me? You can forget about what you wrote in your notes for the police.'

For thirty pieces of silver, she had sold her soul. Such was the price of vanity.

Still, in that wavering sleep between one world and another, Mary Davis kept to her slumbers. While he watched, claiming every moment in this world with her. But now, looking at her once youthful face, what do you say to a dying woman?

'As I was passing, Mrs. Davis,' began Cecelia. 'I thought I would drop in to tell you about Marcia.'

Eyes flickered open, breaking through from her coma; Mrs. Davis wavering eyes fell on Cecelia and held them there. 'Marcia was writing to tell you, but as I was passing, she asked me to tell you myself. It's good news. She has passed her first exam to become top in her class. Her tutor is amazed by her progress; no one has done better than Marcia. And to start so late in the year. Her tutor is putting her down to do research—you know, special research for helping people all over the world. She is likely to find a cure for cancer. You don't know how special your daughter is—'

The gasp came from Mr. Davis's lips. 'Mary,' he called. 'Mary, can you hear what this young lady has just said?'

She looked at her husband.

'Mary, my darling. You've been in such a deep sleep. Did you hear what the lady tells you?'

It was the thinnest of whispers. Her eyes searched about the room until they again fell on Cecelia.

'Marcia,' the candle flickered as she spoke. No gale of breath was being ushered from these lips. 'You've come to see me, child. Oh, how I have missed you.'

Compulsively, Cecelia's eyes were glued to Mary Davis's, trapped under that deadly gaze.

'Marcia, are you afraid of me? Do I look so different? Won't you kiss your mother?'

'Marcia,' the voice from next to her said. The man with angry eyes looked down at Cecelia. 'Go to your mother.'

She looked into Mr. Davis's angry eyes, frightened by his temper, but his needs were bigger than hers. Just do this once for me. Pretend to be Marcia to give this gentle woman her peace.

Almost in tears, Cecelia bent down to kiss this dying woman. The softest and kindest of lips on the veil which hovered between life and death. And love was recorded. Unkind to Cecelia's mind that already she could smell death on this woman. No amount of cleaning would scrub this odor away.

'Oh, my dearest child,' whispered Mary Davis as the brush of Cecelia's lips touched her cheek. 'I had a dream that you were dead to me, Marcia. I have been ill for so long. But, thank God, it's not you who's dying; it's me.'

Tears fell fast from Mr. Davis's face. He was thankful for what Cecelia was doing for his Mary.

'Tell me how you've been, Marcia. Are you happy where you are?'

She didn't know how it came about, but Mrs. Davis's icy hand now sat in Cecelia's.

'Yes, I'm happy. I am the happiest I have ever been, except I am missing you.' That necessary lie.

'No, Marcia. This is your life. You are to do what you want to, whatever it takes to make yourself happy. You don't know what it means to us knowing you are happy. After everything we have been through, you are our success—' Mary's eyes were closing, but in her face was the blessed look of happiness.

Mr. Davis cried, long tears slipping over his cheeks while watching Mary until she succumbed to sleep again. There was no shame in his tears when he looked at Cecelia. She had done something wonderful, and his gratitude was more than he could contain.

'Come,' he said, bidding her to leave Mary's room.

Again, she followed him into the kitchen. In the strangeness of the early evening, Mr. Davis was taking the kettle off the hob to fill with water. Slowly and thoughtfully, the world of penalties was pushing down on his shoulders.

'We need to talk,' he said. Five minutes later, coffee was ready for them to drink.

16

On the way home, Cecelia went through their conversation again, which was more of a confession. They drank their coffee in silence, waiting to be released from this unnatural spell. Image by image dropped into the picture of a slow-growing evening filling with emerging shadows. These shadows came forward, ready for an introduction. Hands outstretched, I am Death. How do you do? You passed me several times; unfortunate for me, but not for you. I needed someone to make up the numbers. The grim reaper smiled. But I will be back for you too in the future.

'First, I want to thank you for what you have done for my wife.'

A much younger man now replaced the old man from five minutes ago; Mr. Davis was no longer sad. How is that so?

'You have given Mary something I could never give her; the peace she needed, knowing that something good had come out of our lives. Marcia will always be a success to her. As a parent, we want this for our children. And I thank you.

I could never have done that, but you did this for Marcia and my Mary. And I will always be grateful. So grateful,' he repeated and nodded, blessing himself with this one good deed.

It was an idea he took with him as he picked up his empty cup to go to the sink, slowly and methodically cradling the notion that this action was beautiful. As if every act had been carved out from wood and needed to be assessed, then loved.

'Will you stay while I go and check on Mary? I'll be only five minutes. Please stay, I have something to tell you.' He was by the door. 'This evening has meant so much to me. You gave Mary and me the understanding that we were still a family again.'

Mr. Davis was out of the room before anything more could be said. The emptiness of his presence certified a release while Cecelia still wondered why she was here. Looking about the bric-à-brac kitchen, the polished pots, a butler's sink, an old Welsh dresser which had seen better days.

Imagining as she sat looking about, it wasn't difficult to think of herself as part of this family, a family of love. A mother and father. A mother turning from her kitchen tops while preparing her children's dinner. Brother and sister were leaning across to each other, pulling faces, poking out tongues, the brother teasing his little sister and the little girl loving it and giggling. This time, a young Mr. Davis came home from work, pulling out his chair to sit down at the table with them. This had been a family, a real family, and nothing like Cecelia's memories. Her vision of their home lives just showed how unhappy and fearful her life had been. But worse things happen to others, Cecelia reminded herself dutifully as she drove herself home.

Her head was clouded with imageries, from Mary's face to Mr. Davis and then to a couple of young girls standing on a corner. Children used for sexual fantasies. Slipping a coin into a slot. For the corrupt, everybody was a commodity. A cruel and immoral world filled with unscrupulous people living off the vulnerable. Her problems, by comparison, were nothing, nothing at all. Nothing she could truly complain about, except her problems hurt.

But now, she had learned valuable lessons from this experience that people like her father, a tall and strong man, can be broken and driven to suicide by the torment of hatred. Her father had been a good-looking man, and an educated one. Someone to be proud of. But Tina took her pleasure in marrying to destroy, for only in that way did she feel superior. So why had her mother hated him so much that she could laugh with derision when she was told he was dead?

This was a strange and cold world.

When Mr. Davis returned from Mary's bedroom, his face, once crippled by grief, had thrown off its props to become something like tranquil, the same she had seen on Mary's face. He was at peace with himself.

'You've got such a long way to go with your life,' he said, retaking his seat. 'You are not as strong as you look, are you?'

Cecelia shrugged, baffled by the change of his conversation.

'I want you to promise me to look after yourself. In many ways, you remind me of Marcia. She was a sweet-natured girl with spirit.' He lowered his eyes again. 'Nothing is going to touch Mary anymore,' he smiled. 'She will never awake from this sleep.'

'You mean she is dead?'

'Yes. I kissed her on the lips, then her forehead, and then

I made the sign of the cross on her. She has gone to our children, Rodin and Marcia. And it won't be long before I follow her.'

That automated response to stretch out her hand and refute this statement would not be welcomed, not by him. He had grown weary of his life; it held no pleasure.

'I, who would have given my life for Mary, who worshipped the ground she walked on, have taken her life. It was best this way.'

Had she heard correctly? Mr. Davis had killed his wife? No, this was not possible.

'It is better she goes now than later; I don't want her to know what I have done.' He spoke with great calmness, as if he had made peace with himself; his hands were on the kitchen table, clasping each other. 'I don't want you to do anything about what I am going to tell you; you will be the only person who will know the truth. It doesn't matter what happens once I am gone.'

Was he well? Cecelia struggled to understand what was going on. Was he saying he had killed his wife, yet there was no regret on his face, no pride, nothing except empty capitulation? It was the same as her father. Before he went on that long walk to his own death, daddy gave her a letter. Read it, he told her, looking at the clock. Read it the following morning. I want you to promise me you will look for happiness, CeCe. Never let anyone be cruel to you. You are special, Cecelia; you should know that.

Now Mr. Davis was staring into his cup of cold coffee as if looking into his destiny.

'I killed Tony Hare, and I am sorry for that. He didn't love our Marcia like she deserved to be loved. It was one reason why I took his life. It was wrong, I know that know, but he wouldn't stop crying and telling me it was all his fault. And because of that, I decided he was guilty. I hadn't planned what I was going to do. I told him I wanted him to make a memorial for Marcia, which reassured him. We went in my car to Elmansor Park; he became optimistic, almost happy. We were going to do something together for the first time. I asked him to choose the place for the memorial. And when he went to find the place, I took an ax from my car and hit him. He never knew he was going to die. Mercifully, it was quick.'

The silence grabbed her, hugging her in a vice-like grip, breathing into her ears that it was never going to let her go. Would she remain suspended in this time-lock forever?

'You can go now, Cecelia Clark. You haven't done anything wrong. Have a good life, Cecelia. You deserve it.'

What was going to happen next was the question that needed answering. But as for her own life, because in telling Cecelia to leave, he was giving it back to her. Glad to run out with her life because, for that brief second, she thought he would claim it. If what he had told her was the truth, she wanted to get home, bury her head, and forget what had happened. But Phoebe would be waiting for her, and seeing her distressed, would demand to know what was wrong.

'Hello Phoebe, it's me, Cecelia,' she had hit the answer-phone and was glad of it. 'I'm running late. I won't be home tonight. I'm staying in a motel. Apologies for letting you know at the last moment. I'll tell you all about it tomorrow. Bye.'

She was going back to her own house to escape the world. Tomorrow she would go to Phoebe's and apologize, but tonight Cecelia needed to be on her own. She needed to sort out what was going on in her head.

The first thing she was going to do tomorrow was to go to the station. It would be difficult because of Mr. Davis's confession. And in that senseless argument of hope against the truth, she wished he had been lying.

Don't think about it anymore tonight. Your head's in a muddle, and you need to sleep. But there was one thing she was sure of. She was going to quit journalism, rent out her house, and move in with Phoebe. She had enough of this disturbing life; it was obvious she wasn't cut out for it. Phoebe and her world of flowers was the place she wanted to be.

Taking sleeping tablets had not been a good idea, especially as Cecelia wanted to make an early start in the morning. But it was a toss-up. Better to get some sleep than none at all, after the day she had been through. Natural sleep would not be possible.

The morning alarm had gone off, and she had slept right through. The sun laying across the bed embellished her face with warmth. After taking that long, luxurious stretch of good sleep, Cecelia realized it wasn't Sunday, and she wasn't on holiday either. She was late!

Leaping out of her bed with a quick tidy-up to get her house ready for renters. Cecelia hurried for the shower. It would be a cold one, but it didn't matter; it freshened her up with a shriek. She had no towels. It also meant her yesterday's clothes had to do for today. But this wasn't unusual.

Nothing to eat, nothing to drink except water. She would get herself something after going to the police station. Her watch told her it was gone eleven in the morning. How long did she sleep?

On a sunny day, the drive to the station was a pleasant one. Unfortunately, the smell of burgers and stuff in the air made Cecelia hungry. If there were time, she would have treated herself to a hotdog with plenty of ketchup, mustard, and onions. Junk food of gourmet standing. And the reason she was so hungry was that she had nothing to eat yesterday.

Reporters waited outside the Alondra Police Department. Cecelia got out of her car to make her way to the front. It made her feel so uneasy having so many people hanging around? Then out of the offices walked Detective Travis with papers in her hands.

'It has been confirmed that the Alondra Slasher has taken a sixth victim,' Detective Travis said to the waiting crowd of news reporters. Again, she was confronted with flashing lights.

Another victim? Came a yell from the crowd.

'I can't comment anymore except that we are closing in on the murderer.'

'Do you have any ideas who it is?' one reporter shouted.

Flashes of lights continued to be triggered.

'I am asking the public to carry on taking precautions. There is a dangerous man still out there. Now, ladies and gentlemen, I'm asking you to let the police get on with what they are good at. Good afternoon.'

Frugal information wasn't enough to satisfy their hungry appetite. Another young woman's death meant panic. What was happening to Alondra?

Walking into the police station, sounds of shock and helplessness bounced off the walls. Her interview with the Davises was worth nothing in the face of what had just happened. A man who killed his dying wife was not top news anymore. Standing over another uniformed man's desk, pointing out something of importance, was Detective Travis.

Seeing Cecelia, Detective Travis nodded. She would be over in a minute.

'What a day?' said Detective Travis, collecting Cecelia with her look. 'Come to my office, and I'll tell you about it.'

'I heard what you had to say outside a few minutes ago,' said Cecelia, closing the door behind her. 'Another victim?'

'Yes, another victim, and this time he has changed his M. O.' Detective Travis went to her filing cabinet to get out a folder. The way she slammed it shut enforced that she was angry. 'But he will not get away forever. This man doesn't work on his own. He has a helper.'

'Do you mean two men are raping and murdering women?'

'No. We've had descriptions of a woman—have you heard about the Moors murderers in England?'

No, she hadn't.

'Child murders, which shocked the world in England in the 1960s.' Detective Travis sat down with the folder. 'Myra Hindley and Ian Brady killed five children, one of them being Lesley Ann Downey. She was taken from a fairground, made to pose naked for photographs, tortured, and then murdered. Why would an attractive blonde-haired woman, Myra Hindley, help her lover do such a sick act as that? She was the one who coaxed the children to their deaths. Charming them, promising them. These children trusted her, and she betrayed their trust. I believe this is what we are looking for. A murderer and his assistant.' She opened her folder and took out the papers.

'The Slasher's female accomplice is doing just what Myra Hindley did. Aiding and abetting this man by helping to set up and kill his victims.'

'But that's monstrous.'

'Yes, it is. I sometimes think that the evilest killers in the world are women. You only need to look at Nazi Germany.'

The upside-down picture was hard to distinguish, which

was just as well. Cecelia didn't want to see the recordings of this death.

'This time, the monster changed his method of working,' she frowned. 'An older woman, and unlike the others, she was not a virgin.' Yet the photograph looked horrifying real. 'I can tell you one thing for free; this man hates women.'

No, she didn't want to see the photographs.

'Did he leave a message?'

'A good question. And yes, he did.' Detective Travis looked up. 'But this time, the message was carved across the victim's chest. He did this while she was still alive. He tied her up with some sort of garden twine. She was also gagged so no one could hear her. The message he wrote was, *I do not love her.* If he didn't love her, why did he kill her? It doesn't make sense.'

'Does she have any family?' Cecelia didn't know what made her ask this question.

'No, she doesn't have any family, at least not in this country. On the other hand, I think she might have a husband.'

'She's a foreigner?' fear was dripping, splashing drops one by one onto Cecelia's forehead. 'Where does she come from?' let it be anywhere but England.

'She's English or was English, and she died horribly. The man had a metal stake. You know, the sort used for pegging down tents. Well, this happened to be a large one. He plunged it into her heart like a vampire after he had raped her. But I don't know when she stopped feeling anything after the way he cut her up. I think he might have used the stake first on her internally.'

The world was starting to move from side to side.

'The shop was a mess. Flowers everywhere.'

'It wasn't a flower shop, was it?'

'Yes, was that a guess?' she paused. 'She was killed late

yesterday afternoon when no one was about. The Slasher locked the door behind him.'

Detective Travis turned the photographs around.

'Twenty-nine years old; it was a wicked and agonizing way to die.'

She lay on the floor of the flower shop with her eyes still open wide, her legs and arms had been tied to four corners of the rooms, and a stake had been pushed into her naked chest. She was dead. Phoebe was dead.

17

In a hospital room by herself, Cecelia was sedated and quarantined from the rest of the world. Whenever she woke from this strange detachment, she looked around the room and wondered where she was and what had happened. In the back of her mind and cut off from her thoughts, she knew something terrible had occurred. So perhaps it wasn't a bad thing to stay unconscious to the truth. The comforting numbness held her like big, friendly arms.

Witnessing Cecelia's meltdown, Detective Travis called for the paramedics. She realized something bad happened. Twice, Detective Travis had visited Cecelia, sitting beside her while wondering what to do. The only work she could do was to find the person who had murdered her friend. If only Travis had known that Phoebe Howard was Cecelia's friend.

Still comforted by the effects of Xanax, the world kept its distance. It was a dream which had happened just recently until she remembered too closely her loss. But this was safely secured and put out of the way with the help of the tranquilizer. And then she would weep for Phoebe and all that she meant to her.

Strange, but this time, it was worse than losing her father. How was that possible when she barely knew Phoebe, but she had come to love her with that special kind of love. A woman's love for another woman is more beautiful than for a man. She had lost someone greater than herself, and no one understood. Don't men love other men with a passion? Doesn't a man understand how another man thinks far better than his love for a woman?

How she loved Phoebe, and how she ached to see her face, the lyric of her English voice when speaking the same language. What will she do without her? Her future had been planned with Phoebe; like twins, they were living the same timeline. Now smashed and deliberately ruined by death. The whole of her life watched her, staring back in judgment.

Did God hate her? He must do. He took the only special person from her again. And then, she would find herself weeping for the loss of happiness. Wait until the night when the sleeping tablets would take away her grief. Now Cecelia understood why people became junkies. And why they took themselves from the ugliness of society to thirst their grief with alcohol to get out of their heads.

But what were her plans going to be for her future? What future? She didn't care.

'If I had known,' it was Detective Travis's voice. These voices came and went with lives of their own in the strange white inhabited dream. 'Will she get over it?' another voice asked. 'It should have been me, not her.' A familiar voice because it was her own. She fell asleep, not wanting to wake anymore.

'Hello Cecelia,' a shape appeared from out of the white haze. A friendly and warm voice.

Somebody was sitting with her and smiling. Had she died? She would be grateful for that; an angel was sitting beside her.

'It's me,' the face still smiled. 'I've been sitting beside you for two hours. You remember me, don't you? Your friend, Mary Ann Leigh. I'm here for you in your hour of need. And I know all about what happened. I know how you are feeling. You are struggling to understand what has happened to your world. But you are not on your own anymore, Cecelia. Please open your eyes and look at me.'

'Go—away.'

'Now, why did I think you would say that? When I know you are not ungrateful.'

'I don't want you here, don't you understand? I want to be left on my own.'

'But the world goes on no matter what has happened, Cecelia. You are feeling sorry for yourself, and it's got to stop. You understand that, don't you? So, no matter how you feel, you've got to carry on living.'

'For fuck's sake, get the hell out of here—' Cecelia had opened her eyes and raised her head in temper. How she hated this woman. It should have been her who was murdered.

'Well, I suppose that's an improvement with interesting language. And you are a scholar,' Mary Ann was smiling.

'Go away. I want to die. Just go away.' Cecelia hated this woman more than she had ever hated her mother. How was that possible? How was anything possible in this cold, cruel world?

'Yes, I know you want to die, Cecelia. It's obvious you

want to die. You've been here for four days, refusing to respond. But you can't stay here forever.'

'Why are you here?' consciousness left out in the cold can suddenly rush back in. 'What are you doing here? How did you know I was in the hospital?'

'Well, is this something like gratitude? I take it as if it is. For the first time, you are interested in me.'

Cecelia's stark eyes looked without comprehension at Mary Ann.

'I suppose you can call it a bit of luck if finding you here in the hospital is lucky. You know I'm housebound because of my fears.' She stared at Cecelia, waiting for her to realize what a momentous act she had made to visit her. 'Yes, well, perhaps you want to forget this for the time being because your grief and problems are far bigger than mine. I heard there was another murder on the news. I was shocked, well I think everyone is shocked. Anyhow, when this sort of news comes out, you always think about yourself and the people in your life, which in this case was you. I thought, my God, I hope the Slasher hadn't got you.'

Cecelia stared hard at Mary Ann, partly hating and partly loathing, but waiting for her to go.

'Cecelia, you can't lie here for the rest of your life, not only because it's not good for you, but also because it's expensive. But, listen, my dear, you've got to live. From what I understand, you hardly knew her.'

'Shut your mouth. You know nothing about me,' Cecelia shouted. The sedation was slipping away.

'Yes, I'm sorry. You are right, except perhaps that I care about you.'

'I don't want you caring about me.'

'There is no one else to care for you, Cecelia, so you can't afford to be too fussy. When I heard about the murder, I was worried. I wondered where you could be, but you seemed to fall off the planet. So, I telephoned your house and left a message. In fact, I left several messages. The voicemail must have got sick of me.'

Would she not go away?

'By now, I was anxious about you. I was convinced the sixth victim was you. Oh, how I said my prayers. And then I remembered you worked with the police, and that's when I told William to find out if you were there. It was over two days ago when we discovered you were in hospital—'

'How did you get to see me?'

Mary Ann put a hand to her mouth to cover it while she laughed. For some reason, she thought what Cecelia said was funny.

'I told the staff on duty that I was your cousin.' Her cheerfulness became confidential. 'If I didn't, I believe they wouldn't have allowed me to see you. You have been very ill, Cecelia. I don't believe you understand the validity of your recent actions. There was talk about sectioning you. And once they put you in a secure area, you'd never get out if that happened. And I mean, never.'

Cecelia refused to look at this giant woman, who resembled more of an angel and not a monster from hell.

'Perhaps, Cecelia, you are too ill to understand what I'm saying. This is where you're vulnerable and why you need to be looked after. As the only friend you have, I have taken it upon myself to do something about your situation. And so, Cecelia, I have saved you.'

What was she talking about?

'Did you know you tried to shoot Detective Travis?'

Shoot Detective Travis?

'I can see by your eyes you didn't. You must have gone

mad, but fortunately for you, the Detective is not pressing charges. You frightened lots of people that day.'

Cecelia heard what she was saying, but didn't understand. This can't be true; Mary Ann was making it up. There was nothing in her memory to remind her of doing it. Something was tapping on her arm, an unseen warning, nudging its nose and staring at her. No, her mind was clear of that accusation.

'I see you don't believe me. And I wouldn't have believed it myself if I had not read your notes. Your actions frightened everyone, which is why you are in this room on your own. The staff is keeping an eye on you, and you can't blame them. You are a dangerous woman, Cecelia, and that is a lot of power to have.'

Looking about her frightened eyes with frightening thoughts, this safe place was not so safe as it was before. A restroom had suddenly become a tomb and prison to contain her. She tried to lift herself, but her limbs would not obey because they had been strapped down. She hadn't noticed before that her wrists were also bound. The cot in which she lay had wrist attachments. Her security had suddenly become a nightmare. The hands of control had taken away her freedom.

'I'm going home now,' said Mary Ann, standing and brightening her face with an overly cheerful smile. 'But I'll come and see you tomorrow.' She went across to the mirror and took an appreciative look at her reflection. 'You need all the friends you can get with the way things are looking for you. But perhaps we can sort something out to help you?'

Coming across, she pecked the top of Cecelia's head with a cold red kiss.

'William is waiting for me in the waiting room. I'm so lucky to have him.' She touched her hair in reassurance.

'He's been so good to me. Funnily enough, he asked to see you,' she laughed. 'But by the look on your face, I am glad I said no. I told him that Cecelia is not well enough, and she won't like anyone seeing her in this state. He's so good, he does everything I say, and I believe he would do anything I asked. You don't look well, Cecelia. You've lost a great deal of weight; your face looks gaunt and haggard. It is not a pleasing effect. But it's nothing which can't be sorted with food and kindness. Well, I'm going before I outstay my welcome. Too-da-loo, as the English say.'

Gloved hands, Mary Ann slowly opened the door, and with a quick look into the corridor, cheerfully left Cecelia.

It was a relief. Two hours later, Detective Travis came to see a conscious Cecelia. She had eyed her resents and passively kept thinking. If this were madness, perhaps she should give in to it. Then, at least, she wouldn't know who she was anymore.

'I was visiting James Patts, and I thought I would see how you are,' said Detective Travis, entering. Her professional eyes scrutinized Cecelia with a detective's mind.

'Did I try to kill you?' this impossible question had been haunting Cecelia.

'Who told you that?'

'Then it's true.'

'Miss Clark, don't be too hard on yourself. You weren't in your right mind, and it was my fault.'

'Why didn't you put me in prison? Surely, trying to kill a law enforcer is tantamount to being a criminal. Therefore, I should have been put in prison.'

'Yes, it is, but—'

'Then why am I not in prison?'

'Do you want to be in prison, girl?' Travis was confused.

'If I deserve it.' Her anger hunted her down. So, had Mr. Davis passed on his bad luck to her?

Taking a deep and necessary breath, Detective Travis redressed her thoughts. 'You saw something you should not have seen, a photograph. It should not have happened, but it did, and I'm sorry. I was thoughtless. I had forgotten you were a civilian. It's as much my fault as yours with what happened—'

'What trying to kill you?' oh, how ridiculous.

'Yes. I needed someone to talk to. You were a good person to exercise out my thoughts, but I went over the limit. I thought we had a good rapport, but I didn't know— not in a thousand years that you knew the victim. So, I showed you a picture you weren't prepared for, especially to see the death of a friend.'

'Is Phoebe dead? Is she really dead?' Cecelia's face screwed into a ball. The nightmare she hoped wasn't true became a fact.

'Yes, she is dead. Yes, Cecelia, cry. Cry for the loss of your friend. But, don't give in to the madness which deprives you of your person. Your English friend wouldn't have wanted that for you.'

Such great and inconsolable tears fell down Cecelia's cheeks. Impossible to hide her face away because of the bands around her wrists. Detective Travis stood awkwardly and tried to put her arm around Cecelia. She was not the most tactile of women.

'I don't want to live anymore without her,' sobbed Cecelia. 'She was my friend, the only real friend I ever had,' her words were mumbled with tears.

'I don't want to hear you talking that way,' clumsily, Travis patted Cecelia's hand. To give up on life when it's so precious. God doesn't give this life to everyone. How could she show Cecelia life was worth living? 'You have had one good friend, and you will have many more—'

'No, you don't understand. I find friendships difficult.'

'Sure, but not impossible. Nothing is impossible if you want it. The art of life is in not giving up. As the skill of love is in not being afraid to be hurt. You are a good person.' Travis looked into Cecelia's eyes to command her grief. 'No one wants to be hurt. I don't, and most of the world doesn't. But you've got to go on and give other people a chance. You've had a good friendship with this woman, so don't throw it away, Cecelia. Rejoice in the time you had with her.'

Travis stayed longer with Cecelia than she should have, knowing she was needed at the station. But her concern for Cecelia demanded that she give more of herself than normal. There was a long journey ahead for this troubled woman.

Comforted now by Xanax, Cecelia settled down into a long and healthy sleep. But, against her will, the healing had started.

Every day, Mary Ann came faithfully to see her, always patient and happy with tales of entertainment about her acting career. At first, Cecelia refused to listen, but she smiled at Mary Ann's stubbornness after the second day. William, she told Cecelia, had made a difference in her life. Perhaps one day Cecelia would meet him. Maybe she would meet someone like William. No, no, no one, not anymore, shuddered Cecelia angrily. Didn't she understand Phoebe was special?

'Yes, I understand,' said Mary Ann gently.

The days became longer, digging into their promises of what they could give. Mary Ann brought Cecelia light reading material to pass her time away in the hospital, while everything about the Alondra Slasher case was kept out of her way. She was not to be taxed on anything until she was well enough.

When Mary Ann arrived a week later, it was to find that Cecelia's wrist bands were off. The first concrete evidence Cecelia was getting better. A psychiatrist had spoken to her and found her grief had made her temporarily insane, and although she was still suffering from loss, Cecelia was now dealing with it. Still reluctant to discharge her from care, he left Cecelia's room just as Mary Ann entered.

The following day brought more news. Mary Ann, glowing with good tidings, entered Cecelia's room.

'The psychiatrist is going to discharge you this weekend with the promise that you must see him three times a week for the first month.' Her lemon-colored dress and long golden blond hair made her look like a Party Princess, especially with those striking blue eyes. Mary Ann promoted strength and vitality with her shoulders back, slim, attractive, and at five feet eight with heels making her five feet eleven. She was obviously still working out. But, more than anything, Mary Ann looked happy. In her happiness, she looked like she had just won Miss America. Mary Ann was in love.

'I understand, Cecelia, that you won't have anywhere to stay when you're discharged.'

'I still have my home.'

In such a short time, so much had happened. Now she knew the bad hand of madness could not claim her. As a different resolve was awakening. What was she going to do with the time she had? Yet no one thought to tell her just what was going to happen to her next.

'You are not going home, Cecelia. That was one condition of your release.' Mary Ann pulled herself up to show the full command of her height. 'You'll be discharged into my care for the first few weeks.'

'To you. I'm not a dog on a license. I might have had a minor breakdown, but I'm still in charge of myself.' A ridiculous idea to stay with Mary Ann when all the time she had tried to resist her.

'Let people help you, Cecelia. You need to let people into your life,' coaxed Mary Ann. 'This was the big mistake you made last time. You put too much trust in this other woman, Phoebe, when you hardly knew her.' Mary Ann's charm had reverted to anger.

'I knew her better than you thought I did—and I loved her. She was the best friend I ever had.'

But Mary Ann wasn't listening. Instead, she had turned her back on Cecelia, clasping her hands together while making plans of her own.

'You will stay in the next room to mine. Do you remember you saw it when you went to the bathroom?'

The picture of Sarah came into Cecelia's mind.

'That's the room you will have. I have been redecorating it. William has been helping me. He is looking forward to you coming to stay with me.'

'I'm not coming to live with you, no matter how temporary,' said Cecelia, fuming, while feeling her life again was being taken out of her hands.

'Then you'll stay in the hospital for a considerable time,' said Mary Ann. 'Don't you see your stubbornness is working against you? It would help if you changed the way you behave, Cecelia. It has already got you into a great deal of trouble. Four weeks, that's all you need to do. Four weeks with me and then you can return to your life. You've got to prove to the psychiatrist you can be trusted.'

Hating the loss of control, Cecelia sealed her lips together. It just wasn't fair.

'Anyhow, think about it. I told the psychiatrist you have agreed to stay with me until you get something sorted out for yourself. William is going to help as well. He said he would do the footwork for you, and look at rooms to rent until your house is vacant again. For goodness' sake, Cecelia, don't be stubborn. You'll only open yourself up to another breakdown,' she was exasperated. 'I know you're not stupid—in fact, far from it. Do something wise for yourself.'

Leaning back in the orthopedic chair, Cecelia eyed Mary Ann with meanness.

'I would like you to think of me as your friend—oh Cecelia, why are you always so stubborn?'

18

———

Despite every caution being taken to keep the news from Cecelia, she heard about the latest reports of the Alondra Slasher. People were coming forward, offering details of sightings. A few people had been interviewed, but none had been detained. On the whole, the police still weren't any the wiser. Someone in their community, perhaps the person living next door, the man stacking the shelves in the supermarket, or even the friendly cop. All were potential rapists until the culprit was caught.

While Cecelia's mind lay dormant, stirred by nothing. Even when she thought of Phoebe, it was from a distance, helped by the Xanax, it kindly clouded her mind. Her thoughts did not progress any further than that. What did it all mean? What was the point of any friendship when it was always taken away? Never in her life had she had any success, not even with Thomas. If there was anyone who was the love of her life, it had to be him. But, oh, what a fool she had been, especially in front of his wife. The rules of the game are they should tell you they are married first before picking the flowers. But, if she had known, would she have walked away from him? Yes, she would.

And yet, when she thought about this amazing romantic affair, there was something poetic about her sordid fling. To lose her virginity to someone handsome gave balm to her bedeviled pride. And she loved him? She loved him with the passionate wildness of her heart. And if he was honest, Thomas truly loved her. So typical wasn't it, that it was Peter who claimed he had fallen in love with her. A man who did not understand love at all. Ironic. Yet, he proved to be the one most loyal. But it wasn't him she wanted. She wanted Thomas every time.

The day came of her hospital discharge. It should have been a day to look forward to, but it was not. Instead, to Cecelia's surprise, she was fearful. A wall of darkness stood before her, impossible in its unknown quantity, waiting and watching and trying to calculate what her next move would be. The world outside had become unpredictable.

Detective James Patts had also made Cecelia a visit. He was going to be discharged to his wife soon, and he was looking forward to it. So it was to him Cecelia told who she was going to stay with. At first, he was pleased. It was good to get out of a place filled only with illness. But then he saw the frown on Cecelia's face, and with his interpretation of her reluctance, suggested she come and stay with them.

'Come and stay with my wife and me. The children have moved out. You can have one of their rooms. My wife will get one ready for you.'

She nearly said yes, nearly said she would have loved to stay with these two. But Mrs. Patts would have enough to do with looking after her husband.

'No,' she smiled sickly. 'Mary Ann is looking forward to me staying with her. It's something she's wanted forever, me living with her.' She stopped in anger. 'It seems to have worked out for her.'

'I am sure,' Patts said, not quite understanding the complexities of female friendship, 'that she will look after you and pamper you. There's no harm in that.'

'Yes, you're right,' said Cecelia, now feeling mean. Mary Ann's offer came from goodwill. 'It's just that sometimes she can be suffocating—'

'I understand,' smiled James. 'A person can go over the top with their good intentions, but you said she has a man in her life?'

Cecelia nodded.

'Then you'll find she will be more eager to spend her time with this new man. I expect she wants to do good by you after all; as I understand it, you've been kind to her.'

'Yes,' Cecelia smiled, but that smile was lost on a sad face.

'I'm being discharged later this afternoon,' James Patts told Cecelia, sitting in his wheelchair while she got her few things together. Mrs. Patts had heard a little of Cecelia's story from her husband, and understanding the nakedness of hospitals, had kindly bought her a few bits of feminine needs in a nice overnight stay bag.

'Yes, it's nice to go home,' smiled Cecelia, hoping the growing stress inside would die. What she would have liked was to go straight to her own house, lock her door, and have that cry she needed.

You will be all right; James Patts wanted to tell Cecelia, but then the door opened, and in walked Mary Ann. She was one hell of an attractive woman and so tall. She was in love, and this made a difference. Automatically, he looked down at her rather large feet and saw she was wearing four-inch heels. The extra height made her look enormous over six feet, while Cecelia in her stocking feet was dwarfed. Mary Ann's size alone was daunting.

'Don't tell me,' Mary Ann said in an unfamiliar voice to Cecelia's ears. 'You are Detective Patts. You came to my house after I reported I had been raped.' There wasn't supposed to be any mention of the Alondra Slasher anymore around Cecelia while her mind was unsettled.

Where had Mary Ann's voice come from? Cecelia frowned. Mary Ann sounded stronger, surer of herself, and with an English accent. But, of course, she was an actress, and an English accent was attractive.

'I am pleased Cecelia has someone she can call her friend,' smiled James Patts. It was strange, as both of them were on their best manners. He felt uncomfortable. Scratching the back of his head, he eyeballed her. It must be those shoes; the woman looked so unbelievably tall.

'Thank you,' said Mary Ann. 'I have always been Cecelia's friend. I care about her greatly. Give me your bag Cecelia, let me carry it for you.'

What was this? Why was she talking this way and treating her like she was a deficient idiot? Or an adult supervising their child. She was so condescending. And yet, nothing was said by Cecelia, who drifted over the supposed insult intoxicated by Xanax.

'I'll see you around,' said James Patts, watching Cecelia's now rather slight frame leave the room. Catching Cecelia's eyes, he had to agree; he wasn't comfortable with the tall woman taking over.

'I see you two are good friends,' smiled Mary Ann, looking from James Patts to Cecelia. 'You and your wife must come to dinner one night. You would like that, wouldn't you, Cecelia?'

Cecelia didn't know anymore, but more than anything else, she had stopped caring.

'And everyone can meet my beau. He's such a nice man. Everyone, I'm sure, will like him. We must arrange a date, of course, only when you are well.' she said, looking from one to the other. 'We must get on now. You're tired, aren't you, Cecelia? I've got to get you home. Oh, she definitely will be spoiled, Mr. Patts, although I should call you Detective Patts.' She smiled a horizontal smile.

'Might not be for long,' he grimaced. 'I believe retirement might be on its way. Which will please the wife? Being a police officer is not a peaceful occupation.'

'No, I shouldn't imagine it isn't.' A disinterested smile crossed her face. 'We are to use that wheelchair to take you out of the hospital, Cecelia.' She pointed to the one which had been brought to the room earlier. 'Think of this as an adventure.'

The collapsed wheelchair was targeted by Mary Ann, who quickly shook it into shape and then waited for Cecelia to climb in.

'Goodbye,' she waved airily to James Patts while pushing Cecelia out through the door.

Hospitals are all the same worldwide, and it doesn't matter if they're private or charity. Impersonal. Even moguls lose their sovereign prestige once they lay horizontal in clothes designed for easy access. An untroubled ride to vulnerability, the steady footsteps carried through while pushing the wheelchair around corners and into the elevator. All so impersonal. When Mary Ann passed nurses and doctors, her confidence rose; she was the adult in charge of the invalid. In contrast, Cecelia felt like a child in its first pushchair.

'I will leave you here,' said Mary Ann, parking the

wheelchair in the spacious reception. Just yards away beyond the glass, the sun shone on a brand-new day. 'William is on his way to collect you.'

From behind Cecelia, Mary Ann applied the brakes.

'I forgot to tell you; I'm killing two birds with one stone while coming to the hospital. I'm going for my cancer checkup. Which I didn't tell you about. I don't want you to feel sorry for me. I had breast cancer last year. Now I'm due for a preliminary scan, which is nothing to worry about, I'm sure. Keep your fingers crossed, Cecelia, and say a prayer if you can afford one. I would be thankful.'

You've had breast cancer. The words leaked out into the silence as Cecelia watched Mary Ann walk away. So, that was the reason for the high heels and smart clothes. Mary Ann was putting on a brave face, and here she was thinking only of herself.

But she wished Mary Ann had stayed to introduce her to William. A man she had never met who was now going to be in charge of her. Only from a distance and briefly had she seen Mary Ann's boyfriend, and it wasn't a good reception. In fact, he was highly strung, which didn't inspire any confidence. But if Mary Ann said he would come and collect her, she was certain William would be there. If not, she would wait until Mary Ann had finished with her appointment.

Would he know who she was? How Cecelia wished she could turn back time and return home to Phoebe instead of going to Mary Ann's house. But the Slasher had already killed Phoebe. He had entered the flower shop not long after Cecelia left. She must have missed this monster by minutes. If she had stayed for ten minutes longer, Phoebe might still be alive, and he would have taken someone else instead. But he didn't. So many ifs and regrets. What had Phoebe done to incite his passion?

Ten minutes passed. It was awkward sitting here, as already two people had come across to find out if she was all right. She smiled; she was okay and waiting for a friend. But she knew these people were also keeping a close eye on her. Nice people, but this was embarrassing.

The front entrance split as sliding doors ran to open, and a man in a navy overcoat on such a warm afternoon entered. He looked from side to side before spotting Cecelia, and without smiling, he strolled over to her. This must be William. Catching Cecelia's eye, he then glanced away. He was either shy or nervous.

'I'm William,' he said, standing in front of her, frowning. 'Mary Ann's friend. I take it you're Cecelia Clark?'

What is that instinct which unjustly sums someone up as being unfavorable? When you know you haven't given them a chance to speak for themselves. It came at once that she did not like him, yet there was no reason for her dislike.

'Yes,' a smile was hard in coming; a smile would be nice.

And then he grinned and nodded. 'It's not easy, is it, being a friend of Mary Ann? You have to do everything she wants. And she's always right. Haven't you noticed how strong she is, mentally? She's a positive person.'

This was a man who understood the lady he loved.

'Come on, let's take you home and make a fuss of you. I'm sure you'll love it.' Then, going behind her, he took hold and pushed the wheelchair. Then, with a jump, he took off the brakes.

'So, no. I didn't get my driving license in this country, does it show?'

He had an accent that Cecelia couldn't place, but she had heard its likeness before. A mixture of everything with the peculiar sound of English. Like all people whose laugh did not match their size, William giggled nervously like a girl. It was so out of context. But then he stopped, embarrassed, an awkward man who was grateful someone like Mary Ann had taken him on. Their reflections on the automatic glass doors showed him pushing her chair, one hand on the frame while the other to his mouth was awkward and self-conscious.

'I'll take the chair back to the hospital.' He was almost apologetic after lifting her out and placing her carefully into the back of the car. 'I won't be a moment.'

Looking through the window, she watched him swagger away. This reminded her of a dog, friendly and endearing, wanting to please, and knowing that she was watching him. He marched quickly back; the good doggy was very obedient.

Oh well, what next?

Did she fancy him? No. He was Mary Ann's, but there was something about him. Nice brown eyes, yet he was nervous as if he weren't sure about himself, which was appealing.

'Shouldn't we wait for Mary Ann?' Cecelia leaned forward as he climbed into the car. 'I'm sure she won't be too long.'

'Yes, I suggested it would be sensible to her.' He had his back to her. Glancing from the driver's mirror was just a pair of eyes. 'But Mary Ann's instruction was to take you home first and make you comfortable before returning for her.'

'Oh, okay.'

Funny, the things you find out about people, the oddly intimate, throwaway details. He did everything Mary Ann told him. The Xanax was wearing off.

She hoped he wouldn't talk to her during the journey. Her nerves were still raw from talking. Just get to bed and forget. It was time to have another one of those tablets. Edgy, sharp corners were sharpening, chaffing her nerves and making those long strides into screaming. Take a tablet, go to bed, and hopefully sleep.

They traveled in silence for the rest of the journey while the miles clicked on carefully until they arrived.

'I'll go and open the door. I won't be a moment.' He turned to look at Cecelia with a wisp of a smile, gentle and carefully hidden behind a well-trained mustache.

She watched him go to the door. He wasn't her taste in men, but to be honest, he wasn't bad looking. In fact, he looked rather cute. Dark short wavy hair and dark brown eyes, which were almost black. Perhaps his nose was too wide, and he really ought to do something about his thick eyebrows because they moved about with a life of their own. Well-dressed, although perhaps not appropriate for this warm weather.

With the house door opened, he walked back to her. Abruptly, he bent down, slid his hand underneath her, and raised her. He moved quickly and deftly.

'I can walk,' Cecelia rose in his arms. 'I'm not helpless—'

'I'm to follow orders, and besides, you don't weigh much. You are as light as a bird.' And then he poked his nose into her hair and sniffed.

What she was feeling was strange and disturbing. He held her with an iron grip.

'Can you put me down, please?'

His fingers curled around her waist as if measuring her.

'Not too far now,' he pushed the door open with his shoulder. 'But first, I'm going to get you a drink. What would you like, coffee or tea? Mary Ann drinks tea.'

'Yes, I know. So please put me down.'

Placing her down, he looked at Cecelia for a moment as if she amused him.

'I'll just switch on the kettle and make you some tea. Mint, Mary Ann suggested mint would be good for you.'

His behavior made her feel uncomfortable, and if he continued taking these familiarities, she would have no other choice but to ask for refuge with Mr. and Mrs. Patts.

'It's so good to see you here,' he murmured under his breath before walking to the kitchen. 'I'll take your bag up to your room—and before you say anything else, I've been ordered to do this.'

When the front door finally went behind him, Cecelia was relieved.

19

─────────

Someone else's house always feels strange. This was Mary Ann's house, and everything about it said Mary Ann's world. Sitting, Cecelia wondered why she allowed this to happen to her and what she should do. She felt so strange in herself, and this William and his familiarity didn't help. So shaky and outside of herself, she wondered when everything would be normal?

She couldn't drink the mint tea. This wasn't her; it was Mary Ann. Mary Ann was everywhere. She was in the decoration, the perfume, and everything was over the top. Throwing away the mint tea, Cecelia drew some water, drank it, and then she felt cold. When will Mary Ann arrive to give her a Xanax? Her dose was well overdue. Cecelia felt stifled, resentful, and out of her comfort zone in this strange world. A world filled with feminine hospitality. With uncertainty, she sat waiting.

Thirty minutes later, the front door opened. Holding the door slightly ajar, Mary Ann called out. 'I will talk to you tomorrow, William. I've got Cecelia to look after. I'll give you a ring at about ten this evening. Thanks for everything. Take care driving home.'

The bright and tall presence of Mary Ann walked in.

'I take it William treated you well.' Mary Ann marched to the kitchen. 'You should have reminded me about your medication.' She called out. 'When I was disrobing for the ex-ray, I realized I hadn't given you your tablet. You must be dying for it. Here, I've got you a glass of water,' she strode back. 'Take the tablet, breathe, and then relax.'

The welcoming capsules were swallowed greedily, waiting for it to sink to her stomach and then into her bloodstream, then the magic would start, and she could breathe.

'Would you like something to eat? I shall rephrase that. You must have something to eat. William said when he held you in his arms, there was nothing to you. He was worried about you. By the way, what did you think of William?'

What a question to ask.

'I don't know him well enough to make any comment.'

'Yes, of course you don't,' Mary Ann smiled, running her eyes quickly over Cecelia; she chewed her bottom lip thoughtfully. 'I've made you some home-cooked chicken soup with the best and freshest ingredients, which won't tax your stomach too much. I'll warm it for us.' And then she stopped. 'It's so good to have you here, Cecelia.' Again, another smile.

Such a transition from the bright disinfectant smell of the hospital into the intimacy of a feminine environment. It was overwhelming in its inconsistency. And with her head everywhere, Cecelia felt giddy. But the soup was hot and pleasant and smoothed a weakened appetite.

'I want you to consider this as your home,' Mary Ann ladled her spoon midway to her mouth. 'Feel free to do whatever you wish here.' She smiled gently. 'This is your home, Cecelia.'

The Xanax had worked its way straight to her brain while the world once again took a comforting step back.

'Do you mind if I go to bed now?'

'Not at all, and you needn't have asked,' said Mary Ann, collecting the bowls. 'Would you like me to give you a hand to undress?'

'No—'

Cecelia's refusal was swift, which caught a laugh from Mary Ann. She nodded, well pleased.

Wonderful to lie in a proper bed again. Clouds replaced the stout hospital disciplinary pillows. So glad to be away from the madness and wearying had, at last, brought her sleep. A perfect night of slumber until the knock came the following morning.

'I brought you some orange juice and scrambled eggs,' said Mary Ann, pushing open the door with her foot while carrying a tray. And then she stopped to look at Cecelia. 'I never expected to have you stay with me. It feels wonderful. And you are to eat your breakfast—no, allow me to spoil you. I've never done this for anyone else before, and I find it fulfilling. Do you want me to feed you?'

'No, thank you.' Cecelia threw up her hand.

'Of course, I'm being too much. William asked about you last night.' Mary Ann had settled herself down to watch Cecelia eating. 'He wanted to know if you were all right. He thought you disapproved of him.'

'I don't know him that well to disapprove.'

'Yes, this was what I said.' Again, her teeth went over her bottom lip. 'Do you think he's handsome? You can tell me. I don't mind.'

'I suppose he is. I'm afraid I am not in the best of place in my head to notice such things.'

'Yes, you're right.'

'I think it's more important for you to think he's handsome.'

'I just wondered if you think there is any room for improvement.'

Such a peculiar question to ask.

'He is himself, and he's kind to you, and that's all that matters.'

'Yes,' said Mary Ann, crossing her leg to look out of the window.

The days passed like shadows under the friendship of Xanax. Resting in bed most of the time and numbed, locked out time and all thoughts of being alive. There was a tree outside the window, and birds collected there briefly as if to say hello. Cecelia felt they were her friends. Sparrows and the beautiful tricolored blackbird, a rare sighting of such an attractive bird. She drew great pleasure in their fleeting passage.

'You have had a settling effect on me, Cecelia. You don't know how much this means to me,' said Mary Ann, while they shared a pot of soup again. Cecelia's appetite still lagged. Everything appeared to be such an effort.

'How's William?'

'William? Well, of course, he is missing me, but he's a grown man, and he can do without me for a while.'

'Aren't you afraid you might lose him? An attractive man like that might find someone else.'

'Oh, my dear,' she clamped her hand over her mouth. 'You don't know William, as if you did, you would laugh with me. He is such an unbelievably shy man; it took all his energy to meet me. He is so nervous about women. There,

I've finished.' She took her bowl to the sink. 'William is taking me out tomorrow to do some shopping; I don't think it's a good thing to have food delivered; they give you products which are due to expire. Will you be all right? I need to fill your prescription. I must admit, though, you seem a lot calmer on it.'

There was no need for a verbal answer, but a nod.

Life was running smoothly. The sedatives were wonderful, but they were only a temporary measure, as was Mary Ann's hospitality. Next, Cecelia needed to make plans for her future.

These ideas formed during the last three days. She was now thinking about her future, and it couldn't be done, doped up and out of it. Bravery was necessary if Cecelia wanted to claim back her life. And it had to be done without Xanax. Leaving one of her doses out, thoughts and memories she had tried to avoid surfaced once again. Slowly at first, then as if in a rush.

Now with longer lengths of consciousness, the truth of what Mary Ann had been telling her over dinner and her pointing out the good and bad side of relationships, especially about Phoebe, was becoming prone to questions.

In Mary Ann's opinion, Phoebe had been using her. Did Cecelia really want to give up her ambition of being a writer? No, she didn't think so. Being a florist was nothing when someone like Cecelia had skills. Cecelia was a born writer. Phoebe, to be honest, was a bad influence.

Listening, Cecelia kept her thoughts to herself. The passive agreement didn't do any harm. There would be no arguments if she didn't reveal to Mary Ann how she felt. Yet, in a way, Mary Ann had a point. In the greater part of her life, Phoebe was still unknown. As Mary Ann had said, painting out a broader canvas of this so-called friend, she was a character whose surface Cecelia hadn't penetrated.

But did she know the reason Phoebe left England? Mary Ann nodded, keeping her eyes fixed on Cecelia's. Was it because she was evading prison? No, Cecelia didn't think so, judging by the look on her face. She nearly killed her husband, stabbed him so close to his heart that he almost died. No wonder she fled. Not such a nice person then, was she? Mary Ann raised her eyebrow. She hated to say it, but in one way, it was just as well Phoebe was dead. Poor Cecelia, to be taken in by this woman. Again, those startling blue eyes fell upon Cecelia; let this be a lesson to you not to trust those people who come with false smiles.

But how did Mary Ann find out? Disbelief took its toll. Didn't Cecelia remember she had told her she lived in England for a while? Yes, she did. It was in the newspapers and on the front page. And there, you see, it was a lucky escape for Cecelia.

No, they couldn't be talking about the same person—it wasn't possible. What Phoebe told her about her husband was completely different. Seconds traveled through the conversations they had about Phoebe's husband. There hadn't been many; Phoebe passed over it quickly, not wanting to talk about him except for the facts. He was a bully, and he beat her; no one believed her when she told them about him. She figured he would kill her in the end, which was why she ran away. Cecelia frowned. And if you were critical and looked at it from Mary Ann's way, if a man was after you and you believed he would kill you, then Phoebe was casual. But that was what she liked about her. Phoebe never took life seriously; she was not afraid.

This shock lasted a couple of days as a new grieving took hold. Loving and missing her friend now had to take second place in her life. Was it always to be like this? Choosing the wrong love and now her best friend was not who she said she was.

And yet, she still missed Phoebe or the person she had wanted her to be.

Inevitably, time moves on, sprinkling its dust behind it to cover the way back. A week with Phoebe, a few evenings. It amounted to nothing, not compared to Mr. Davis's life-long love for his wife.

The occupation of her time was slowly being absorbed by Mary Ann, who was tiresomely thoughtful, unobtrusive, and always there. The comfortable routine of days came with dependency. It suddenly struck Cecelia that Mary Ann was swallowing her up. Then another panic set in. She had to get away, and soon, before she lost herself completely.

It happened when Mary Ann went for another follow-up appointment, an opportunity for Cecelia to telephone Detective Travis and find out what was happening with the Alondra Slasher. The strangest thing about survival was if you were still curious, you still enjoyed life.

'How are you?' Detective Travis was pleased to hear from Cecelia.

'Getting back on my feet and in my mind. I can't imagine what you must have thought of me. I don't know what exactly happened. And now, I am sensationally embarrassed.'

'Don't worry about it. I had a similar effect when I saw my first murder. I think it's because we have a greater sense of self-righteousness. That's why I became a police officer, to serve my fellow man and woman.'

Itching to ask, wanting to know what was going on, this was the time to do it across the impersonal demands of the telephone.

'It's gone quiet,' said Detective Travis. 'It's like the Slasher has gone on holiday. There hasn't been another murder for over six weeks now, which is how I like it. But I would also like it if we found this murderous serial killer, perhaps even the two of them. He has an accomplice, and this is a fact. I took the notes you made from your visits to the victim's house, and they have proved interesting. I feel we are on to something positive. You're at your friend's house, Mary Ann. How long do you think you'll be staying there for?'

'Perhaps another week or maybe two, no longer. Has Detective Patts returned to duty?'

'As far as I know, they have retired him. So, take care of yourself, Cecelia, and call me whenever you want.'

Her cloudy head was wearing itself clear; the fear Cecelia had of falling apart didn't happen. She was a lot stronger than first tested. It was like Detective Travis had advised; you've just got to get on with your life because it's the only one you got.

The photograph of Sarah, which sat on the dresser, had thoughtfully been put out of the way, not that her likeness upset Cecelia; it was an act of thoughtfulness. The strangest idea was why Mary Ann should keep her picture for all those years. There were no other pictures around the house, and it was bereft of any other relationships. It was as if Mary Ann had been dropped from another dimension with no family.

Of course, this wasn't the right thing to do, but Cecelia was going to do it anyhow. After all, she was pretty sure that Mary Ann had gone through her stuff because a couple of pages were missing from her notebook. Carefully sliced from the edges, Mary Ann must have used a knife, as there were no serrated fringes.

Curious to know what Mary Ann had deleted from her life, Cecelia flicked the pages backward and forward. From a sense of annoyance, her memory credited her with only a few possibilities. Over and over, Cecelia exercised her mind, calling upon her memories from a fog until, finally, it awoke. There were a few notes on Phoebe and the last things they did together. Had she written it or had fancy created it? No, she remembered those written musings.

Odd how curiosity claims attention to other aspects happening in life. If she hadn't known Phoebe, what did she know of Mary Ann? Only what Mary Ann told her about herself.

You should not poke into kindness, especially when someone has done everything for you to get you well. Yet Cecelia wanted to know about this woman whose hospitality was fathomless. Creeping around Mary Ann's house, she knew she was doing a disservice to her hostess.

A room in this house was where the actress lived. Going into another person's private room always came with a clause. Be respectful and don't let her know you have entered. Cecelia opened the porthole into another life.

One side of the room was covered with mirrors: a flamboyant gesture to Mary Ann as an actress. A person who thought a great deal of themselves, and one who liked to be noticed. Thick red carpet on one side, wooden boards on the other, and above, the actor's best friend, lights. What a fantasy this room was. And in here, Mary Ann was a star. An alcove was fitted with a makeup table and a mirror framed with lights added to the glamor.

Often luck produced a star by being in the right place and at the right time. So it was a shame Mary Ann had just missed out.

But what exactly was she looking for? This was a kind

of treachery on a friend who had done everything that was kind. Everyone has things in their lives they are ashamed of, Cecelia thought, looking at the makeup. Her idiotic duplicity to Mary Ann was to allow her to believe she was still a virgin. When Mary Ann confessed she was a virgin at one of those dinners, she said she was the same. It was said to please Mary Ann. But what did it matter?

'William is pleased I am a virgin; he tells me he is a virgin as well,' said Mary Ann.

How naïve she was. This man was never a virgin. She could tell by the way he held her tight, his fingers measuring her waist and then slipping down to her butt. William was familiar with women. Should she warn Mary Ann of him? Perhaps not. Poor Mary Ann, to get to nearly twenty-six and not to have made love.

The small walk-in closet held a variety of clothes, all sectioned off. These were the daytime frocks that Cecelia remembered seeing Mary Ann in. But what were these? Long dresses, not the gowns one would wear in everyday life. They are more like ones for the theater. But of course, again, she was an actress.

Looking out the bedroom window, she saw a car pull up outside the house. There was only one person in the vehicle. Cecelia jerked back her head, closed the open doors, and hurried back into her bedroom. Her alibi was sleeping.

'Cecelia, are you awake?' the door opened after a light tap five minutes later. 'I've made us some tea. Oh, you're dressed.' She had placed the tray on the little table and brought it across to the bed.

'I can't live in nightclothes for the rest of my life.'

'And that is precisely what I was thinking, which is why I have bought you something to wear. Let me open it for you.

I thought green was your color to go with your pretty brown hair. Don't you think it's lovely?' she held it up.

No, this was not Cecelia; this was not her style, a long green dress, silky to the touch and exotic and open at the side.

'It's so nice and thank you—'

'But—'

'I don't know what to say because it would only come across as being ungenerous—'

'But it's not you—is it? I told William you wouldn't be comfortable in it, but he insisted. I'm sorry. I'll take it back to the shop.'

Oh dear, she had disappointed Mary Ann. 'No, please, don't. It's not you; It's me. I find change difficult. I like to stick to the clothes I know; they make me feel safe. But you shouldn't have. You've done enough for me.' Cecelia looked at this dress with caution. 'I will wear this dress sometime soon. Just give me a while to get used to it.'

'I don't know,' Mary Ann held on to the dress; she wasn't sure. 'I don't want to force you into any awkward decision; your friendship is too valuable to me.'

'Mary Ann,' began Cecelia sitting down with her for their evening meal. 'I was thinking.'

Mary Ann looked up from her plate.

'It's been nearly three weeks now; it's time I moved on with my life. I want to get back to work—'

'What, leave? But why? You can do your work from here. Cecelia, you may feel better.' Mary Ann held her fingers in quote marks. 'But you have been ill, seriously ill. You've had a bad breakdown. Trust me, I know.'

'I can't impose myself on you any longer. You've also got your life to live and someone else to consider. William. Isn't William unhappy about this arrangement? You hardly spend any time with him. He cares about you, but there is only so much caring can stretch to.'

'Are you saying you have had enough of me?'

'No, I'm not saying that. But it was never going to be forever, was it? You've helped me a great deal, and I appreciate your care—'

Mary Ann wasn't taking this well. It wasn't all about the dress.

'My house is now free,' continued Cecelia. Her voice became stronger as she became more resolved. 'The people who rented it have now gone back to Europe, which means I can move back.'

'Friendship, I thought we had a wonderful friendship.'

'We do. But I can't keep on living off you; I need to get back to my life. But we still can keep in contact.'

'When were you going to tell me this? Or was I going to wake up one day, knock on your door to find you had gone?' in short, stiff steps, Mary Ann left the small dining room.

She realized that Mary Ann would take it badly? But she never imagined it would be as bad as this. An uncomfortable atmosphere stood in the way; she had been ungrateful. But why? And how much did gratitude cost? Did it mean giving up the rest of her life for the cost of a month?

'I'm sorry, you're right,' Mary Ann returned to the table, this time carrying a bottle of wine. 'It's been a hard time for me. Having you here was a great help; it took my mind off things. The cancer is clear, which is a relief. That was another thing I had to do today. I didn't want to worry you because you are still vulnerable.' She smiled. 'I bought us a bottle of wine—an expensive French one to celebrate,' she sighed. This wasn't going as well as she planned. 'What I am trying to do is apologize. I've behaved badly. Will you accept my apology?'

'Yes, of course, I accept your apology, but there's no reason for you to apologize. It's me who should be grateful to you. Oh, Mary Ann, you understand that I've got to get out before I lose my confidence. Please understand. My entire world has been turned upside-down, and I must claim it back.' She clasped her hands imploringly together. 'Phoebe was a dear, dear friend to me—She was special.'

In submission, Mary Ann lowered her head, and then she looked up impassionedly.

'I understand, and you are right. My problem is I can be needy and grasping. I thought it was this which hurried you away.'

'No, no, it's nothing like that, Mary Ann.' Cecelia put her hand on top of Mary Ann's, assuring her.

'Well,' said Mary Ann, looking down at Cecelia's hand. 'Let's have a nice evening and celebrate. We need one night at least to let our hair down.'

She went to the kitchen to open the bottle.

20

When Cecelia woke, it was with a pounding headache and a scattering of fragmented memories. For those few seconds, she thought she was back home and in her own bed, but she was still there. Disturbing to find an entire night had passed with no recollection. Getting out of bed, she found herself in her nightclothes. How did that happen?

Where are the memories when you look for them? And what were these weird thoughts doing in her head? The sum total of bad dreams. Two of them toasting and drinking —was it only one bottle of wine? You had better take this, Mary Ann said. Now, looking into her hand from that small square window in her mind, was a Xanax tablet.

Slowly taking a shower, she saw a face from her hazy memories. A man watched her, standing by the shower door and smiling. His eyes were going up and down her naked body with admiration.

'You are beautiful, Cecelia. Has anyone told you that before?'

No, this had to be a dream. It wasn't possible. But from

the shadows, something else came forward. He picked her up to take her to her bed, and then he ran his hands all over her.

'I have been waiting for this all of my life,' he moaned.

Could it have been the effect of the Xanax tablet? Mixing this medication had produced some worrying side effects. But when she had come out of the shower and was dressing, she suddenly felt uncomfortable pains. How could it be a dream when her insides were painful?

'I don't remember what happened last night,' said Cecelia, entering the living room. Mary Ann was seated as she looked up.

'And I thought I was the only one. Do you know where I found myself this morning? Outside in the yard with my coat on. I don't usually drink, and this has never happened to me before. I found two empty bottles in the kitchen this morning.'

Cecelia bit her nails and stared at Mary Ann. 'Was William here last night?'

'Not that I remember. I still don't know how I got outside in the yard—and with my coat on, which was just as well. Last night wasn't cold, yet—'

'Has William got your house key?'

'Yes, of course. Why?'

'Nothing,' and now she was nibbling at her thumb. 'Mary Ann, do you remember when you said about knowing people?'

'Yes.'

'I just wondered. Does William work?'

'No, he doesn't have to, although he works to keep himself busy. He is independently wealthy. Why? Are you suddenly interested in him? Do you want to meet him?'

'No—'

Dreams which turned into nightmares pelted images in her mind.

'I've got your Xanax for you. Do you want to take it now?'

'Yes, please.' Cecelia took the tablet and palmed it into her pocket. 'I've never told you how grateful I am for taking care of me.'

'No problem, Cecelia; it's been a pleasure having you here. Oh yes, William is all very well, but those special chats we have had are impossible with a man, especially William. Would you like anything to eat?'

'No. No, thank you. I'm going to take a trip home this afternoon to make an inventory of what I need, stock up the cupboards, and get some more linen. My stuff is still unavailable to me in Phoebe's apartment until they've cleared it from the investigation.'

'Yes, I understand. Do you want William to drive you home?'

'No, thanks,' and then she thought. 'Why? Is he here now?'

'Yes, now I remember. When I eventually came in from the yard, I found him sleeping on the sofa. Though I don't remember him entering the house.' She frowned, struggling with her thoughts. 'When he left me just ten minutes before you came in, he said he couldn't find me anywhere when he arrived. I told him he should have looked in the yard. Oh, Cecelia, I think we went over the top. I had a terrible headache. But serves me right, I suppose.'

It was creepy how dreams sometimes feel so real, yet they were only dreams? Dreams which run as real-life were the worst, teasing seductively. William was the problem; he made her feel uncomfortable. There was something about him that was abnormal. Mary Ann might be forgiving of his eccentricities, but it didn't mean she should as well.

'I'm going now,' Cecelia came back into the kitchen, but no one was there. 'Mary Ann.' A figure passed across the kitchen window. It had to be William, or was it her imagination toying with her?

Leaving a quick note, Cecelia stepped out into the blinding sunlight to escape.

'Do you want a ride?' William leaned against his car, long legs crossed at his heels. He grinned. He liked her.

'No. I'll be fine, thank you.'

'How are you going to get home, then?'

So, Mary Ann had spoken to William about this.

'By taxi.' She didn't look at him, but neither did she move. Was he mentally undressing her? Holding his head back and imagining how she looked, she knew the signs. 'I didn't see Mary Ann.'

'No, you wouldn't. You know Mary Ann.' He grinned, still admiring her. 'Look, I can give you a ride—it's no problem to me unless you find me offensive.'

'No, it's not that. I just—I just want to try myself out. I've been dependent for far too long.'

'Look,' he said, straightening himself up. 'Giving you a ride is hardly going to take away your independence, is it? Besides, Mary Ann suggested I should offer. She's really upset, as you know, but she still wants to make certain you're okay.'

Hounded into a corner.

'Very well—and thank you.' Her independence was making her appear stupid.

Swiftly, he came around and opened the rear door.

'I thought you would like to sit in the back. There'll be more room for you.'

He was laughing at her, openly mocking her. She didn't trust him. He grinned, but that was okay with him.

Just a car journey, nothing more. Many are the time she had stepped inside a cab with an unknown driver. If Mary Ann knew about the trip, then he shouldn't do anything to her. Rapists work on surprise.

Rapist? Could he be the Alondra Slasher?

Let's be sensible about this. For goodness' sake, she still wasn't in her right mind and prone to hysteria. William was Mary Ann's boyfriend, the man she trusted. The Xanax had really messed up her head.

For a while, the two traveled in silence. Eyes on stalks, Cecelia watched the journey, still not reassured when William took the familiar roads to her house. Just how did he know where she lived? Once in a while, he glanced at his mirror. Dark brown eyes separated from the rest of him made him look surreal. But this was a perception from a damaged mind, drugged and mutilated, and bound by distortion.

Oh, God, help me.

'I've done well this far.' He looked into his mirror to catch her reflection. 'Now you are going to have to tell me exactly where you live.'

She was sure he was smiling at her. This was a big joke to him.

'If you take a right here, three blocks to the traffic lights,' she said, leaning forward.

'So, this is your home turf,' he turned the wheel. They were getting closer.

'If you don't mind, you can drop me off here. I've seen a person I know. I want to have a quick word with her. If you don't mind.'

He looked in his mirror again and smiled. He knew she was lying.

'What the lady wants, the lady gets,' he carried on grinning as he moved his car over to the sidewalk. And then he pulled over. 'You don't like me, do you?'

'I don't know you enough to make a comment like that.'

'I know you don't like me.'

'It's nothing to do with me. Like I said before, you are Mary Ann's friend, and as long as you are good to her and take care of her, that's all that should matter.'

'Do you think you could tell me why you don't like me?' he was leaning to take a better look at her.

Last night's dream now drew a brighter vision. While she and Mary Ann were intoxicated, he had taken his opportunity. Slipped up to her room to watch the free show, enjoying her undressing and then staggering into the shower. He was in the room with her, knowing she was drunk and drugged. It was then he decided he would have her.

'If you value your relationship with Mary Ann, I suggest you keep your hands to yourself.'

He shrugged.

'Better let you get out to catch up with your friend.'

She couldn't get the door open quick enough. But before she climbed out, he stretched across and grabbed hold of her hand.

'It was completely innocent,' he said. 'Nothing happened except a little appreciation.'

Her eyes matched his, but hers were dangerous. So, it wasn't a dream. He had run his creepy hands over her and gratified himself within her. Was it when she screamed, he withdrew? Oh, how dirty she now felt.

'Do you want me to pick you up tonight?' he called just before she slammed the door.

'No—'

'You're coming back tonight, aren't you?' William reversed the car to talk to her.

'I don't know.' She didn't want to look at him. He had touched her without her consent. This was rape—

'Cecelia, please don't do this—'

Those mellow notes in his voice which lay caresses one after another were wearing thin. It made Cecelia think. Did she have the power to make him worry? Was he now concerned she would tell Mary Ann? He should be anxious.

'Cecelia, I'm sorry. But don't do this to Mary Ann. She genuinely cares about you.'

'You should have thought about it before. There is something seriously wrong with you.'

'You don't understand. Mary Ann goes so far, and then she freezes.'

'Which to you means you can do as you like to others—and without their permission. Do you know what that makes you?' Cecelia bent down hissed through the open window. That word was on her lip, but denied access. 'If only she knew what you've been doing—'

'Yes, you're right. I've been stupid. It was only a bit of fun.'

'I'm not laughing. If I were to mention it to certain people—'

'Okay, I get your meaning. Though I thought,' he frowned, eyeing her with uncertainty. 'I thought—I'm attracted to you, Cecelia.'

'I don't care. You don't do things like that—'

'Okay, I get the message. But please don't tell Mary Ann,' William called after her fast—disappearing angry figure.

How disgustingly dirty she felt. Touching her everywhere—hands everywhere.

Loud noise from the traffic and indignation covered up

the footsteps running behind her. William chased after Cecelia.

'Wait,' he pulled her around.

Under attack, Cecelia's reaction was quick. Raising her hand, she slapped William's face, leaving a large red mark on his cheek. Shocked, his hand went automatically to his face before tottering backward.

'You hit me—'

'Yes, and if you don't leave me alone, I'll do it again. And I don't care what Mary Ann says or does to you; I'll be going to the police.' Shaking from anger and fear, Cecelia meant every word she said.

People passing stopped to stare at this warring couple. Aware of the gathering crowd, William didn't like the attention. It wasn't his thing.

'I am so sorry, Cecelia, I can explain myself. Please let me.' His hand was still on his cheek, but his brown eyes were frightened. With his other hand, he needed to diffuse this situation. Worried, he pawed the air without touching her, trying to calm her down. 'Just come with me for a drink, a coffee?'

'You think I would go with you after what you had tried to do to me? I wasn't so out of it that I didn't remember what you did. You'd better be careful with what is happening now, especially with the Alondra Slasher.'

'Are you all right, mam?' a passerby, a tall man, square shoulders whose dark face stole a wealth of injuries, was taking a serious look at William.

'Yes, she's my girlfriend. We are having a fight,' said William, now smiling with the confidence of conceit. This man should mind his own business.

'I am not his girlfriend, and neither am I all right,'

Cecelia turned her frightened and angry eyes to the passerby.

'You should leave the lady alone,' the man drawled. He was taller and more well-built. An oak keel belonging to a ship stood between Cecelia and William.

'Cecelia, please. I'm sorry. Don't tell Mary Ann; it will break her heart.' Once more glancing up at the man, William walked steadily and angrily back to his car. Punching footsteps of defeat.

'Are you sure you are all right now?' asked the concerned man, whose troubled eyes reminded her of Mr. Davis's. 'Do you know him?' his deep voice was soft yet tangible, taking every word with kindness and laying it to rest.

'Yes, I thought I knew him, but I will be all right now. And thank you for your kindness.'

He stood there watching her like a good shepherd who watches his sheep through the night while she hurried embarrassingly away.

She wanted to get home and have a shower, to rid herself of his touch. Whatever Mary Ann might think, William was dangerous. There was no way that she was going back to stay with Mary Ann. If she did, then she would be an idiot by putting herself right back into his hands. He needed reporting. But she couldn't be the one.

As she walked along the sideway, hysterical with fear, her imagination took over that William was still watching her. Perhaps he had followed her. Maybe he had feigned he was going off, but turned around and doubled back. He could have parked his car to stalk her.

'This was how it was meant to be,' she remembered the man from her dream telling her as he rubbed himself up and down her naked body. 'None of the others meant anything to me, I promise you.' His brown eyes stared into hers. 'We will be together until the end of time, Cecelia. And you will be my woman, and I will be your man.'

He ran his hands favorably around her small but ample breast, lips mouthing her nipples where an appetite for her started by slow sucking. It was pleasurable at first, believing it was a dream until she looked down to find his dark head at her breast. Once again, she shuddered. She could see him now. He had touched her where she should not have been handled without her permission.

'Oh,' she cried, her footsteps hurrying until she was running. 'Get out of my mind,' she ran her hand in front of her eyes to rid herself of his stalking eyes.

Cars screeched, a sure collision course, but they missed her. In the road, Cecelia looked about, mystified by what had happened.

'What's going on with you, Cecelia?' asked Detective Travis, eyes curled with anger and then exasperation.

She was in the Alondra Police Department, one of the off-duty officers who had witnessed the incident, had recognized Cecelia. Taking control of the near accident, he brought Cecelia in.

'Haven't you already put yourself in as much danger as you possibly can?' Detective Travis sighed and then shook her head. 'You know, you are more trouble than the criminals. You've tried to kill me, and now you are trying to kill yourself. Is this some sort of record? What are we going to do with you? In this state of mind, you are without doubt destructive, and I can't think what to do with you.' She was tapping her pen on top of her notebook. 'But I know I can talk to you because you're a good listener, Cecelia.' Detective Travis dropped the formalities. 'You've got that rare and unexplained quality where people open up to you.'

'I'm sorry,' whispered Cecelia.

'No, no, don't apologize. Sometimes we have to respect each other's inadequacies. Do you know what's wrong with the world? It's color. People don't see people; they see color. I see you as white, and I know you see me as black, but I'm also female.'

Cecelia smiled.

'I'm also awkward. I like to do things my way because I believe it is the right way. I'm not as clever as some, but I'm a lot smarter than most. I believe in God as I believe in justice. Some bad people in this world dance to their own tune—for whatever reasons. I sometimes wonder if people will ever get along with each other. Anyhow, I'm troubled.'

This wasn't the right time for Cecelia to enter her voice.

Travis looked to see if Cecelia was paying attention to her.

'We didn't tell the public that one child, the thirteen-year-old, survived the attack. Perhaps we should have done. And if we did, two innocent but stupid men, John Wanton and Art Perry, would still be alive. Oh,' she slunk her head into her hand. 'Yes, we make mistakes too.'

Surely, to Cecelia's thinking, this was good news that a young girl had survived the madman's attack.

'She awoke from her induced coma just yesterday evening, and we were able to get a description of her attacker this morning.'

'That is good, isn't it?'

Detective Travis's sorrowful eyes looked up at Cecelia.

'I shouldn't mind that he's a black man, but somehow, I do. But evil is evil, I suppose, except that it seems to be another winning point for the whites to score against the blacks.'

'No, I disagree with you there; people are people. I believe we still are afraid of each other, and even ourselves.

But I must admit, I never thought the Slasher would be a black person. I always instinctively felt he would be white. Are you certain about this?'

'Yes, the thirteen-year-old white girl came too for a little while,' said Detective Travis, staring down at her notes, 'and she saw a black man holding her in his arms staring down at her. Well, she gave us a fair description of him. I never thought he would ever be black.'

'But that doesn't make any sense. Cradling a young girl when his intentions are always to murder.'

'He was almost caught that time. Perhaps that's the explanation.'

21

The Alondra Slasher's profile was now in all the newspapers across the West Coast. One half of the page was devoted to his face, a black and white sketch. Let every black man beware. Detective Travis was doodling a heavy-lined box on her notepad; it was a potential coffin for all the black men in Alondra.

The Slasher was estimated to be around six feet tall, prematurely lined, and put in his thirties with short, gray-tinted black hair with brown eyes, a square chin, a broad nose, and full lips. His color was described to be mid-brown. A face that looked to be intelligent and gentle, but that's where everyone had been fooled, because he's a killer.

Staring at the likeness, Cecelia felt she had seen this face before and not so long ago. It was the face of the man who had stepped in to help Cecelia with William. No, he was no killer, and yet, he had been sighted after every murder. A black man and a white woman. Was there some connection? Were they working together?

So much had happened just lately, and none of it was good. As if life had got stuck in one long groove of disaster.

Looking at the faces in everyday life, everyone looked depressed. Or was it because she felt depressed?

Her opportunity to speak to Detective Travis again about her concern with Mary Ann was out; Detective Travis already had enough on her plate, and besides, her problems compared to the rest of the world were trivial. Rationally, she should leave Mary Ann alone; there were only so many problems Cecelia could take on her back. An involvement that had its roots based firmly on guilt. Look after yourself, girl, she heard this voice telling her. The voice was right, but conscience dictated otherwise. If anything, she should alert Mary Ann about William. He was dangerous; angry thoughts strayed to the idea that he might be the Alondra Slasher. Yet, it was a leap in the dark and an ill-conceived notion with nothing to back up her thinking. Was it also because the young girl had now given the identification of the Slasher, and he was black?

'Why don't you stay a few days in one of our cells?' offered Travis on impulse.

'What?'

'It just came to mind that you might feel safe in the police station. It's a pretty basic cell, but it will serve you until you get your head together. At least I'll know where you are,' she grinned. 'It would please me and stop me from worrying about you. Although worrying about you seems to be an occupational pass time.'

This sounded like a good idea to be around people who Cecelia knew were guaranteed to be safe. She should take this sensible offer, but she wasn't going to, was she? For one, she hadn't been on her own for at least two months. Don't be a fool, Cecelia, take it. She reconsidered her options; it wouldn't be forever, just until she got her head straight. So, if this was a genuine offer, then it looked like she was going to accept. Feeling safe came higher than comfort.

On the plus side, a police cell was handy, and she could use the police's database. Everything she wanted would be at her fingertips. Of course, all this was just between Detective Travis and herself.

'If you can see what I can't see, I need you to point it out to me.' Travis's very own words as she left her office. 'I am making you a temporary police officer—unofficially, of course. But dammit, I'm going to do everything I can to get that son of a bitch killer.'

A table had been installed for Cecelia as a desk, so placed to have her back towards Travis. Likewise, Travis was doing the same. Two women's minds both tackling the Slasher. They must come up with something between them.

Women's minds worked differently from a man's logical process, sometimes skipping the obvious to something which could be outrageous but which suddenly makes sense. Is this why a gay person's mind has the best of both worlds?

Mapping the list of events as they came to Cecelia on her pad. The problem was, why was the Slasher murdering these women? Except for Phoebe, every girl was a virgin. Poor Phoebe. But why had he raped Phoebe and then carved across her chest? What was it he carved on her chest? Her mind had been blessed not to remember, but these gruesome details must be known. The only way she could honor her friend was to find out who her murderer was and bring him to justice. Somehow, Cecelia didn't believe that it was the black suspect.

From the office computer, Cecelia went into the police files, terrified of facing the truth. Down into the report, there were photographs. Dead eyes stared out at Cecelia, revealing the last moments spent in agony, while this monster was the only witness to her death.

'Phoebe,' Cecelia whispered in pain, renewing the torment she had felt just weeks ago. 'I am so sorry. So sorry.' The sharpest of tears fell from her face, weaving their way and dropping to her shirt.

'Are you all right over there?' called out Detective Travis, as if she had heard Cecelia ushered her whispers.

'Yes, thank you. I'm good.' quickly she poked out the tears onto a tissue. 'I'm good.'

'That's what I want to hear. Fighting back is not always easy.' Travis's chair creaked as she turned back to her desk. 'I'm proud of you, Cecelia Clark.'

It was difficult to make out the word whore, in blooded letters across her breasts just above the stake driven into her heart. Tears without words, Cecelia stared at the monitor with insoluble sadness. Somebody that wicked could deprive Phoebe and herself of happiness. It was as if the murderer went out of their way to destroy their love and friendship.

Was this a plausible motive for these murderers? The Slasher couldn't stand others being happy when he was not. What could have happened to him to begrudge other people's hopes for the future? Desperation, Cecelia's mind kept on returning to the photograph. She must not give in to the anger of her tears. It had become essential that she work her way through it. And vital she survived and lived, and lived well, if only for the memory of Phoebe.

But could it have been Phoebe's husband who had kitted his anger and found where his wife was? Another tangent off the radar, another possibility.

Yet, to kill children was to kill innocence and everyone's hopes for the future. Was this a message? Sarah.

'What have you got?' asked Travis after two hours of recorded silence.

'I don't know what to make of it,' said Cecelia, turning around. 'From what I have found, there is always a black man and a white woman seen in the vicinity of the murders, but there is no indication or anything about a white rapist.'

'So, you think it's a white man who's the Slasher?'

'Yes, and I have no reason for it other than the way I feel.'

'The same here. But the thirteen-year-old described a black man, and it's the only profile we have.'

'Not the only one. Don't you remember, Mary Ann Leigh also gave you a description—'

'Oh yeah,' Detective Travis was not impressed.

'Why haven't you taken her description seriously?'

Turning back to Cecelia, Travis changed her attitude. 'Let's say it's personal.'

Frowning, Cecelia waited for Travis to continue.

'I met Mary Ann once when I was off duty. She's a big woman, and if you remember. I dropped my notebook and bent down to retrieve it when she walked into me. I said, excuse me, mam. When I stood up, she said to me, you people are all the same.'

'What do you think she meant by that?'

'I don't know, except I guess I was angry. An officer came across to us and asked if we were okay. I said yes, while Miss Leigh said I had been offensive, which I hadn't. So, you see, it's personal. I don't like the woman, and I don't trust her, and that is why I don't believe she wasn't raped. She likes to be taken notice of—you know, one of those narcissistic types. The people who disappear when the camera isn't on them.'

She carried on, while staring at Cecelia's unjudging face.

'But perhaps I can take another look at the description she gave us.'

Stepping up to her filing cabinet, Travis pulled out her notes and returned smoothly to her chair.

'It's a white assailant, that's for sure.' With her glasses on, Travis read the notes. 'Sometimes, I wonder if we are going to catch this man at all.' Travis looked up. 'For the last six weeks, there hasn't been a peep from him. It's as if he's done enough killing to satisfy his lust.' She began drumming her thumb on the desk. 'God knows, I don't want there to be another murder, but it would be satisfying if only to catch this murdering rapist serial killer in the act.'

Eating herself up with her thoughts, Cecelia tried to keep her head down. But there was one name that kept coming to the surface—William.

'What did you think of Mary Ann, other than you don't like her?'

'Why are you asking this?'

'Just curious. No particular reason.'

'You were the one staying with her. You mentioned she has a man friend.'

'Yes, I did.'

Odd, or would it be more appropriate to say that she was being contrary? What happened to sharing her suspicions with Detective Travis? Was it loyalty? No, she didn't think so, and certainly not to William. He didn't deserve it. Mary Ann, then? It was apparent that Mary Ann didn't know about the darker side of William and how dangerous he was. Maybe because it was embarrassing for herself, but had she been raped? Yes, she felt she had. He used her without her consent. It made Cecelia shudder and feel dirty just thinking about it.

If there was anyone she should warn, it should be Mary

Ann. The pervert. But what would she say to her? That her boyfriend had almost successfully raped her? And if she hadn't come to her senses, he surely would have penetrated fully. How he made her skin creep.

'You're doing a lot of thinking over there,' said Detective Travis. 'Want to share?'

'No, not just yet.'

It was during one of those late-night conversations while the candles burned down, flickering on their last ebbs, that Mary Ann told another side to her story about how she met William. Apparently, he too was also an actor, and then Mary Ann laughed.

'And not a good one. More of an amateur. It was his good looks which got him parts.'

Cecelia couldn't help giving Mary Ann a sidelong look. Yet what was beautiful to one person is ugly to the next. Mary Ann thought he was good-looking, and that's all she needed from her partner.

'We were doing this play called *Sixth Victim* in a theater in Edmonton, London,' said Mary Ann, leaning forward confidentially, moving one lip over the other. There was something in this which she was exceptionally pleased about. 'In essence, it was about someone that couldn't see the obvious. It wasn't a good play. At least, I didn't think so. This was the first time I was introduced to William Parker. He was nicknamed nosy-parker because he was always seeing things he wasn't supposed to see—although I don't know what.' she smiled slyly.

And then Mary Ann's conversation trailed into the wide web of platitudes.

Parker, so his last name was Parker, and he was also English. The town of Edmonton was also some help. Putting theaters in Edmonton, London, into the search engine came up with one place: the Millfield Theatre, Edmonton, London.

What a find. The Millfield Theatre actually existed. A time for rejoicing, Cecelia felt like jumping up and down and clapping her hands. This was a success. Sometimes, life was like that, failures and triumphs. With the spirit of winning, Cecelia continued her search.

Now it was a question of dates, but at least she knew the name of the unsuccessful play, *Sixth Victim*. A telephone number on the website suggested she should call. Cecelia glanced at Detective Travis, who was busy with her own searches. A better idea was to call tonight. The Millfield Theatre was still open in the evening with their new show.

Gone ten o'clock before Detective Travis called it a day. She ordered pizza for them both, a meal which Cecelia didn't enjoy because she didn't approve of it; she ate only one slice. These were the little things which she missed about home, eating what she wanted and when.

But ten o'clock in the evening in Alondra was six in the morning in London, an important time factor which Cecelia had forgotten. The telephone kept ringing, but just as she was going to hang up, someone picked up the phone. It was security.

'I'm sorry, I'm ringing from America, and I forgot about the time difference,' she hurried excitedly to be connecting to a world she had never been to but had only dreamed of. 'I wonder if you could help me.'

He couldn't help the lady if she wanted to book tickets; she would have to call back tomorrow.

'You had a play called *Sixth Victim*. I understood it was performed about five years ago.' Cecelia continued, unperturbed.

He could not help her with this, either. His shift would be over in an hour and a half.

'I would be so grateful if you could,' she gasped hopefully, desperate not to let him go. Do anything, say anything, in fact, lie. 'It's my brother, you see. We're trying to trace him. There was an argument in the family, but now my mother is dying, and mom wants to make it up. She wants to speak to him before she dies.'

Now, this put a different slant on her request. It brought the hero out in him. He had the keys to the office and would have a look. Listening in, she could hear doors being opened and shut, crunching footsteps. A corridor with echoes suggested he must be passing through the theater itself. And the muffled sound of an office entered to be followed by drawers opening, metal against metal. They say it rains a great deal in England.

'Ah, this is the one.'

She could almost see his finger running down the ledger.

'Got the play. What did you say your brother's name is?'

'William Parker.'

'William Parker,' he repeated under his breath. 'Nope. There was no William Parker in the show.'

Was her trial going to stop here?

'Try Mary Ann Leigh?'

'Mary Ann Leigh?' what had this got to do with looking for your brother, he was thinking.

'We understand she was his girlfriend and the reason he went to London.'

'Hmm,' he muttered. 'Let's see if she's on the list. No, I can't see her. Hang on. She's right at the bottom of the cast, but she hasn't got a character name, except she's listed as *Sixth Victim*. Whatever that's supposed to mean.'

'Thank you,' said Cecelia, about to replace the receiver. 'You've been extremely helpful.'

'Just a moment. Can you tell me what part of America you're calling from?'

'Alondra, California.'

'The land of the sun.'

'Yes,' smiled Cecelia. The price of his help was the dream of everlasting sunshine.

There was nothing substantial but proved again that Mary Ann was lying.

William wasn't an actor, but he could have been one of the stagehands, a drop in status for Mary Ann and her independently wealthy lover. Ticking this off, Cecelia went down to the next entrance on her list. Think Cecelia, think. You've got a brain, now use it.

Try databases. There must be one that holds a record of rapists. Again, to the search engine, she tapped in her request. The FBI had created one over thirty years ago to catch nationwide criminals. Strangely, it wasn't anything to do with genetic coding, but with behavioral traits. The organization was called the Violent Criminal Apprehension Program or better known as ViCAP. Putting William's name in the register, Cecelia ran it through the system. It was a hope, but the chances were low as this program was hardly used. Disappointing, but this was another search that also was crossed off.

Methodically, Cecelia had never been this systematic before. An exercise of almost deliberate slowness and the only profile she was building up was of a man whose existence was difficult to prove. But this didn't mean anything; a clever man would always fall off the radar, even though it was becoming more difficult these days, which was all the more reason to look deeper.

Steadily, Cecelia worked into the early hours of the morning and was surprised to realize that she had not taken any Xanax since yesterday. It must be the hours she had spent staring at the screen which had interfered with her vision. An ache in her temple moved into her mind and broke the rhyme of her thinking. Exhausted now, and no wonder. Not so long ago, she'd suffered a major breakdown. Time to get some sleep. But sleep was not draping its winged charm around her. A long night ahead was promised, which was made worse by the thought of the cell bed.

Came the morning, she might have had two hours' sleep, but that had been beaten up with dreaming. Tomorrow night, no matter what happens, she was going home.

'I have a feeling,' said Detective Travis as she entered her office and seeing Cecelia there. 'That we haven't heard the last of the Alondra Slasher,' she tossed several copies of the newspapers on Cecelia's desk. 'Last night, there were at least a hundred calls about sightings of the rapist. People are becoming nervous. It's like a national attack of fear with people spooked by their own shadow. But what do you expect when the papers have splashed his picture all across the front page? Here, take one and tell me what you think. What on earth's wrong with you? Are you sick? Are you ailing for something?'

'I'm trying to go cold turkey from the medication which the hospital prescribed for me. But it's not easy, it's a fight with the devil, and at times it feels like the hands of the addiction are going to win.'

'No, don't ever give in, not to that monster. I never thought highly of taking anyone offline by drugging them out of their heads. You need to get through this—and don't run away from it. So, how are you feeling now?'

'Pretty shaky and rather nauseous, but apart from that, okay.' Cecelia didn't like to admit strange thoughts were running through her head. It must be the withdrawal process.

This was received with a nod and a smile from Detective Travis. 'Hang on there, gal. It will pass, everything passes,' she returned to her desk. 'Oh, while I remember it, we've had a call from Phoebe Howard's husband, a Harold Hardaker. Did she ever mention anything to you about her husband?'

'He was the reason she left England. Phoebe said he used to beat her badly, and she was terrified of him. So, what does he want?'

'He wants to take the body back to England.'

'He can't do that to her. She was happy here.'

'I'm afraid he can do whatever he likes. She was still legally married to him.'

'Is there no way we can stop him? She was terrified of him.'

'Guess it doesn't matter anymore since she's dead. Her body belongs to him. She has no use for it anymore.'

'No one can own your body. I won't let him.'

'So, what will you do to him?' Detective Travis grinned and turned her head. This was a fight she could not win.

'Is he here now?'

'Yes, he is.'

'Where is he? I would like to meet him.' Suddenly, this seemed to be the most important deed that Cecelia had ever wanted to do, to meet the man who had nearly killed her friend.

'He's staying in one of those Travelodge places, just on the outskirts of Roseland. I'm not sure that it's a good idea for you to meet him. Whatever you think about him, they were still officially married. And besides Cecelia, she's dead. So, no one can hurt her anymore.'

No, but I can hurt him. She felt unreasonably aggressive.

'Most of the sighting,' continued Travis, looking down her list. 'Are unproductive; people were overreacting, which is understandable. But I suppose it's better than not receiving any information. This black guy is turning up everywhere. I just don't understand how he disappears,' she sighed. 'It's putting a strain on the relationships between folk.'

'How is the girl?'

'Yeah, she is recovering slowly, but he's made a mess of her. I can't see her having any children when she's older. People like him are sick. He decided this time not to penetrate her with his penis, but to use some other instrument. It might even have been an adult toy or even a crowbar, judging by the internal examinations carried out on the other victims. This man hates women, and the sooner we get him off the streets, the better.'

To Cecelia, the police station was becoming noisy. A side effect perhaps from coming off Xanax was affecting her sensitivity. Another reason to get out of this place and return home.

22

———

Weak and haunted by memories, Cecelia saw Phoebe in one sudden image, alive and chatting to her about their plans. Then in a flash, she was lying dead with the word whore etched into her naked breasts and above a stake that had cleft her heart in two. If she took just one of those tablets, this image would go away, just for a little while, until she could deal with it.

'I think I've got a link from the reports,' said Detective Travis, her eyes fixed on her computer. 'I think we are on the wrong trail with the black man. I don't know what this Jackson man is all about because there is no history of him on the records. The only information I can find on this man's identity is that he comes from San Luis Obispo. He's thirty-seven and a lawyer—a much-respected man who has gone on the wander. But why? Except that ten years ago, he lost someone. But that doesn't give him any reason to rape and murder women if he is the right person.'

'That's interesting,' replied Cecelia, fighting to concentrate.

'We need to get hold of this man and talk to him, but

somehow, I doubt he is the murderer. But I don't know. I just don't know. It's all guesswork.'

Hours passed slowly for Cecelia. Someone had been brought in drunk from a family domestic while his partner was now being treated in hospital. What was wrong with people? They married someone they were supposed to love, and then they tried their damnedest to destroy them. People just like her mother. When her mother dies, she won't rejoice. As far as Cecelia could see, hers had been a wasted life.

Everywhere Cecelia looked, people were trying to destroy each other. Why? It just didn't make sense.

Another emergency, and if Cecelia calculated right, she might not be on her own this evening. A man tried to stab his wife, and now his wife was terrified, and rightly so. He said she had incited him. This was a bible fearing city. Did they not read their bibles any longer?

'I'm going home,' Cecelia told Detective Travis, who looked up from her desk with surprise.

Nodding her head gently and thoughtfully, Detective Travis would not prevent Cecelia from going. After all, it's still a free country.

'I've got to go.' It was seven o'clock in the evening, picking up her light jacket. The world had turned ugly as page after page threw itself down on her vision, now distorting her reality. Her life was a mess. She couldn't get anything right, and she had killed her father with words. Her mother was right; she was a waste of time while Thomas used her. Phoebe, the only friend she ever had, was murdered. Isn't that telling you something, Cecelia? I feel like I am going mad.

How fragile Cecelia felt, probably to do with the fact that she hadn't eaten anything substantial for the last three days, and neither had she slept, which must be why she shook. Coming off the drugs had given her hallucinations. Shadows turned into monsters, sneaking out from corners, unknown and threatening to beat her. Several times, she thought she had seen William from the edge of her vision. A double look revealed a poster of a man advertising toothpaste. Was she going mad again?

People who had been to the bleak slope of madness will find themselves traveling again down the same warped route. An inevitability that was prophetically horrendous. Why not give up and walk straight into deformed reality instead of avoiding the detours? After all, you will go there in the end, so make it easy on yourself, don't fight it. Another person—William? Watching her? But no. Turning back, this time it was a cat staring at her from the fence.

Let's be sensible. There is no way William would know where she lived unless Mary Ann told him, but Mary Ann didn't know where she lived either. Logic and rationality were clever, but they didn't offload Cecelia's well-constructed fear. She caught the shuttle bus to Huntingdon and then walked the rest of the journey.

Her house was still the same, and nothing appeared to have changed in the last six weeks. Strange to be back here when so much in her life had been altered. Nothing significant had happened to her house. Did the wood and bricks not miss her as much as she had missed them? But of course, it wouldn't. Mortar and bricks, the sturdy substance in life, feel nothing, not even when pulled down.

The telephone started ringing just as Cecelia closed her door. Shut the door to keep the world out, keep the noise and the flashy lights away; the world was already running down for the night. There was a kind of poetry in this understanding. A sort of fatalistic harmony.

Well, now, she had two choices on whether or not to answer the telephone. The luxury of choice. This was her world, and she was in control. She would answer the phone, but two steps towards it, and it rang off. Now she didn't have to worry about it. That world could stay outside.

The people who had rented her house left nothing of themselves. A strange sensation to understand how people can quickly disappear as if they had never been. Just over a week ago, other people had walked about here, talking and perhaps laughing, sharing their feelings with one another. Their footsteps from a week ago, if not in a physical form, became another type of knowledge, an imprint on this life. A peculiar possession to build up a picture from nothing. It was the same feeling she had when she first moved into her house. Other people had been there making their lives. If she listened hard enough, she was sure she could hear them talking.

Did her living make any impact on other people? Do we make an impact on others while we are alive? Perhaps some people do. Cecelia went to the kitchen. Although it was warm in the house, she still felt cold.

Don't be unhappy. Phoebe; was sitting in the chair by the window. Her shoulder-length hair was again multi-colored.

We were supposed to do life together, at least set up the flower business, and then you died.

Yes, I know, and I am sorry for that.

Couldn't you have put up a fight and tried to get away from him?

I'm sorry. She was fading fast into the chair as if she had never been.

'Wait, Phoebe, don't go. Please don't go. I'm sorry, I didn't mean to get at you. But I'm left on my own here. You have deserted me. Phoebe.'

You will get over me. Just give it time, Cecelia. Just give it time.

'Phoebe,' Cecelia ran to the chair, but the image was gone.

The kettle boiling hollered out in a temper. In a hurry, her tired body moved slowly, bothered that it was being made to do so. It was imperative to turn off the gas. And then the world was thrown back into silence, the hush Cecelia had longed for when she was in the station cell. Suddenly, the house felt like a tomb, with everything watching and listening to her.

Someone had thoughtfully left their instant coffee at the front of the cupboard, a little thoughtful expression of welcome. Such consideration. Obviously, the last people who couldn't take it with them on their journey back to the UK had left it. How kind of them, a reminder that there are some good people in this world. A heaped spoon of granules and hot water; this would have to sustain her until tomorrow when she would go to the shops to get herself some groceries.

How very cold she was.

No, Phoebe had never been here; never left the morgue where she was still being kept until she was collected by her husband, Harold Hardaker. What right had he to be alive when she was not? If he had never beaten her, she would never have fled to America, and she would not be dead. But then, she would never have known Phoebe.

Going to the chair by the window, Cecelia sat down, imagining it was still warm from Phoebe's cold body. The pain of losing Phoebe was the biggest agony she had ever encountered, far bigger than losing her father. Wasn't that strange?

'Your father's dead at last.' And mom getting ready to go

out on a date.

No, that wasn't right. Mom was stuffing dad's clothes into a garbage bag.

'What are you doing?'

'Your dad's dead. He won't need these anymore.'

No, that wasn't true either. She was the one who had killed dad. It didn't matter that he had abandoned her. Thirteen, and carrying the weight of a juggernaut on her shoulders, and still reliving these memories.

'You had better behave yourself,' Tina had warned her after the funeral. 'If you don't behave yourself, then you're off to a home unless someone adopts you. But who would do that? Look at you; you're fat and ugly. No one would want you—'

Sipping her cooling coffee, Cecelia looked out of the window. The night was drifting in faster and blacking out the world. Was this her imagination, or was someone standing by the bushes outside the house opposite? The bush rustled from the low creeping breeze, picking this figure out and then concealing him between the movement of the light wind.

Yet, there was definitely someone waiting at the front of the house opposite, and this time, it was not her imagination.

Just coincidence, that was all, don't read too much into anything. It's just someone hanging around, waiting for a friend. You know where your mind is? It's not in a good place.

But there was definitely somebody there. Not everything was in her imagination. Eyes clung to the silhouette, holding on to him in the certainty that he was real. She was certain that the man across the road was black. There was no reason as to why except because of his build and the way he stood. By his confident stance, he looked like the sort of man who was not afraid of anything. He was young, although not so young. Someone with that kind of confidence had to be in his mid-thirties, and he held himself proud with shoulders held back as if waiting for something to happen. With the light still off, Cecelia could observe him undetected. Alone in this house, she had nothing else to do except to be paranoid. Just recently, she had put plenty of time into practicing paranoia.

Now came the questions—you see, she had not avoided paranoia. Had he followed her home? If he had, why was he stalking her? Was this to get Cecelia or to make her go mad? And another question. Why had Phoebe been killed? Hadn't he guessed she wasn't a virgin? The Slasher couldn't have done his homework.

Something crashed on the floor above with a thud. This was all she needed. Something to go bang in the night. Well, was she going to see what it was to find that imaginary rapist waiting for her upstairs in the bedroom?

She laughed. Hearing her voice in the house gave her power. This was her house, and she was safe. And yet, she still felt afraid. This was no way to live, always in fear as her father had lived, terrified, demoralized until he killed himself.

'Dad, I'm afraid. Tell me, was the only way to stop being afraid was by killing yourself? Why didn't you tell me? Weren't we supposed to be friends? I thought you were better than mom. I wanted you to stand up for yourself— you know, have some self-respect. I thought you were worth it. Why didn't you?'

Well, you had better do something about the noise. This was Phoebe now. *Just because I am not here for you is no excuse for you to give up. But that is the thing with you, any old reason to give up. Why don't you try surviving, and not only just surviving, but making a success of your life? So, I am dead, so what? It's only you who can make yourself happy. Haven't you worked this one out yet?* And then she laughed and disappeared.

Was she going mad?

Look out to the road again. The man had gone. Frowning at the place where he should have been. Was he the Alondra Slasher?

Tonight, she would sleep well in her bed, which reminded Cecelia that her leather bag containing her notes was still at the crime scene. There was a possibility that next week her things would be returned. Nothing she could do about it now. But she had a mind, didn't she? She would recall most of what she had written. It would be like editing.

Time to get herself ready for bed. A long night of sleeping wouldn't do any harm. Half-finished black coffee on the kitchen side. And now to tackle her bed for, of course, it wouldn't be made.

Now you've made your bed, lie in it. Tina's voice echoed in her head.

Cecelia turned her back and began walking upstairs. Laughing in the background was mom. Why can't you grow up and leave me alone? Look, Mom, what sort of person takes pleasure in hurting their daughter? *I'm only doing it for your own good. If you can face up to me, you'll be able to deal with anyone.*

Yes, without a doubt, the renters would have walked up and down these same stairs. Lowering her eyes, treading the steps, she could sense their presence from their lives in the past now laid down and sleeping.

Sworn that her bedroom door was closed. Strange, in fact, scary. Oh, dear, here we go again, spooking herself. Take one of her tablets just for tonight and sleep.

Deal with your feelings, girl. This time, it was Detective Travis's voice. You will have to do it sometime. *It's better to get it over with now instead of leaving it until later. Pain has to come out one way or another.*

Her room smelled heavily of perfume, the scent reminding Cecelia of flowers. Had Phoebe passed this way and lay a ghostly wreath on her bed? Enough to make her shudder. Someone dies, and the entire world becomes dead.

In a locked cupboard were stashed spare pillows and covers. Freshly laundered sheets on the shelf waited. So grateful to be used, so wonderfully fresh. There's nothing like physical work to purify the terror and despair. Cecelia picked up her bedding and carried them back into her room.

Damn it. The door closed behind her. Sometimes Cecelia felt like kicking hard at life for being so awkward. Why couldn't it give her just one break?

Open the bedroom and allow the fresh air to come in. But what has happened here? The windows have stuck; it couldn't have been the renters. Tomorrow, she would have to get it sorted out, or if not tomorrow, another day.

When one action is satisfactorily carried out, the world ticks over with pleasure. With one success, another will follow. This was going to be a positive—no, brilliant evening. She was home, safe, and getting on with life.

Finish her coffee, find herself a nightie, and then write out a list of things to do tomorrow. Ticking things off a list shows results, positive marks that prove her sanity.

Too quiet in this house. To solve this, she would sing to herself. Okay, not sing, but at least hum. Perhaps the evil spirits would quit her home if they could tell she wasn't afraid—well, she wasn't, was she?

As Cecelia was drinking the rest of her coffee, she

pretended she had taken two sleepers instead of one. After all, it's about fooling your mind. Tell your mind, the part monitoring your life, that everything is good and you are happy. After a while, your mind has no choice but to believe it is happy. Coffee tastes stale. Tomorrow, she would get fresh coffee.

With the light on and the curtains pulled, Cecelia sat at the table with an unused notebook, making notes on what she would do tomorrow. God, that coffee was foul.

Quickly penned notes covered the blank sheet of paper, strides of letters proposing her life in a series of actions. She was going to rewrite her notes on the Davis's, but this time they have to be done more sensitively because of their deaths. How would she put it across sympathetically about the murder of Tony Hare? This needed some consideration, but she had the advantage in this climate of fear and paranoia.

Scrawling more notes, long loops covering over the page, and then sliding off onto the table. Tired? Exhausted. She could hardly keep her eyes open. But then, she'd barely slept last night, and now sleep came gratefully, slipping long fingers through her hair, over her eyes, and pulling her eyelids down. For a couple of weeks, the effect of tiredness had forgotten to touch her. Erratic thoughts covered in madness. But now, it was coming over her fast.

So heavy trying to climb the stairs, and the ghosts waiting for her, laying their baited forms in tight corners, had vanished. So, it was wonderful not to care anymore, not to be checked with fearful superstitions. The bed, how she loved the bed, and how her bed loved her. Pulling open her covers, she climbed into it and fell gratefully and heavily asleep.

23

———

Thomas was looking down, lying beside her, and smiling at her.

'Did you really think I would drop you just like that? You obviously don't know me well enough. You are my love, Cecelia; you always have been. As soon as I saw you when you were at my door, I fell hook, line, and sinker, in love with you.'

'But you stayed with your wife,' Cecelia smiled dreamily, trying to stretch up and touch him.

But he took her hand and gently bit her finger, rounding his lips over her soft digit and pulling her hand to his face, where he nuzzled his nose tenderly. She was so precious to him.

'You are my wife.' He moved closer towards her, now stroking her face. 'We will always be together. No one is ever going to come between us. I want to touch you everywhere, Cecelia. I am obsessed with you.'

She laughed. These were the most pleasant dreams she had ever had. To have a man you love, love you back, is surely the answer to every woman's dreams.

And then his breath was on her neck, lips touching her flesh, sending thrills of sensation down her body. This was what she had always dreamed of. His soft hands now so carefully pulling off her sheet, she felt the cooler air taking its cognizance, checking out her body.

'But what about your wife?'

'My wife? Think nothing of her. She's gone from my life.'

The strings of her nightie were being slipped off and down her shoulders. He gasped when her breasts were exposed. Such sweetness, she felt his full soft mouth over her nipple as he began sucking and sucking, the softer down pulling. This was so wonderful. Thomas was better than he had ever been before. She giggled softly to herself.

Naked now, he was going down on her. Such ecstasy as the tongue flickering from one side to the other. She pushed her pelvis up, ready for him.

'Go in now and take me. Quickly. I can't stand it any longer. Mount me.'

'Oh, Cecelia. I never thought it would be like this. Wait for me.'

Smiling, Cecelia's eyes flickered open for the briefest of seconds. She wanted to see her naked lover, to see Thomas's beautiful, tanned form reared up and ready for her.

'Take me now, my darling,' Cecelia stretched out to his head. But the soft silky hair of her lover became coarse, thicker, and wavy.

Had his hair changed? This was not how she remembered him. But their lovemaking had been so long ago, so long ago he was not as she had imagined him. Or was it? Why couldn't she open her eyes? Was she asleep? Was this the reason? But how did Thomas know where she was?

Love. He knew where she was because he loved her. Love will always find the person they love.

My God, what was he doing to her?

'Thomas, Thomas, please don't. You're hurting me—'

Despite her yells, he was pushing, hitting the base of her pelvis, riding her hard. No rhythm, but eager to complete. This was not how she remembered it. This was not love—it was pain.

'Thomas, you're hurting me. Stop it. I want you to stop.'

But he carried on pushing, thrusting, and now the pain was becoming more intense. She had to do something before he tore her apart. Was this pain because she had not had sex for what seemed years? No, it should not be as bad as this. Love is gentle.

'Stop Thomas.' Cecelia pulled herself out of this drugged-up stupor.

Thrashing to put on her bedside light, the burning fires entering her and causing panic. She hurt as she had never hurt before. And this frightened her. What was he doing to her? She had to stop this now. He was holding down her legs to prevent her from kicking.

The light booted open the room, and the dark fell back like a rat caught weaseling back into the corners. This rat, which had been caught, was staring at her. Still fully clothed with his zipper open, he witnessed her shock. William was staring down at her.

In those few frozen seconds, Cecelia contemplated everything she must do, and then he smiled at her, for he had won.

'You have hurt me, William. Please stop,' she said calmly, finding a new sanity from within. 'This is not how we make love; don't you remember?' he should not see how terrified she was, as this was the best part of his pleasure.

He cocked his head to one side. Just a little jerk, but it

was enough to show that he was surprised. She had surprised him.

'Don't you remember how we did it before?'

Her roaring pain was subsiding just sufficient to hold on to her mind. Don't show him you are frantic. Even if you want to scream, and don't become hysterical. Another thought tumbled in. Mary Ann's boyfriend was not the person she thought he was, and Cecelia was now finding this out.

'Do you want me to kiss you?' she smiled, raising her chest with hands held out towards him. 'Remember the tenderness we shared? Me in your arms, our lips meeting— that was the most beautiful love I have ever experienced. You and I together, William. There is no other one but you.'

Keeping her eyes on his. It was a magic ring that kept her safe as long as she didn't take her eyes off him.

'Why don't you undress, and we can lie together? Look.' Cecelia patted the bed beside her, not taking her eyes off him. An open invitation. 'Come on, don't be shy.'

This was a mistake because he veered back from her.

'I'm sorry. I didn't mean—I mean I'm attracted to you—I desire you, William.'

'I wish I could believe you.' His eyes had moved to her chest.

'Believe it.'

'You rejected me every time I came close to you.'

'And do you know why?' her voice gambled with panic. 'Let me tell you why.'

His eyes traveled down between her breasts and now making their way ever downwards. He wasn't listening to her.

'Because of Mary Ann—that's the reason I rejected you. I didn't want to upset her.'

'You shouldn't worry about her anymore.'

'Why, what have you done to her?'

'You're just like the rest. Pretending to be interested in me. I thought you were different, but you are not. They all promise me things when they are scared. Yes, you will love me forever. You will do anything for me because you don't want to die.' William mimicked a girl's voice sounding like Mary Ann. 'All of you are whores.'

'But Mary Ann loves you—' the panic was setting in fast and fierce. Was he threatening to kill her if she didn't do what he wanted?

The Alondra Slasher. It fell into place like a rattler writhing in a bag, waiting to be released. But he had visited Phoebe to find that she wasn't there. He had gone into Phoebe's shop while she was busy, turned the open notice to closed, and killed Phoebe for pleasure.

That red light flew into her eyes, pounded into her heart, and blew a fit into her soul. William had killed Phoebe because Phoebe wasn't him.

She screamed with rage, and in that tempest of temper, sprung up from the bed to smash his face. Her hand, seemed to move in slow-motion, grabbed hold of him. His dark shark like eyes, dead from within, drilled into hers because now he was going to kill her. This was her time to die.

'No,' Cecelia screamed. The few kickboxing lessons she had must be of some use.

He was bending her arm back and delighting in his power.

She didn't want to die now. Her thirst for living had not been quenched. She wanted to live and to breathe and to be like she had never been before. She thought she had finished with life, but she hadn't.

Take your life, Cecelia. It was Phoebe. *And don't let him take it like he took mine.*

'He will not kill me, Phoebe,' Cecelia yelled to the ghost that had appeared by William's side.

It was that strange unquiet visitation that caught the lost mind of its axis. William turned to look at the waif that Cecelia was talking to. It was enough. Cecelia kicked him in the stomach, and he fell back, stunned and winded.

Strange, the need to make certain her kick had met its mark. Those few seconds, which she should have taken to get away, had been badly spent. Too late, Cecelia turned to run away. Suddenly feeling her nakedness, she looked for her cover. All those habits of modesty were against her, and an extravagant folly had cost her dearly.

She was going to live, and the future had opened its arms to welcome her. She was going to live, not die, certainly not die yet. Not too far to the closed door when a hot gloved hand grabbed hold of her ankle and pulled her to the floor.

'No, no,' Cecelia screamed, now crying.

Legs that had once been running to escape were now floundering, paddling the air, but had hit something. William used her legs to pull himself upon her. Grabbing her arms and bringing them to the floor. She was his to do with what he wanted.

She stared at him, puzzled, confounded. William looked different. And still staring at him. Did she not understand she was going to die? That he was going to kill her. He could not kill her successfully if she was not afraid. He wanted her afraid. This was part of the event; this was what gave him that extra high, the violence.

It was his nose Cecelia was looking at. A nose is just a nose. She shook her head with irony and then smiled.

'You are wearing a false nose,' although still naked, Cecelia laughed.

She was laughing at him. He leaned back and stared at her.

'Who are you that you should need to cover yourself?' tears crumpled quickly and ran from her eyes. Irony and madness had produced this strange reaction. An invitation to death, and Cecelia had forgotten to be scared.

'Don't laugh at me.' The owner of those dangerous eyes was now frantic for recognition. 'Don't you realize you are going to die?'

'Don't you realize how foolish you look?' hysteria had made her throw back her head into the madness of laughter. 'A man who has to dress up to pretend that he is someone important. How funny is that?'

'You should be scared. You should be terrified.'

'And you should wear better prosthetics.' Uncontrollably, Cecelia carried on laughing.

William touched his face. The rubber nose, which had once been secure, had now peeled off completely. He had been humiliated.

Madness had turned to laughter. For Cecelia, laughter is the best anesthetic in the world. To die laughing was a wonderful way to go. And she had rolled over in an outburst of laughter.

It was there on the floor. It had dropped from his belt. In the scramble, it had become dislodged from his person, and there it was, his strap-on penis, a dildo, and William had been wearing it. That made sense why it was painful. Cecelia roared with another scream of laughter. Was there anything real about this man?

She should have feared him. She should have cowered when he stood above her, begging him for mercy, but

Cecelia wouldn't stop laughing. Raised full height, William hated her with a vanity. Coming across, he dragged her up to his face. Despite that, Cecelia carried on laughing.

When he slapped her, Cecelia slapped him back. He couldn't get her to take him seriously. But she would.

'You whore,' William said. His venom was like a rattlesnake that was about to strike.

'A man with a false nose and who can't even fuck. Is there anything you can do for yourself?'

And then she stared at his thin pencil line of a mustache. Hypnotized, bobbing her head to one side and frowning. Lifting her bruised arm, she plucked at the hair and removed it.

'Who are you?' the soberness of her retrieval had given her equal status.

The game was up. Cecelia had seen him, and the brightness of identification traveled wide into her eyes.

'Mary Ann, is that you? What are you doing dressed up as William? I thought William had killed you.' She hid her mouth with her hand. 'My God, I should have recognized who you really were before now. You and William are one and the same.'

Her head was flying across the room, slapped into orbit while Cecelia's cheekbone took the full impact from the wall, breaking the tender mask of her flesh and smearing the wall with her blood.

Mary Ann? Why hadn't she seen through the disguise? All the time when she was talking to William's nervous face, it was Mary Ann. Her mind was tumbling with confusion as she hit the floor. The wall stretched up into infinity, and Cecelia didn't hear the stomp of feet until Mary Ann's hands grabbed hold of her arm to pull her upwards.

Was Mary Ann wearing contact lenses? Cecelia was once again staring into her eyes.

'You lied to me.'

Faces changed in anger; features alter with the rivets of temper. Mary Ann was ugly. Ugly, ugly, oh so ugly.

'You told me you were a virgin.'

Her teeth were so near Cecelia's nose that she wondered if she would bite it off. How absurd.

'Well, I was a virgin once,' Cecelia drawled, tasting the metallic flavor of her blood.

'Did you lose it to Thomas? Or was it someone else? I read your diaries. You whore. You're no different from your friend. Pretending to be something you're not—have you no respect for yourself?'

A shock of electric intelligence came buzzing, waking up Cecelia's befuddled mind. Phoebe?

'You killed Phoebe?'

'She begged me to die in the end. I shall never forget the look on her face when I told her you were in love with me, not her.'

'You killed Phoebe?' Cecelia repeated.

'I would have given you the world. I would have treated you like a princess. You would have wanted for nothing.'

'You're mad—no, insane. What made you think I ever wanted you?'

'It was you who came to me, remember?' now it was Mary Ann's turn to be baffled and insulted. Then, with a sudden jerk, she grabbed hold of Cecelia's face to take that last kiss from her lips. But she was angry and bit hard into Cecelia's lips and pushing her tongue into Cecelia's mouth.

'Get off me. Get off, you bitch,' Cecelia pulled her head back with narrowed eyes. Then, repulsed by this intrusion, she spat out Mary Ann's saliva into her face.

'You tramp. I'm going to take you even if you don't want it.'

'Take me, how? You have nothing to give me. You're not a man, and you're not even a proper woman. Go on, take what you want because you don't understand love. You are a poor excuse for a human being—'

And the rest of her words remained irrelevant because Mary Ann was dragging Cecelia across the room to the bed. Throwing Cecelia on the bed with hatred, she pulled open her legs. There was going to be justice for Mary Ann from her own misguided making.

'No,' Cecelia moaned, now sorry that she had mocked her.

With horror, Cecelia saw her kitchen knife lying on the side table. What the hell was she going to do with it? And then Cecelia knew telepathy shared minds. The strap-on still lay on the floor, but Mary Ann had a replacement.

'Oh my God, no. Please don't.'

'So, you're scared now? When I've finished with you, you won't be a woman either.'

Screaming, oh, how she screamed. Whistling up hell and damnation, Mary Ann was going to cut her from within. Kicking her legs, but they didn't do anything because Mary Ann held them down with her large hands.

'Please, have mercy. I beg you.'

Words which would remain idle, judging by the look on Mary Ann's face. Struggling to sit, Mary Ann pushed Cecelia back down.

It was the doorbell followed by heavy beatings, which signified a sudden change. Cecelia's screams had been answered. In that moment of sharpened tension, taken by surprise, Mary Ann spun around. An opportunity was created for Cecelia to kick Mary Ann off. One high kick was all it took to send Mary Ann tumbling backward onto the floor.

Out of the bedroom, running down the stairs. This time Cecelia gave no thought to her nakedness. Running to the door. Whoever heard would save her. But the front door was locked.

Thunder pounded on the stairs. Mary Ann was in fast pursuit and gaining upon Cecelia.

'You won't get away from me,' Mary Ann yelled with hard determination, half-man, half-woman, transmogrifying.

What to do? Where to go? Cecelia saw her jacket; inside the pocket was the gift that Detective Travis had given her. She screamed with panic, pitying her life. Then, running for her jacket, she prayed to God for His favor. This was her only hope.

Screaming, Cecelia's voice peeled with agony when the knife came slicing across her back. Ripping her from one shoulder to the other. The pain was agony. Her time was short. She grabbed her coat just as Cecelia was kicked to the ground with a fierce roundhouse kick, but she still had her jacket. With her hand in the pocket, Cecelia squeezed the trigger. Mary Ann stopped suddenly and fell backward.

24

There is always an investigation when someone is killed, even if it is in self-defense, because the formalities of death still have to be recorded. The Alondra Slasher was dead. It was official. Life had been taken, and this time it was the victim who took it, Cecelia Clark.

It was a strange and uncomfortable moment when she returned to the Alondra Police Department. Cecelia stayed in a hotel, free of charge from a grateful owner. And now, climbing out of the cab, still tender from the stitches across her slashed back, there was a crowd of Alondra people waiting. Arriving early in the morning, bringing flowers to cheer her. Lights were flashing to welcoming applause. A respected killer who had killed the right person.

'So, I see you've got yourself a crowd of appreciation,' smiled Detective Travis, who heard the arrival and had come out to greet Cecelia herself.

Showing Cecelia into her office, Detective Travis noted how Cecelia held herself. This had been one hell of a time for this peculiarly diffident kind of freelance investigative journalist. Quickly, Detective Travis pulled out a chair and waited until Cecelia sat down.

'How're you feeling?' Detective Travis asked, now sitting on the other side of her desk.

'Alive and grateful.' Yet still, with every moment passing, Cecelia wanted to cry.

Every sound made her shake, every sudden movement, not because of the withdrawal symptoms, but because her nerves were shot to pieces. Now she was trembling, and those tears were already bubbling to the surface. Gulping them back, Cecelia stole a quick look at the Detective.

'I thought I was dead,' she whispered while looking down at her hands, trying desperately not to cry.

'You thought you were dead? I was sure you were dead when we broke into your house. You were lying on the floor in a pool of blood, girl. And I saw myself going to your funeral.' Detective Travis was incredulous.

Now biting her lips fiercely and trembling, Cecelia could not look at Travis.

'I was naked.'

'Yes, you were naked. But it doesn't matter.' She pushed a box of paper tissues across her desk to her. A recent acquisition. Had she anticipated this kind of scene?

Gratefully, Cecelia took one and applied it to those swollen tears, hating she was making a fool of herself.

'We were just grateful you were alive—that's how you must think of it. Life is good, Cecelia, and you were determined to hold tight on it. And while I remember—not that I would forget—did you know there was a reward for the Alondra Slasher? Ten thousand dollars,' she smiled and nodded. 'But perhaps not enough for what you've done. But it's a start from a grateful people. But, my God, I just can't believe we got the Slasher and finished her reign of terror just as much as I can't believe that it turned out to be a woman. Mary Ann Leigh was some sort of mixed-up lesbian.'

'Who called for the police?' Cecelia kept having to remind herself that she was alive, and she was alive now and for years to come.

'Isiah Jackson.' Detective Travis was waiting to see if Cecelia recognized the name. But evidently, she didn't. 'His sister was Sarah Jackson.'

None the wiser, Detective Travis was going to have to explain it to her.

'Just over twelve years ago, a young girl was found dead, drowned, the coroner recorded. The case was dismissed as a tragic accident, or suicide. But the family refused the findings. Instead, they believed she had been murdered by her friend, Mary Ann Leigh.'

'Mary Ann Leigh?' Cecelia softly repeated.

'Yep, Sarah Jackson. She was the one in the photograph on the bedroom table. She missed out on her fifteenth birthday by one week.' Detective Travis paused in reflection to wait for this idea to be assimilated. 'The medical examiner had found marks on her shoulders, as if she had been pushed and held down to keep her under the water. The coroner dismissed this as bruising caused by struggle. I am not sure what he meant by that.'

Worried eyes were fixed on Detective Travis.

'Isiah Jackson was ten years older than Sarah; he studied law at Yale University and one of their brightest alumni. But he put his life on hold when he found his sister dead. Only the week before Sarah's death, he received a letter from his little sister saying she wasn't sure what to do with her friend, Mary Ann Leigh. She had become frightened of her. Sarah Jackson felt Mary Ann

Leigh had become possessive by making plans for their future.'

Cecelia held her mouth with her hand. The coincidence was frightening.

'The crux was getting to prove that Mary Ann Leigh killed Sarah, and although he knew it would never be easy, he wanted justice. He made it his life's business to keep an eye on Mary Ann Leigh by tracing her around the country.'

'She went to England to study acting at RADA.'

'She went briefly to England, but the Brits didn't accept her. She wasn't good enough. But it looked good on her resume. She lived in L.A. when Isiah Jackson tracked her down. He needed proof Mary Ann was his sister's murderer. He was building quite a profile on her. He followed her from job to job. Jobs that included waitressing, billboard walker, and money collector. She was also on a show with many other young women as a hostess wearing a skimpy dress. But she didn't last long because she didn't want to do the low work. She found it demeaning.'

It was hard to believe the well-mannered Mary Ann did any of these things. It must have hurt her vanity immensely.

'It was during this time when she was a game's hostess, one of the women on the show went missing. She was going out with a man called David. David disappeared, and two weeks later, Merrilee's badly decomposed body was found. Merrilee's suicide notes said that she thought she was pregnant, which was why she killed herself. The poor girl was found hanging in a motel, but the bruising around her neck was inconsistent with the hanging. So it remains one of those unsolved crimes. Now all evidence points to Mary Ann as being her lover and murderer.' Detective Travis shrugged; she had been through this evidence some fifty times before.

It wasn't easy to believe what Detective Travis was saying.

'When Isiah Jackson heard you screaming, he banged on the door. He had seen lights go on, then off, and imagined what was happening to you. So he rang the station, and the rest is history.'

'So, I've got Mr. Jackson to thank for my life?'

'To a great extent, yes, but don't forget, Cecelia, it was you who kept your head together. Mary Ann Leigh was certain that you were the one for her. We kept records of every moment she had with you. There were also tape recordings of the last minute of each of her victim's deaths. She always got them to tell her they loved her. It was important, they said it. It was a part of her M.O. Once they had told her they loved her, Mary Ann was free to kill them satisfactorily.'

Cecelia had to know because she would carry this for the rest of her life. 'Mary Ann recorded every one of them telling her they loved her?'

'Yes.'

'Did Phoebe tell Mary Ann she loved her?'

'Yes. It was what secured her death.' Detective Travis watched Cecelia catch her breath.

'I'm glad I killed Mary Ann now. I wish she had taken her longer to die—I wish I could have tortured her.' Imagining how Phoebe died again brought fury and rage chased with guilt. Someone had to die, and these were the hands which had killed.

'You did torture Mary Ann, Cecelia. She loved you and jealousy drove her to hatred. She had a passion for you like no one else.' Travis smiled at the irony. 'I believe if you had become her lover, she would have stopped raping and murdering. Everyone she had tried to court turned against her, which was why she killed them. She couldn't stand to be rejected. Unfortunately, she never loved Phoebe; she killed her because of you. Mary Ann believed you were having an affair with Phoebe.'

'Me? Having an affair with Phoebe? She was my friend.'

'Mary Ann was incapable of distinguishing a lover from a friend.' Travis's elbows lay on the table, fingers linked. 'You've got to get on with your life, Cecelia. Take a holiday from this—enjoy yourself and put this all behind you.'

Detective Travis watched Cecelia's changing expression. From bafflement to confusion and then to anger at what had happened, it was pointless and sad. After that, nothing could be done but to pick up on one's life and go forward.

But she will write this piece and write it honestly for the victims of the Alondra Slasher.

REVIEW

I would appreciate it if you reviewed my book as this would make my day.

Thank You...